UNRAVELED
BOOK 9.5

Also by Shannon Messenger

The KEEPER OF THE LOST CITIES Series
Keeper of the Lost Cities
Exile
Everblaze
Neverseen
Lodestar
Nightfall
Flashback
Legacy
Unlocked Book 8.5
Stellarlune

The SKY FALL Series
Let the Sky Fall
Let the Storm Break
Let the Wind Rise

KEEPER OF THE LOST CITIES

UNRAVELED

BOOK 9.5

SHANNON MESSENGER

Aladdin

New York London Toronto Sydney New Delhi

ALADDIN

An imprint of Simon & Schuster Children's Publishing Division
1230 Avenue of the Americas, New York, New York 10020
First Aladdin hardcover edition December 2024
Text copyright © 2024 by Shannon Messenger
Jacket illustration copyright © 2024 by Jason Chan
Simon & Schuster: Celebrating 100 Years of Publishing in 2024
For information about special discounts for bulk purchases, please contact
Simon & Schuster Special Sales at 1-866-506-1949 or business@simonandschuster.com.
The Simon & Schuster Speakers Bureau can bring authors to your live event.
For more information or to book an event contact the Simon & Schuster Speakers Bureau
at 1-866-248-3049 or visit our website at www.simonspeakers.com.
Jacket designed by Karin Paprocki
Interior designed by Mike Rosamilia
The text of this book was set in Scala Pro.
Manufactured in the United States of America 1024 BVG
2 4 6 8 10 9 7 5 3 1
Library of Congress Control Number 2024942224
ISBN 9781665967419 (hc)
ISBN 9781665967433 (ebook)

For Team Keefe.

How could I dedicate this book to anyone else?

Dear intrepid Keeper readers,

Right now, I have a feeling that many of you are thinking, *Wait—why is this book 9.5? Why not just call it book 10?* Or possibly: *Where's Sophie?* And I don't blame you! I realize that I'm following a slightly unconventional writing path with this series, and I promise that I'm not trying to mess with you!

(Even though messing with readers is one of the great joys that comes with being an author . . .) 😊

The truth is that the Keeper story is a massive puzzle with all kinds of crucial pieces that don't always fit together the way I think they will. And this piece has been especially stubborn— which I suppose isn't surprising, since it's connected to our infamously stubborn Lord Hunkyhair.

Surely you had to know that Keefe wasn't just sitting around feasting on bizarre human foods for the thirty-six chapters that he was missing from *Stellarlune*. He was busy with a lot of Very Important Things that I'd planned to tell you all about when he finally reunited with Sophie. But when I attempted to write those chapters, they refused to cooperate. There were too many other urgent problems for Sophie and Keefe to deal with at that moment, and too many reasons why Keefe wasn't quite ready to share his secrets. So I left book 9 with Keefe's vague promise of "someday I'll tell you all about my adventures in Humanland" and planned to write it all into book 10. But that plan hasn't worked either—and after *lots* of deleting, I finally realized what was wrong.

Keefe's "adventures in Humanland" are *his* story—and the only way for us to fully appreciate what happened is to live those moments *with him*. We need to see what he sees, feel what he feels, hear what he thinks as the plot unravels.

(See what I did there???)

And since the main Keeper books are limited to Sophie's POV, that meant I needed to add this bonus-book-of-sorts to the series. It picks up right after Keefe leaps away at the end of *Unlocked Book 8.5* and covers everything he did while he lived in the Forbidden Cities.

Don't worry—*Unraveled Book 9.5* has plenty of shocking reveals and twists, like any other Keeper book. It's also absolutely essential to read this book before reading Keeper #10. (And not *just* because I'm currently still writing book 10 . . .)

And for all of you Keefe fans out there, it's totally *KEEFE! KEEFE! KEEFE!* (Though I suspect you'll also find that Sophie and your other favorite characters aren't nearly as far away as you might think.)

So settle into a nice comfy chair, grab your favorite snack, and get ready to spend some quality time in our world with the Keefster!

xoxo

PS: If you haven't read *Stellarlune* yet, STOP RIGHT HERE. Otherwise it's massive spoilers ahead.

PREFACE

"THIS IS A BAD IDEA."

Keefe hadn't meant to say the words out loud.

But it didn't matter.

He'd run out of good ideas long ago.

Maybe he'd never had any to begin with.

His life had been too coordinated.

Too manipulated.

Everything building, building, building to this moment.

This choice that wasn't really a choice.

This unavoidable risk.

This test of who he was and what he could do and who he wanted to be.

So it was time to trust himself.

Time to get some answers.

Time to embrace his new reality.

"Are you ready?"

He hadn't meant to say that out loud either—and it wasn't really a question.

Ready or not, this was happening.

So Keefe did what he always did when he was in over his head.

He pretended like he had some idea what he was doing.

Then he dived in, hoping for the best.

Maybe he'd look back on this moment, knowing it was where everything unraveled.

Maybe it was the new beginning he'd been fighting for.

Either way, it was much too late to turn back.

ONE

"OKAY. NOW WHAT?"

Keefe made himself ask the question out loud.

He needed to start using his voice again. After all, that's why he was doing this.

Or part of the reason, anyway—and he didn't have time to think about the other scary, stressful things he was running away from.

He had more than enough scary, stressful stuff to deal with already.

Like the fact that he had no idea where he was, or where he wanted to go, and all he had was a small backpack crammed with elf-y things that probably weren't going to be very useful now that he was in Humanland.

Or the fact that human emotions were *WAY* more overwhelming than elvin emotions.

He'd figured they would be—and thought he'd mentally prepared for the onslaught.

But whoa.

This was a thousand times worse than when he woke up in the Healing Center after surviving his mom's lovely experiment.

Every possible sensation kept punching his senses over and over and over, like he was caught in the middle of a fistfight with a bunch of angry ogres.

Sharp irritation. Tingly joy. Burning frustration. Itchy impatience. Sour regret. Warm affection. Bubbly glee—plus a zillion other zings and zaps and prickles and pains mixed with a ton of loud noises and weird smells.

It made him want to claw at his skin and tear at his hair and cough and sneeze and barf up everything in his stomach.

Instead, he wrapped his arms around his waist and tried sucking in a deep breath.

Didn't help.

Neither did squeezing his eyes shut and covering his ears—which also didn't fit with the whole "blending in" thing he was supposed to be going for.

He pried his eyes open and tried to focus.

The too-bright sunlight washed everything to a blur, but when he squinted, he could make out a stretch of desert and a few triangular structures. Keefe was pretty sure they were the pyramids he'd learned about in elvin history—the ones the elves helped the humans build back in the days when elves and humans were trying to be the bestest of buddies.

The buildings looked old and crumbly now—but that didn't seem to bother the huge crowd that had gathered in the sweltering heat, mostly to record themselves pretending to balance the pyramids on their heads, for some bizarre reason.

They were also talking.

And laughing.

And *feeling*.

So. Many. Feelings.

Too many.

It was too much.

The pressure in Keefe's brain kept building and building and building—but that wasn't nearly as terrifying as the word taking shape in the back of his throat.

A heavy lump he couldn't choke down but refused to spit out.

He didn't know what the word was—but he knew if he said it, his misery would vanish.

Everything would be perfectly calm and blissfully quiet and . . .

Seriously creepy.

Keefe locked his jaw and shook his head, trying to knock the word loose.

When that didn't work, he replayed his memories of the day he'd given his first *command*.

The way everyone stood frozen with their mouths dropped open, with dull, unblinking eyes.

Empty shells of the people he cared about.

He'd barely found a way to snap them out of it—and he had no idea if he'd be able to fix that kind of mess again.

Especially with humans, who didn't have any mental defenses.

He tried picturing that, too.

All the innocent people around him, frozen like a bunch of sweaty statues.

Grown-ups.

Kids.

Even a few tiny babies.

The lump in his throat deflated with the image—but it sprang right back when a group wearing shirts that said EASTLAKE HIGH SCHOOL! GO, FIGHTING LLAMAS! blasted him with a hurricane of nauseating angst.

Time to move.

There had to be somewhere nearby that wasn't so chaotic.

Somewhere he could think.

Breathe.

Get control.

But when he tried to weave through the crowd, their annoyance pelted him like goblin throwing stars—and the unspoken command slid across his tongue and pressed against his lips.

Keefe gritted his teeth and spun around, searching for somewhere he'd be able to light leap without being noticed.

All he found was people, people, and more people—plus a few grumpy camels and some smug cats flicking their tails.

It's fine.

I'll be fine.

He chanted the words in his head, hoping that would make them true.

But the crowd closed in tighter, forcing him to start shoving to make any headway—and their anger felt like a gorgodon chewing on his skull.

His ears rang and his knees wobbled—but right when everything got spinny, he finally spotted a way out of there.

The ugly contraption—was it called a bus? He couldn't remember—was spewing out smoke and chemicals. But it was big enough for him to hide behind.

He ducked by one of the back wheels and dug out his pathfinder, wishing he knew where any of the facets on the blue crystal would take him.

He'd stolen the pathfinder from his father, and it annoyingly hadn't come with any instructions.

Please be somewhere quiet, he begged as he randomly locked the crystal into place and held it up to the sun. *Somewhere less crowded.*

He repeated the pleas as the light whisked him away.

Then there was nothing but rushing warmth and tingly freedom—until he re-formed.

The sounds hit him first.

Shouts and whoops and cheers and boos.

Followed by OVERWHELMING DELIGHT and FURIOUS RAGE.

He was standing outside an enormous arena that was swarming with people who were mostly wearing bright red, but some were wearing deep blue. The two groups were feeling ALL THE THINGS while shouting at each other about points and referees and penalties. Then a whistle blew, and pandemonium erupted.

The word on Keefe's tongue turned to boiling lava.

He couldn't hold the eruption back any longer—but with the last of his strength, he spun the pathfinder and tumbled into the light, not caring if anyone saw him.

Maybe they wouldn't believe their eyes.

Or maybe there'd be stories about a miserable, wild-haired boy who'd "magically" disappeared.

It didn't matter.

Anything was better than what would've happened if he'd stayed any longer.

He just wished he knew where he was going.

Another crowd would probably shatter him.

Even leaping felt too exhausting.

The light kept battering his senses, and he could feel his concentration slipping, slipping, slipping.

It would've been so much easier to just . . . let go.

Stay in the bright, twinkly warmth and never have to worry about who he could hurt or what might happen if—

NO!

Keefe dragged himself back together and held on as tight as he could.

He had to keep fighting.

No matter how tired he was.

If Foster could keep going after everything she'd been through, so could he—and as soon as he thought the name, he found a whole other reason to fight.

Gold-flecked brown eyes with a tiny crinkle between them.

She tended to have that cute little worry crease whenever she looked at him.

Because she cared.

Maybe not the way he wished she would.

But a whole lot more than he deserved.

He owed it to her to fight as hard as he could, for as long as he could.

And honestly?

He owed that to himself, too.

So he rallied his concentration and braced for another emotional tidal wave as his body re-formed again.

TWO

OOL, CRISP AIR BRUSHED KEEFE'S skin.

Branches creaked and cracked.

A nearby river gurgled.

And . . .

That was it.

Keefe collapsed to the ground in a heap and buried his face in his hands.

He might've teared up a little too—especially when he peeked out from his cocoon of patheticness and found himself in the middle of a forest, surrounded by red, orange, and yellow trees.

No humans.

No elves.

No obnoxious ogre bodyguard.

He was finally alone.

It was such an incredible relief.

Also super depressing.

Was this the only way he'd be able to function now?

Had that been part of his mom's horrible plan all along?

Cut him off from everyone he cared about and wait for him to break?

"Forget that."

Keefe said the words out loud, glad to have his voice back.

The command had retreated to whatever dark mental corner it came from—and it was going to stay there.

He cleared his throat and sat up taller. "I *will* control these abilities."

It almost sounded like he believed it.

But he *had* to believe it—even though Dex hadn't been able to come up with any gadgets to help him, and Elwin's and Kesler's gross concoctions had only made him worse.

There had to be a way to beat this.

Otherwise his mom won.

The thought of her smug, callous expression when she'd told him to *embrace the change* was enough to get him back on his feet, dusting crunched bits of leaves off his tunic as he slung his backpack over his shoulder.

He hadn't fled the Lost Cities because he was giving up.

He'd left to keep everyone safe while he figured out what was happening to him and either found a way to stop it or made sure no one would ever know what he was capable of.

And if the Black Swan had been able to keep Foster's existence secret for more than twelve years by hiding her with humans, the same trick should work for him.

It was a solid plan.

He just had to stick to it.

Yeah, it was probably going to be harder than he'd imagined—but what else was new?

He grew up with a cold, judgmental father and an evil, unstable mother who kept trying to murder his friends.

He could handle *anything*.

In fact, he was looking forward to the final showdown with Mommy Dearest.

After all, wasn't that how this was supposed to end?

Some sort of epic battle where he proved once and for all that she'd never be able to make her little Legacy Boy do what she wanted him to?

And bonus: He'd get to use his awful new powers to destroy everything she'd built.

Then he'd finish her, too.

A chill rippled down his spine at the thought—but it wasn't fear.

Or dread.

Or guilt.

It wasn't even doubt.

It felt more like . . . anticipation.

He used to worry he wouldn't be strong enough. Or that his elf-y instincts—as Ro liked to call them—would slow his hand before he could deliver the final blow.

But that was one change he *had* embraced.

He was too angry now to hesitate.

Too aware of how much his mom deserved what was coming.

He was ready to fight her with everything he had.

No restraint.

No mercy.

And if he survived . . .

He didn't know how to finish that sentence.

There were too many what-ifs in the way.

Too many risky possibilities.

But that didn't stop his brain from picturing those beautiful brown eyes again—and imagining a happy twinkle shining in the corners.

Foster didn't smile nearly as much as she deserved to—but when she did?

It was absolute perfection.

Then again . . . after reading his letter, she might not have a whole lot of smiles for him.

She'd already been super mad that he'd agreed to the Council's order to stay away from her until he mastered his new abilities. And she definitely wouldn't be a fan of his Hide-with-Humans Plan.

He couldn't blame her for that, since the last time he'd run away had been a massive disaster.

But he had really good reasons this time!

He just . . . hadn't been able to explain them.

He'd wanted to—but that would've involved revealing a secret that wasn't *his*.

So he'd kept his message vague and begged her to trust him. Which probably meant she'd ignore everything he said and try to track him down and drag him back to the Lost Cities.

He actually wouldn't be surprised if she was already looking for him.

How long had he been gone?

He took a quick count and . . .

Wow.

Had it really been less than fifteen minutes since he'd left Havenfield?

He counted again and . . . yep.

He didn't know the *exact* timing, since he hadn't looked at any clocks. But he couldn't have been at the pyramids for more than ten minutes before the emotions had overwhelmed him. Then he'd only been able to stay at the arena for a few seconds before he'd had to flee. And there was no way he'd been in this forest for more than five minutes.

So . . . yeah.

He sank to the ground and curled into a cocoon of patheticness again.

No point standing there, pretending to look confident when he couldn't even last fifteen minutes around humans without almost losing control—*twice*.

But . . . he *hadn't* lost control.

That had to count for something, right?

Plus, the fact that it all happened so fast might even be *why* it was such a struggle.

He hadn't had a chance to get his bearings.

If he was able to stay somewhere long enough to actually adjust and settle in, his next leap should go a lot smoother.

He wasn't totally sold by that little pep talk—but it was enough to get him back on his feet.

And hey, not being gone very long also meant he didn't have to worry about anyone looking for him yet.

Grady had made it sound like Foster might not be home for a while.

Goose bumps prickled Keefe's skin as he remembered *why*.

She burned down one of the Neverseen's storehouses.

Keefe honestly had no idea how to process that development— but he'd never forget the fear clouding Grady's eyes when he'd told him.

Grady even asked him to stay in the Lost Cities in case Foster needed help.

He was *that* freaked out.

That's why Keefe agreed to take Grady's Imparter with him—and promised to answer if Grady actually used it to hail him.

But he couldn't imagine that was going to happen.

Foster could handle herself.

In fact, Keefe wished the Councillors would make big banners that said *Our moonlark's on FIRE!* and hang them from their castles.

This was a whole other kind of victory.

Who knew how many of his mom's careful plans had just gone up in flames?

But . . .

There *would* be consequences.

Keefe tried to imagine how his mom would react to the news.

Would she scream and swear and throw things?

No.

She'd stand, perfectly calm. Tilt up her chin and smooth her hair. Probably smile as she planned her revenge.

And something about that image made an old piece of memory drift back to Keefe's consciousness.

He couldn't tell if his mom had tried to erase it—or if his brain had buried it with the other unsettling pieces of his childhood to protect him.

Either way, he could now see every detail in sharp focus.

He looked about eight years old and was sitting hunched over the dressing table in his bedroom, watching his father stomp away with all his favorite tunics. His father claimed they looked sloppy and plain. *Not fit for a Sencen*. He'd also smeared thick goop in Keefe's hair and plastered it to his skull. And he'd made Keefe put on a jeweled cape, even though they weren't going anywhere—and when Keefe pointed out that he didn't have a Sencen crest to fasten it, his father told him, *You don't deserve one yet.*

Keefe waited until he heard the vortinator start spinning—then snatched the jar of hair gel and hurled it against the mirror.

Sticky gunk splattered everywhere, and cracks fanned out across the glass.

Keefe grinned—until he realized his mom was standing right behind him.

He braced for her to shout for his father.

But she just clicked her tongue and said, *Better clean up this mess.*

As she turned to leave, she added, *You're wasting your rage.*

Keefe snorted. *What does that mean?*

She stepped closer, studying her fractured reflection in the broken mirror. *It means anger is the greatest power any of us have. Save it. You're going to need it.*

His mouth went dry when he saw the intensity in her eyes. *For what?*

It's hard to say. She smiled, but it looked more like she was baring her teeth when she added, *But someday you and I will do incredible things together, Keefe. And when we do, we'll need that rage for anyone who gets in our way.*

THREE

"MOM OF THE YEAR STRIKES AGAIN," Keefe muttered, not sure why he was talking out loud.

Maybe he needed to remind himself that he wasn't still that confused little eight-year-old boy wondering why Mommy suddenly seemed extra scary.

He also didn't know why he was so surprised.

He was *very* aware that his mom was the absolute worst.

But . . . he couldn't understand why she always seemed so convinced that he'd be on her side.

She'd never been a good mother.

She didn't even *like* him.

Did she think he wouldn't care about that because she believed her plan was *that* brilliant?

Or maybe she really did expect her experiments to transform him into an obedient little puppet.

"Never gonna happen," he told the trees, and anything else willing to listen. "You hear me? I'LL NEVER DO WHAT YOU WANT!"

He knew his mom wouldn't hear him, of course.

But it felt good to say it.

And in a weird way, he was glad his brain had dredged up that depressing memory.

It proved he'd been right to disappear.

His mom had *way* too many plans for him.

Until he knew what they were—and had a foolproof plan of his own—he had to stay far, far away.

Which meant he also needed to be able to hang around humans for more than a few minutes without wanting to numb everybody.

"You will," he told himself. "You just need to get some rest. Start fresh tomorrow."

It sounded so simple when he said it.

Like he wasn't all alone in a strange forest, staring down a night of sleeping with a lumpy backpack for a pillow and a blanket of soggy leaves because his brain went into creepy-control-freak mode when he was anywhere that had actual beds.

Hopefully nothing would wander by and think he smelled tasty. . . .

He spun around, scanning the shadows for glowing eyes.

None so far—but that didn't mean they weren't there.

He sighed and dragged his hands down his face—and found a whole new reason to panic when his fingers brushed a metal cord resting at the base of his neck.

His registry pendant.

He'd planned to leave it on top of his note in Foster's room as another way of saying, *Don't try to find me.* But then he'd gotten distracted by Iggy and Grady and his own wishy-washy doubts and had forgotten all about it.

The cord broke with an audible *snap*, and he flung the crystal as hard as he could at the nearest tree.

It bounced off without a scratch.

Stomping on it didn't do any damage either.

It just sank into the leaves.

He finally had to smash it between a couple of rocks until it was nothing but sparkly dust.

But anyone with access to his feed—like oh, say, his mom's little Technopath buddy, or the Council, or Dex—would still be able to track him to his last recorded location.

Keefe unleashed a string of words that Ro would've given him a high five for saying.

Looked like his foresty campout wasn't an option anymore.

Nope!

He had to go back to random light leaping.

Maybe I'll find somewhere better, he tried to tell himself as he dug out his pathfinder. *A deserted tropical island would be awesome.*

He could build himself a giant sand castle and call it Keefetopia!

But of course he wasn't that lucky.

In fact, the universe clearly had it in for him, because he reappeared in the brightest, noisiest, most overwhelming city he'd ever seen.

The buildings were a hodgepodge of different styles and shapes, all smashed together and covered in blinking neon lights. Music blared from every direction. Cars honked. Giant signs flashed advertisements for circus-like shows or things called POKER and BLACKJACK and ALL-YOU-CAN-EAT BUFFETS. People in sparkly clothes stumbled around carrying cups that were almost as tall as them, filled with colorful liquids. And the emotions in the air were somehow ramped up *and* fuzzy.

Keefe's skin buzzed, and his head filled with a thick, murky fog as a new command formed on his tongue—a word that felt slippery and smooth and ready to slide out his lips with his next breath.

He took one wobbly step and almost face-planted onto the sticky, trash-covered ground, and he knew he couldn't risk staying any longer.

The good news was, he doubted anyone noticed him raise his pathfinder and leap away.

But the place where he re-formed was a whole new kind of miserable.

He didn't have to worry about controlling anybody—but only because he'd reappeared in the middle of a blizzard, and the swirling ice and snow had whited out the world.

The wind clawed at his skin as he trudged through the knee-high snowdrifts, wondering if his body temperature regulation could keep him from turning into a Keefesicle. But the cold seeped deep into his bones, making his heart race and his limbs go numb.

"C-c-c-come o-o-on," he grumbled through chattering teeth as his shaky hands struggled to adjust the pathfinder again. "Th-th-th-there h-h-has t-t-to b-b-b-be s-s-s-somewh-wh-wh-where th-th-th-that is-is-is-isn't t-t-t-terrible."

He didn't care if the place was ugly.

Or smelly.

He just needed to be alone—and not freeze to death.

And maybe the universe finally took pity on him, because the warm, rushing light dropped him off in the middle of another quiet forest.

It was grayer and colder than the last one, with hard, frosty ground covered in prickly pine needles. But Keefe still threw his arms around the nearest tree and hugged as hard as he could.

"I'm never leaping again," he mumbled into the scratchy bark. "That's it. I live here now."

He was only half joking—and he snuggled the tree for longer than he was proud of before he stepped back and surveyed his surroundings.

Snowcapped mountains in the distance.

Early glints of sunset streaking the sky.

It was stark and beautiful—but he could also feel the temperature dropping, so it was going to be a very long, very cold, very lonely night.

Or maybe not lonely enough.

The ground was dotted with animal tracks—and they did not look like tiny, cuddly creatures.

Keefe crossed his arms, trying to save whatever body heat he could as he searched for some sort of shelter.

Best he could find was a tree covered with a few less icicles than the others.

If he levitated to the taller branches, he could camp out there and hope nothing climbed up to get him. But he'd have to make sure he didn't move in his sleep; otherwise he'd go *splat!*

At least he didn't have to worry about anyone finding him now.

He tried to think of any other trackers he might've missed, but he was pretty sure he had it covered.

He hadn't worn a nexus in years.

Dex had never given him one of those panic-switch rings

he'd made for everyone else—which Keefe had always meant to call him out on.

And Ro had agreed to keep her freaky ogre bacteria off his skin.

So unless Grady had a way of homing in on the signal for his Imparter—which seemed unlikely—he should be totally untraceable.

Well.

Foster could still go all Super Telepath on him and transmit a bunch of messages into his brain—but she wouldn't be able to tell where he was.

Unless she poked around his recent memories and found enough clues to guess his location . . .

She didn't usually break the rules of telepathy like that—but she might tell herself she was doing it to protect him.

Keefe sighed and closed his eyes, imagining a giant stone wall around his mind.

He poured every last drop of his mental energy into making that barrier as thick and impenetrable as possible—but he knew he wouldn't be able to block her.

No one could.

He'd have to ignore her—which made his chest tighten and his heart turn heavy and cold.

Telepathic chats with Foster were one of his absolute favorite things in the entire world.

Every time her voice filled his head, he couldn't help

smiling—even when she was reaching out to yell at him.

But nothing good would come from talking to her right now.

She wouldn't be able to convince him to come back.

And he'd already said everything he could say in his note.

In fact, he honestly couldn't believe some of the things he'd told her.

His cheeks heated up as he pictured his hastily scribbled confession.

You mean a lot to me, Foster. More than you'll ever know.

Part of him still didn't know why he'd felt the need to add those words.

He just . . . couldn't leave without finally telling her the truth—after keeping it in for so many years.

And yes, this was Foster, so it was possible she'd convince herself he only meant it "as a friend."

She had a gift for taking "oblivious" to adorable new levels.

But Keefe was pretty sure she'd know exactly what he was trying to say.

He just had no idea how she'd react.

Maybe she'd blush.

Maybe she'd cringe.

Maybe she'd laugh so hard, she'd pee through her leggings.

Or maybe she'd crumple the paper and throw it away, hoping he'd stay in Humanland and they'd never have to deal with the mountain of awkward he'd heaped on their friendship.

Or maybe she'd run straight to Fitz and tell him everything—

and Fitzy would get jealous and finally realize what a fool he'd been for letting her go. Then he'd beg for forgiveness—and after lots and lots of groveling, Foster would tell him he'd always been the one who made her heart go pitter-patter.

And Fitzy would tuck her hair behind her ears, and she'd bite her lip as he leaned toward her and—

Keefe didn't try to hide his shudder.

No one was around to call him out on his jealousy—or shame him for sitting back and letting Fitzphie happen. As if he was supposed to shove his way between them screaming, *NO! PICK ME!*

Sophie deserved better than that.

She should get to choose whoever she wanted, without anyone fighting for her like she was the latest prize in the Ultimate Splotching Championship.

And . . . she wanted Fitz.

Keefe knew that for a fact.

That was the brutal little perk that came with being an Empath.

He understood Foster's feelings even better than she did.

Then again, the last few times he'd been around her, her emotions about Fitzy had been . . . different.

A little hurt.

A little sad.

Definitely disappointed.

Even a little angry.

Almost like her crush was starting to fade.

But there had still been plenty of mushy stuff underneath all that. So Keefe was pretty sure it was only a matter of time before Fitzy found a way to fix things.

A few of those sappy gifts he'd gotten so good at giving. An abundance of apologies. And Fitzphie would be back with a vengeance.

Keefe's hands curled into fists at the thought—which was ridiculous!

This whole thought process was ridiculous!

How much time had he just wasted obsessing about his silly unrequited crush?

A whole lot longer than he'd spent trying to figure out how to get through the night without ending up a Keefe-snack for a hungry beast.

And definitely longer than he'd been able to hang with humans before trying to unleash his mind control.

That's what he needed to be focusing on.

Solving *those* problems.

Not this pathetic angst.

Then again . . . thinking about Foster was a *really* good distraction.

The whole time he'd been standing there obsessing about what she might or might not be feeling, he hadn't shivered, or felt the wind picking up, or realized his teeth were chattering.

What if that was the trick to solving the whole human-emotional-overload issue?

Maybe if he kept his mind focused on Foster the next time he was around a bunch of humans, he'd be able to tune out all the other noise that kept messing with his senses and pushing him over the edge.

The plan seemed worth a try—especially since it might be his ticket to a warm bed instead of a snowy mountain campout, trying not to fall out of a tree or get eaten.

But just to be safe, he memorized which facet had brought him there on his pathfinder. That way, he'd have a guaranteed crowd-free escape if Operation Foster Distraction turned out to be an epic fail.

"Wow, am I really doing this?" he asked as he spun the crystal to another random facet.

Seemed like a pretty horrible idea.

But those were kind of his specialty.

And it might just be reckless enough to work.

He took one last calming breath as he held the pathfinder up to the light.

"Here goes nothing," he whispered as the warmth carried him away. "Bring on the Foster-Feels!"

FOUR

THINK ABOUT FOSTER, KEEFE reminded himself as he re-formed somewhere very cold and loud and wet—and a stampede of emotions immediately tried to trample him like a herd of angry stegosauruses.

Think about Foster.

Think about Foster.

But not in a clingy way, he felt the need to clarify. *No reason to make this extra weird.*

He was just a guy thinking about a friend who also happened to be sweet and beautiful and brave and brilliant and a million other things that made her his favorite person ever—you know, so he wouldn't be tempted to unleash his creepy powers all over a bunch of innocent people.

A sad laugh bubbled up his throat, and he choked it back in case any commands tried to sneak out with it.

Think about Foster.

Think about Foster.

Think about Foster.

She'd probably know where he was, since the big greenish-blue tower and enormous waterfalls in the distance seemed like pretty significant landmarks. A huge crowd wearing bright blue capelike covers over their clothes had gathered to ooh and aah at the magnitude of it all—or that's what Keefe assumed they were doing.

He couldn't hear anything over the roar of the falling water.

But a buzzy sense of awe hung heavy in the air, thicker than the mist drenching everything.

He could also feel a twitchy sort of impatience, as if everyone was waiting for something to happen.

And plenty of stinging annoyance—probably because the howling wind did *not* feel good with everything all soggy and shivery.

There was also a hint of fluttery nervousness that made his stomach a little squirmy.

And—

That's not thinking about Foster!

Keefe shook his damp hair out of his eyes and took a slow, steadying breath.

Okay. If Foster were here, she'd probably say we should figure out why everyone's wearing those ugly blue things.

Maybe to keep their clothes dry?

If that's what it was, it didn't look like the covers were working.

His gaze shifted to the soaked crowd, and his head started spinning, spinning, spinning.

So many people.

So many feelings.

So much mist and wind and noise.

It was too much.

He—

Nope!

Clearly, thinking of Foster in terms of "if" and "probably" wasn't going to be enough.

If he wanted Operation Foster Distraction to work, he needed to go full delusional-daydream mode.

So he took another long breath and pictured Foster standing right beside him with a shy smile.

Her hair whipped against her cheeks, and she reached up and tucked it behind her ears before offering him her hand.

"Hold on to me," she shouted over the thundering water. *"We don't want to get separated."*

Keefe focused on his palm, imagining how warm and soft her fingers would feel as they twined around his—and rolled his eyes when his heart skipped the next few beats.

This was definitely a new level of pathetic.

But . . . it actually seemed to be helping!

The more he made himself believe that Foster was right there with him, the easier it was to tune out everything else.

He pictured the way her cape would stick to her arms—just like his soaked tunic was now suctioned against his shoulders—and imagined her reaching up with her free hand and tugging gently on her eyelashes.

She always did that when she was nervous—though sometimes she'd try to stop herself, so no one could tell what she was feeling.

But Keefe *always* knew.

That was one of the things that had caught his attention the first time he'd met her.

He'd been hanging out in his favorite ditching spot when a hurricane of panic came blasting down the corridor, followed by a prodigy he'd never seen before—and he couldn't decide which was cooler: being able to feel her emotions without needing contact, or getting a chance to meet the mysterious new girl.

He'd been the president of the Foster Fan Club ever since.

And maybe someday . . .

He didn't let himself finish the thought. But hope still swelled in his chest, drowning out every other sensation—which was super ridiculous, but also kind of a win.

Keep it up! Keefe told himself as the crowd shuffled forward. *Think about Foster!*

He tried to see where everyone was going—but widening his gaze made him too aware of reality. So he narrowed his focus to his hand and imagined Foster pulling him along, telling him, *"Let's go this way."*

The crowd grew thicker as they walked, and everyone seemed to be following each other.

"We should figure out where to get one of those blue covers," Foster suggested. *"You need to blend in."*

Keefe risked a glance around, trying to see if there was a booth or a store selling them—but he couldn't see past the crowd.

He did notice a group that looked like they were mostly his age, though—and several of them had their blue covers draped over their shoulders instead of actually wearing them. So he caught up and matched their pace, trying to look like he belonged.

Just keep your head down and don't draw any attention.

Seemed easy enough—until he slipped on a puddle and almost face-planted into a lamppost.

Keefe's cheeks burned, and he imagined Foster cracking up—though after all the times he'd teased her for being clumsy, he totally deserved it.

Watch your step.

At this point he couldn't tell if the voice in his head was his or Foster's—but that was perfect.

Bring on the delusions!

He imagined draping an arm around her shoulders—to help his balance, of course—as he tried to figure out where he was going. But it was hard to piece together the scene from scattered glances.

He knew there was a metal railing lining the path. And a river on one side of him. And a crowd that kept getting bigger and bigger and bigger.

"Don't think about them," Foster's voice ordered. *"Look at the sky. See how bright it is?"*

Even with the thick gray clouds blocking the sun, Keefe could tell it was much earlier in the day than in the forest he'd just left—which felt super weird.

He'd forgotten that humans hadn't figured out how to get all their cities on the same time zone.

"You'll get used to it," Foster promised.

Keefe doubted that. But maybe—

He tripped again, this time over someone's feet.

Their irritation scraped across his senses as he stumbled back and grabbed the rail to keep his balance.

He hadn't realized the crowd had stopped moving.

Or that they'd formed into a line.

"We need to figure out what they're waiting for," Foster told him.

All he could find was a sign that said MAID OF THE MIST, which didn't make a whole lot of sense.

Was that what one of the waterfalls was called?

Seemed like a strange name—but humans did have a ton of

bizarre myths and legends, so maybe they believed some sort of magical maiden lived in the water.

His mind flashed to an image he'd seen somewhere—a human drawing of a red-haired girl with a green fish tail—and he wished he could ask Foster if that's really what humans thought mermaids looked like.

But she *wasn't* there—and as soon as he thought those words, reality came crashing down harder than the falling water.

Emotions battered him from every angle, making his head throb and his stomach churn as his throat closed off with a searing new command.

NO!

THINK ABOUT FOSTER!

Keefe closed his eyes and pictured her face, letting his photographic memory fill in every tiny detail.

Every glint of gold in her eyes.

Every warm shade of brown.

He'd had to draw Foster a few times—part of his whole "recording his memories" project, trying to find what his mom had hidden from him.

But he'd never been able to capture the depth of her stare.

Her eyes radiated too much power.

And wonder.

And intensity.

They truly were breathtaking.

So was she—but she had absolutely no idea.

Keefe understood *why*.

She'd grown up with her head filled with the thoughts of a bunch of jealous kids who hated her for being different. And all those insults felt true over time.

That's why Keefe wished he could punch the Black Swan for what they'd put her through.

Leaving her alone in a world where she'd never belong, giving her powers she couldn't understand or control, and letting her believe it was her fault that she didn't fit in.

Sure, they'd put her with a family who cared about her—but they also knew that family would be ripped away, and she'd have to leave everything behind and start over in a place where nothing made sense and tons of people wanted to kill her.

And then they expected her to save everyone.

Fix several millennia's worth of problems without any actual plan for how to do it.

Made her risk her life over and over and over.

The crowd moved forward, and Keefe kept his eyes on his feet as he followed, trying to count how many times Foster had almost died, to keep himself distracted.

She'd been kidnapped.

Attacked with Silveny outside the Black Swan's hideout.

And who could forget the freezing battle on Mount Everest, when he'd first found out Mommy Dearest was behind everything?

Then King Dimitar had tried to kill them in Ravagog.

And Fintan and Brant made the castle in Lumenaria crumble around her.

And his mom tried to drown everyone in Atlantis.

He didn't want to think about Umber's attack, or how long Foster was stuck in the Healing Center battling those horrible echoes.

Then they had to battle a small army of bloodthirsty mutant newborn trolls.

And then of course there was all the creepy stuff that happened in Loamnore.

None of that counted the times her allergy had almost taken her out.

Or when the Black Swan made her reset her abilities.

Honestly, those last few made Keefe angrier than anything the Neverseen had done.

Sure, his mom and her black-cloaked minions were cruel and evil—but at least everyone agreed they were the villains.

The Black Swan were supposed to be the heroes.

Everyone was expected to trust them and follow their orders—even though they mostly wanted everyone to sit back and read a bunch of boring books while the Neverseen ran wild.

Keefe wondered how Forkle and crew felt about Foster's little firestorm at the Neverseen's storehouse.

Were they celebrating, like they should be?

Or lecturing her for being too reckless?

Probably both.

And if he was right, he hoped Foster stood up for herself and told them exactly why she—

A voice snapped him back to the present, and it took his brain a second to piece together that someone was talking to him.

A human.

Keefe looked up and realized he was about to cross through some sort of narrow structure—but the path was blocked by a guy in a dark blue shirt.

The guy's skin was all droopy and wrinkly, and he had big, bushy white eyebrows and a shiny bald head—and if Keefe hadn't had his jaw clenched so tight, he probably would've blurted out, *Whoa, I forgot how weird humans look when they get old!*

So maybe it was better that he was fighting back a command.

Then again, the guy had clearly asked him a question, and Keefe had no way to respond—and nowhere to go.

The crowd had pressed in behind him, and there were metal rails closing in both sides of his path.

If Foster was there—

WAIT, NO "IF"—KEEP UP THE DAYDREAM!

But Keefe couldn't picture her anymore.

His brain was racing in too many different directions, most of which wanted him to leap over those rails and *RUN, RUN, RUN!*

At least his panic seemed to drown out the other emotions.

All he could feel was his racing heart and his shaky breaths.

All he could hear was his pounding pulse—and a few garbled words that sounded like "ticket" and "poncho."

And yes, he could grab his pathfinder and leap away—create the kind of spectacle that would turn him into a human legend and make it way easier for his mom to pick up his trail.

But if this plan was ever going to work, he *had* to find a way to actually interact with people.

So he forced himself to make eye contact and slowly cupped one of his hands around his ear, hoping the old guy would take that to mean, "Uh, didn't hear what you said."

The guy nodded and said something that got drowned out by a particularly loud gust of wind—then pointed to the group Keefe had been trying to blend in with and shouted, "ARE YOU WITH THEM?"

The group was now crossing some sort of ramp—and they all had their blue coverings on.

Keefe chewed his lip.

Lying probably wasn't a smart idea—but the only other option was fleeing. So he gave a quick nod and held his breath.

The guy studied him for a long second. Then shrugged. "BETTER HURRY! WE'RE ABOUT TO TAKE OFF."

Keefe had no idea what that meant. But the guy moved aside to let him pass, so he rushed to catch up with the others.

The moment he stepped onto the ramp, he regretted all his life choices.

The floor dipped under his feet, and he recognized the sensation much too well.

A boat.

He'd boarded a boat.

A HUMAN boat.

Weren't there a bunch of those at the bottom of the ocean???

"Welcome to the Maid of the Mist," a voice blared from some sort of hidden speakers.

Keefe spun around, but the old guy had blocked off the path.

It's fine.

It's a totally sturdy boat.

Heading toward three giant waterfalls . . .

"Welcome to the Maid of the Mist," the voice repeated.

Relax, Keefe told himself. *Feel how excited everyone is?*

The nervousness he'd picked up earlier had vanished, replaced with an almost audible hum of anticipation.

Would people be feeling like that if they were worried about drowning?

Probably not.

But they also trusted their technology way more than he did.

Plus, they probably didn't get seasick. . . .

His stomach squirmed and soured as he remembered his miserable journey in Lady Cadence's weird houseboat contraption.

He'd ended up collapsed on the deck in a shaky, sweaty Keefe-ball—and that was after he'd choked down a bilepod.

How was he supposed to survive without even a basic nausea elixir?

A horn blared as the boat lurched forward, and Keefe barely managed to grab one of the rails before toppling over.

No way was he letting go—even to reach for his pathfinder.

"Please keep your hands and arms inside at all times," the voice told him.

Keefe tightened his grip.

The boat steered toward the falls, and the mist thickened into a downpour.

This wasn't going to end well.

FIVE

HE GOOD NEWS WAS, KEEFE survived—and he only barfed once before the boat lurched back to the dock and he could release his death grip on the railing long enough to leap back to the nice, solid mountain.

Okay, fine, he barfed twice.

Well . . . three times, if he counted the little bit he accidentally swallowed before he burped it up again—but he was trying very hard not to think about that.

Just like he was trying super hard not to think about the bad news . . .

Operation Foster Distraction had turned out to be an epic fail.

Yeah, he'd made it through the unexpected river adventure without unleashing any commands on unsuspecting humans— but he'd also accidentally ended up on a crowded boat, weaving around enormous waterfalls and getting so drenched that his boots were now *squish, squish, squish*ing with every step.

Clearly, thinking about Foster only worked when he ignored everything else. And how was he supposed to function— or accomplish anything he needed to—if he had to wander around completely oblivious to the rest of the world?

Plus, it probably wasn't going to help his sanity if he spent all his time hanging out with an Imaginary Sophie.

I'll find another way, he promised, even though he mostly wanted to bury himself in pine needles and sulk at the stars.

Didn't help that his head was now filled with a constant chorus of *KEEFE! KEEFE! KEEFE!*

It started a few seconds after he reappeared on the mountain, and the call was so loud, he'd whipped around, expecting to find Silveny soaring through the sky.

But there was no sign of his favorite sparkly alicorn.

He hadn't realized Silveny could transmit to him—and for a second he'd been tempted to let her past his blocking to make sure Foster wasn't in trouble.

Then he'd realized the calls didn't feel frantic enough.

They felt annoyed and concerned, as if Silveny was planning to lecture him like an overprotective mama—and he didn't have the energy for that.

So he ignored her.

Well, he was trying to.

Silveny was *not* making it easy.

Even the twins had joined in, rattling his brain with their high-pitched shrieks of *KEEFE! KEEFE! KEEFE!*

Part of him wanted to smile.

Another part wanted to cover his ears and bang his head against the nearest tree.

And a teeny, tiny part he wasn't proud of couldn't help wondering why he was hearing from Silveny instead of Foster.

Did she sic the alicorns on him to make him worry that something bad had happened?

Or was she too furious to talk to him?

Or worse—too embarrassed after reading his note?

Or maybe she was with Fitz, and they were too busy getting back together for her to bother with—

"Stop it!" he told himself, shutting down those thoughts before they could spin out of control. "No more thinking about Foster."

He'd already learned the hard way that it didn't help—and now he was alone on a dark mountain in the middle of nowhere with no idea how to get through the night without turning into a Keefe-sicle.

The air was cold enough for him to see little clouds of his breath—which felt extra awesome in soaking-wet clothes. And he could hear way too much rustling and scurrying—plus some ominous howling in the distance.

The trees also looked a whole lot shakier now that he was staring down the reality of trying to sleep while balancing on their branches.

"Why does the pathfinder even go to this place?" he grumbled, kicking the frosty ground with his soggy boot.

It was a restricted blue-crystal pathfinder issued to his father by the Council for official assignments in the Forbidden Cities. Shouldn't that mean the facets went to places in the human world that were actually important?

Unless there was something special about the mountain and he just hadn't noticed it yet . . .

He turned in a slow circle, but he couldn't see very far in the dark.

Maybe if he explored a little, he'd find something useful— preferably a nice, warm house with an extra-fluffy bed, a kitchen full of amazing food, and a huge sign that said WELCOME, GUESTS!

Though Keefe would've settled for an abandoned shack.

Or an empty cave.

He hugged his arms to his chest, but all it did was press his cold, wet clothes against his skin. And the *squish, squish, squish* of his boots sounded a whole lot louder as he trudged down the icy slope.

Every time a branch cracked, he braced for a rabid beast to tackle him.

Nothing did.

In fact, the hike was miserable—but relatively uneventful.

No creatures.

No landmarks.

Just freezing wind and a whole lot of trees.

And more trees.

And oh, hey, look—more trees!

And over there, who would've guessed it?

EVEN MORE TREES!

And up ahead?

Wait.

Keefe skidded to a stop, huffing out a huge cloud of breath.

It was possible the shadows were playing tricks on him, but . . .

It almost looked like there was a small stone structure hidden by the branches.

He tiptoed closer and . . .

A cabin!

He'd found a cabin!

A very dark, very quiet cabin—though whether that was because no one was home or because whoever lived there was currently asleep was impossible to tell.

Thick curtains covered the small front windows, and the door was shut tight.

But when Keefe closed his eyes and searched for nearby emotions, all he felt was his own silly hope that he'd actually found somewhere warm!

And when he crept over to the door and pressed his ear against the wood . . .

Silence.

So . . .

Now what?

He was pretty sure there were human laws against entering a house he didn't own without permission—and if someone *was* there, they'd totally wake up and freak out.

But what was he supposed to do?

Knock?

Stare at anyone who answered with his sad, desperate eyes and hope they decide to invite in the strange, non-talking guy who kept rubbing his temples because he couldn't block a bunch of obnoxious alicorn transmissions?

If he could at least use his voice, he'd tell them . . .

Actually, he wasn't sure what kind of story would motivate a human to invite him into their home in the middle of the night.

Stranger Danger was a much bigger thing in the Forbidden Cities.

And he probably looked extra suspicious in his elvin clothes.

Sure, it was just a plain blue tunic and basic gray pants—but to human eyes, they'd still look a little off.

But none of that would matter if the cabin was empty.

Only one way to find out.

He stared at the door, needing several deep breaths before he raised his arm and gave a quick knock.

The sound was barely audible—but it still made him jump.

It'll be fine. I can handle this.

He repeated the pep talk as he waited.

And waited.

And waited some more.

Another long minute passed—which could mean the place was empty.

Or it could mean his pathetic knock wasn't loud enough to wake whoever lived there. . . .

Keefe sighed and rubbed his hands together, trying to generate a little warmth before he forced himself to knock louder.

Silence stretched on again, and he cleared his throat and croaked out a raspy "Hello?"

Maybe the fact that he could use his voice without any struggle proved his senses knew there was no one around to hear him.

Or maybe he was just getting desperate.

The temperature kept dropping, and he swore he could feel ice crystals forming in his hair.

"Anyone here?" he tried again as he wiggled his toes, hoping to regain some feeling.

No response.

No footsteps.

No sound of any kind.

"I guess no one's home."

Somehow saying it out loud made it feel more like a fact.

Keefe reached for the door—then paused with his fingers just above the polished brass doorknob.

What if it was locked?

It probably was.

Humans were known for being super private.

And even though he couldn't stop shivering, he also couldn't justify breaking a window to get in.

But what if the cabin *wasn't* locked?

Seemed worth checking.

Then again . . . was he really going to walk into a strange house, kick off his shoes, hang his clothes to dry, and crawl into bed?

YES, his freezing brain shouted. *It would just be for one night—and if I try not to touch very much and I clean up before I leave, they probably won't even know I was here!*

Though it'd be kind of weird if they didn't know he'd stopped by . . . wouldn't it?

Seemed like he should at least leave a note to thank them or something.

> *Sorry for letting myself in! Don't worry, I didn't*
> *steal any of your stuff!*
> *—Random Dude Who Slept in Your House*

Okay, yeah.

Probably not the best idea.

But there had to be something he could do to make amends for invading their privacy.

He stood a little taller when he remembered he'd filled his backpack with some of his mom's jewelry.

He was planning to sell it so he'd have money to buy food and stuff—but he took a *bunch*, so he could definitely spare a piece.

Whoever owned the house would probably still think it was odd to find a necklace on their table along with a vague note saying, *Thanks!*—but Keefe had a feeling they'd get over it once they saw the sparkly jewels.

Plus, a fresh round of howls was echoing through the dark—and they sounded much closer.

"Okay," Keefe decided, blowing out another huge cloud of breath as he hitched his backpack farther up his shoulders. "One night here, and then I'll figure out a new plan in the morning."

He turned the doorknob before he could change his mind.

SIX

"HELLO?" KEEFE CALLED, SURPRISED his voice sounded so steady.

He was even more surprised that the cabin really was unlocked.

The doorknob had stopped midturn, and he'd thought that was the end of it—but then he'd heard a soft *click*, and the door creaked open.

He leaned his head inside. "Um . . . I hope it's okay if I come in. It's really cold out here—and I think I just heard a bunch of yetis howling."

He wanted to smack himself when he remembered that humans thought yetis were imaginary.

Great.

Why couldn't he have said "wolves"?

"Um, what I meant was—AHHHHHHHHHHHHHHH-HHHHH!"

Bright lights flooded the room, and Keefe scrambled to shield his eyes.

When his vision adjusted, he expected to find an angry human aiming some sort of weapon at his head.

But the cabin was empty.

He must've triggered a motion sensor and turned on the giant silver chandelier.

He collapsed against the doorframe, waiting for his heart to feel a little less like exploding.

"At least it's safe to say no one's here," he mumbled.

His scream could've woken a sleeping gulon.

In fact, he wouldn't have been surprised if Silveny heard it all the way back at Havenfield.

Plus, he could see the cabin clearly now, and it looked like no one had been there for a while. Everything was dusty, and the air had a stale smell, like the windows hadn't been opened in months.

Hopefully that meant no one would be showing up while he was crashing there.

"Okay," Keefe said as the door swung shut and the full warmth of the cabin enveloped him. "I guess this is home for the night. Who knew it'd be so . . . fancy?"

He'd been expecting rugged wood furniture and a couple

of tacky knickknacks. Not sleek glass tables and pristine white armchairs, white woven rugs, and giant silver vases filled with carefully arranged branches.

Even the shoes by the door weren't hiking boots.

They were carefully arranged on a shiny metal rack and looked like the kind of shoes a guy would wear with dressy clothes.

And the cabin was much bigger on the inside.

From the front, it looked like it was just a tiny, single room. But the space stretched toward a huge wall of windows overlooking a moonlit lake. There was also a staircase in one of the corners, which led up to a loft tucked under the wood-beamed eaves.

But no sign of a kitchen.

His stomach gurgled in frustration.

"There must be snacks in here somewhere," he said, wishing he'd thought to pack at least a little food before he'd left. "Whoever owns this place has to eat, right?"

Actually, it seemed like the guy mostly went there to paint.

Easels and stools were set up against the wall of windows, and there was a row of silver shelves filled with bins of brushes and paint tubes and stacks of blank canvases in all different sizes.

Keefe set his backpack on the floor and kicked off his wet boots so he wouldn't get mud on the rugs as he made his way over to one of the paintings-in-progress—a half-finished landscape of the lake at sunrise.

It was actually pretty good.

A weird style, where the brushstrokes were thick and blobby, but somehow that captured the light perfectly. Keefe could almost feel the early rays of sunshine dancing across the mirrored surface of the water.

"Cass," he murmured, reading the signature at the bottom of one of the finished canvases stacked underneath the easel— a snowy scene of the same lake. "Well . . . thanks for letting me stay here, Cass. I promise I won't mess anything up."

He probably should've been embarrassed by how much he was talking to himself, but it wasn't like anyone could hear him.

And it was awesome to have his voice come so easily.

He *almost* felt normal.

His head was even blissfully quiet.

Silveny's transmissions had stopped, so either she gave up on him, or she was rallying for another assault.

He couldn't decide which would be worse.

"All right," he said, running his fingers through his wet hair, trying to shape it back into his carefully mussed style. "Time to focus."

He was still drenched and starving and exhausted, and finding food seemed like the easiest problem to tackle—even if it felt kinda wrong to poke around Cass's cabinets.

Was it stealing if he ate the food he found?

His stomach unleashed a particularly desperate growl.

"I'll leave *two* pieces of jewelry," he promised as he turned to study the room, noting that Cass hadn't hung any of his paintings.

The only decorations on the walls were gleaming silver mirrors, so maybe he didn't think any of his paintings were good enough yet.

Or he preferred looking at himself.

"So, if I were Cass," Keefe said, trying to see the cabin through new eyes, "I'd probably keep my food in . . . *there*."

He made his way over to a large silver cabinet and carefully opened the mirrored doors.

"No, apparently I'd use this to store a bunch of boring books."

Most of them were about Impressionism—whatever that was. But there were also several shelves full of sketchbooks, each with a different year written on the spine.

"Huh, I guess Cass is an old dude."

There had to be at least sixty years' worth of sketchbooks, along with several still-sealed books waiting for Cass to fill them.

Keefe couldn't resist taking a peek at one of the older ones. "Wow, he *really* likes this lake."

He'd drawn it in pencil.

And ink.

And watercolor.

And charcoal.

And pastel.

The next sketchbook was more of the same.

So was the next one.

And the one after that.

The art improved from book to book, so clearly the practice was paying off. But Cass had spent a *lot* of time drawing the same place—which felt like a strange decision, since humans only lived about eighty years.

Keefe would've thought he'd want to cram in as many new experiences as possible, not repeat the same thing over and over.

But maybe having limited time made him really want to focus.

And, boy, did he focus.

Keefe flipped through a few more sketchbooks, and it was all lake, lake, and more lake.

Meanwhile, his insides were clenching into a tiny, crampy ball.

"Okay, I get it—enough with the sketchbooks," he told his stomach, reaching what was probably a new low in the Talking to Himself department. "There has to be a snack stash *somewhere*."

He headed toward the stairs, hoping the loft was a giant pantry—or maybe a closet with some dry clothes, even though it felt weird borrowing them without permission.

"I'm leaving him *two* pieces of jewelry," Keefe reminded himself. "And I'll leave the clothes folded next to the note. Plus, I'll try to pick something ugly that he probably never wears anyway."

Seemed like a fair enough trade—not that it really mattered, since all he found in the loft was a bed.

A gigantic, amazing bed with a soft white comforter and a mountain of fluffy pillows that made him want to forget the whole food quest and burrow straight under the covers.

But his stomach gave a sloshy, gurgley rumble that almost sounded like a threat.

He'd also spotted a nightstand tucked into the corner, with three drawers that seemed worth checking.

"Oh wow. More sketchbooks," Keefe groaned as he opened the top drawer. "Bet that means I can guess what's in here."

He grabbed the middle drawer's handle and . . .

"HANG ON—I THINK WE HAVE SOME FOOD!"

It was hard to tell.

Both of the bags had drawings of little tube-shaped things that looked kind of edible—so that seemed promising. And they were called Cheetos, which sorta sounded food-ish.

But they also had a drawing of a cheetah wearing sunglasses, so who knew what kind of madness he was about to experience.

If Foster were there, she'd be able to tell him if he should try the Flamin' Hots or the Puffs—but he was going to have to figure this one out on his own. And since the Flamin' Hots had little flames on the bag, the Puffs seemed like the safer bet.

"Remember, I'm leaving sparkly jewels to pay him back," Keefe said as he wrestled with the crinkly package. "Sparkles make everything better, right?"

It took more strength than he expected to pry the top seam apart, and a soft *hissssssssss* unleashed a plume that smelled way too much like feet.

"Not the best start to the whole Cheetos experience—and wow, these things are *orange!*"

The bright powder stuck to his fingers as he grabbed one and gave it a quick sniff.

His stomach growled.

"Okay, stomach, I'm trusting you," he said as he popped it into his mouth. "Huh."

He couldn't think of a better response.

It looked like a giant caterpillar and tasted salty and sharp—kind of like cheese, but way drier and tangier and crunchier.

He munched on another and shrugged.

"No idea what I'm eating—but it's good."

He polished off the whole bag in a couple of minutes. Even licked the Cheeto dust off his fingers. Then he stared at the Flamin' Hots, trying to figure out how brave he felt.

"I think I'll save that adventure for tomorrow."

The nightstand still had one more drawer he hadn't checked, and he was hoping that's where Cass kept the desserts—preferably some of those Ding Dongs he'd been dying to try, because how could anyone not love a food called a Ding Dong?

Sadly, all he found was more sketchbooks.

"Okay, Cass—you *might* need to get another hobby."

He was about to slam the drawer when he spotted a silver

zipped pouch at the bottom. And when he peeked inside . . .

"Whoa. That's a lot of human money."

The stack had to be at least an inch thick—and the bills were all different colors, so it was probably a mix of different human currencies.

There was also a small rectangle with a string of numbers printed on it, along with the name CASS LORDEMAN—probably Cass's way of saying, *Back off, this money's mine!*

Keefe set the card aside and counted the bills, telling himself he was just trying to get familiar with the different denominations.

After all, he needed to know how to count human money if he was going to use it, right?

But the more he flipped through the stack, the more he couldn't help wondering . . .

Exactly how bad would it be if I took a little bit with me?

He could leave a *third* piece of jewelry—surely that'd be worth more than the tiny amount of cash he'd be taking.

He definitely wouldn't take it all.

Just . . . *enough.*

But when he imagined stuffing the bills in his pocket, his insides turned twisty and sour.

"I already ate the guy's Cheetos," Keefe mumbled. "And I'm about to sleep in his bed."

It sure would've been nice to have some money, though. . . .

He was going to need to buy more food.

And human clothes.

And he still had no idea how to be around humans for more than a few minutes—much less how to find someone who bought jewelry and negotiate a fair sale.

And that would only get him one kind of money.

He'd probably need more, since he'd be moving around a bunch.

Keefe sighed. "Why is doing the right thing sometimes the worst?"

The cabin had no answer.

But he stuffed the money back inside the pouch—along with the weird card—and dropped it back into the drawer so he wouldn't be tempted.

He even piled the sketchbooks on top of it to make it harder to find.

"It's better this way," he told himself. "I'll . . ."

His voice trailed off as he noticed a word on the cover of one of the sketchbooks.

Portraits.

"So Cass *does* draw other stuff!"

Maybe he'd get to see what Cass looked like.

Keefe had been picturing a pale, wrinkly guy with wild gray hair—but when he skimmed the sketchbook, the portraits were all of a much younger, very stuffy-looking blond man.

And they were annoyingly artsy.

The face was always turned away or obscured by hands or clothing.

He'd also done some portraits of a woman, but he'd drawn her from behind and focused all the detail on her tight, intricate updo.

And he'd drawn a teenager looking down, with his features hidden in smudgy shadows.

"Guess he doesn't like drawing faces," Keefe said, flipping to another sketch of the teenager. "I get it. But . . ."

He frowned.

Something about the teenager's hair looked . . . *familiar.*

Messy in a very specific way.

But that had to be a bizarre coincidence.

Except . . .

Now that he was thinking about it, the updo the woman was wearing was the same style his mom usually wore.

And the blond guy had his father's short, rigidly styled hair.

"Cass Lordeman," Keefe said as the book slipped from his hands.

It could be a real human name, of course.

But.

It could also be a pseudonym, referencing his *real* name.

Lord Cassius.

SEVEN

BUT . . . MY FATHER HATES ART."

Keefe let the words hang there, hoping they'd block out the other evidence.

But now that he knew what to look for, there was no way he could call it a coincidence.

The faceless blond guy in the portraits had his father's stiff posture.

And the cabin's fancy decorating was totally the same stuffy style as his father's other houses.

Keefe had also found the place by using his father's pathfinder.

It even explained why there was so little food and so many different kinds of human money.

Plus, that name.

Cass Lordeman.

It almost seemed *too* obvious.

A laugh lodged in Keefe's throat—bitter and cold.

After all the lectures he'd had to sit through about how pointless art was, and how he needed to focus on his studies.

All the drawings his father had crumpled up and thrown away.

All of that, and the whole time his father was sneaking away to paint a boring lake over and over and over—for *decades*.

He tried to picture his father sitting by one of those easels, dabbing little blobs of color onto the canvas while munching on Cheetos.

Calling himself *Cass*.

It just . . . didn't make any sense.

Why hide a love of art?

Why punish his son for sharing that interest?

Actually, no—he didn't want to know.

He'd given up trying to understand his father forever ago.

He'd given up trying to understand either of his parents.

The only things he needed to know were that they were horrible people and brilliant liars.

And he was done with them.

He jumped to his feet, not sure if he wanted to grab his stuff and flee—or trash the place.

Ro would definitely vote for All the Smashing!

Especially the giant mirrors and vases.

But . . . that sounded super exhausting.

And leaving sounded even worse.

It was still dark and cold outside—and his clothes were still soaked.

He also still had no idea how to be around humans without risking an interspeciesial incident.

The smartest move would be to get a good night's sleep in the amazing-looking bed and spend the morning working out a plan for where to go next.

"At least I don't have to worry about keeping the place clean anymore," Keefe reminded himself. "In fact . . ."

He yanked open the bottom nightstand drawer and snatched the pouch of money.

"Don't need to feel bad about taking stuff either—and I'm not leaving any jewelry!" he told the empty room. "And let's see. . . ."

Now he could snoop around as much as he wanted—and there had to be human clothes stashed somewhere.

His father would want to blend in when he went to buy art supplies and Cheetos—and he wouldn't risk being seen in the Lost Cities in anything remotely human.

Keefe peeked under the bed.

"Ha—thought so."

He hauled out two stacks of neatly folded shirts and pants and a pair of white lace-up shoes, which looked way more comfortable than the dressy shoes downstairs.

"Let's hope this one's your favorite," he said as he pulled on a pale blue sweater made from some sort of ridiculously soft fabric.

Keefe was sure every piece of clothing had been super expensive by human standards.

That's how Lord Pretentiouspants rolled.

Only the best of everything—as long as it was for himself.

The jeans had clearly been custom-tailored—which meant they were a little loose and a little long, but Keefe could make them work. And the check-mark symbol on the shoes probably meant they were rare somehow.

"Huh. Very springy." He bounced on the balls of his feet. "I feel like I should be playing a human sport in these."

He glanced in the mirror and frowned.

"Ugh, I look like him." He messed up his hair even more, which didn't really help. "Whatever. I also look way more human, and that's what matters—and you can keep my soggy laundry!"

He kicked his wet clothes into the corner. It wasn't like he was going to need anything elvin.

He'd use his father's cash stash to buy some better stuff as soon as he got a chance. But just in case that took a while, he brought the rest of the clothes downstairs to see how much he could squeeze into his backpack.

"Okay . . . what else?"

He grabbed one of the sealed blank sketchbooks and a pen, since it'd probably be smart to keep notes on anything he learned during his investigations.

"Lesson number one," he said as he flipped to the first page and wrote, *My father is the World's Most Boring Artist.*

He added a quick sketch of the lake his father was obsessed with to prove his point—and honestly?

His drawing was way better than anything his father had done.

Was *that* why he was always trying to stop him from making art?

Keefe wouldn't be surprised if his father was jealous of him.

But it was probably better not to think about it.

He shut the sketchbook and stared at the blank cover, wondering if he should give it a title.

Important Discoveries.

He crossed that out as soon as he wrote it, since it was almost as boring as his father's lake drawings.

The Astonishing Revelations of a Breathtakingly Handsome Genius?

He crossed that out too.

He'd dealt with enough unrealistic expectations in his life— no need to dump a bunch more on himself.

Musings and Other General Shenanigans.

Eh.

Not horrible, but he could do better.

He scratched that out, wondering if he should start over with a fresh sketchbook since the cover was now a total mess.

But that actually seemed fitting for a book chronicling his

chaotic time in the human world—and suddenly he knew exactly what to call it.

Adventures in Humanland.

He underlined it for emphasis—then turned the lines into little shooting stars, because why not?

And while he was being fancy, he turned the dot over the *i* into another star and doodled a quick little globe off to one side.

"It's a start," he told himself as he shoved the sketchbook into his backpack, followed by the money pouch and most of the human clothes. "Actually, this worked out pretty well."

He could've spun the pathfinder to any of the other zillions of facets. But he'd ended up in the one place where it was totally okay for him to grab anything he wanted.

Maybe that was proof that things were about to get a little easier.

He doubted it—but it was nice to have a tiny bit of hope.

Keefe took another long look around the cabin to make sure he hadn't missed anything useful before he kicked off his new shoes, switched off the chandelier, and headed back upstairs.

The bed was even softer than it looked.

In fact, it might've been the most comfortable bed he'd ever lain on.

But . . . he couldn't sleep.

Don't think, he told his brain—but it only made his thoughts spiral faster, dredging up memories of his father shredding his sketchbooks and shouting about wasted potential.

He tossed and turned and tossed some more before he finally gave up and went back downstairs, staring at the canvases in the fading moonlight.

It didn't make a whole lot of sense, but . . .

"I need to finish one."

He grabbed a handful of paint tubes, a palette, and a couple of brushes and sat on the stool in front of the painting with the lake at sunrise.

He didn't bother trying to emulate his father's blotchy style, so the final piece looked incredibly disconnected.

But that was fitting.

And his sections were way better.

He signed *The Keefster* at the bottom.

"All right. That's . . . done. Time to sleep."

But his legs didn't want to stand.

He sighed and grabbed the finished painting of the snowy lake, smeared a layer of white on top of it to give him a blank space, and painted a quick self-portrait.

He didn't need to look in a mirror.

His photographic memory knew what to draw.

But he still checked his reflection in the dark windows and made a few tweaks to the expression.

His portrait stared straight forward—no hiding his features like his father's drawings of him. And he'd planned to make himself look defiant, but . . .

He looked sad.

And lost.

It was the Keefe he tried hard not to let his father see, because it was easier to act like nothing mattered.

But maybe it was time to stop letting his father off the hook.

Maybe Daddy Dearest should have to face the mess he'd created.

So Keefe didn't paint over it.

He even signed it *Your son*.

"Whoa, when did I start crying?" he asked, swiping the tears away with the backs of his shaking hands.

At this rate he was going to need to re-title his sketchbook *The Slow Unraveling of a Boy with Awesome Hair*.

The joke wasn't great—but it still gave him a small smile.

Humor always helped.

"Aaaaaaaaaaaaaaaaaaaaaaaaaaaaand—that's enough of that," he said, setting the paints and brushes aside. "This might be the last night I get to sleep in a bed for a while. I'm not going to waste it."

But as soon as he lay down again, his brain went back to spinning, spinning, spinning.

And no matter how hard he tried to block it, his deepest, darkest worry rose to the surface.

The question he could never joke away because he was too afraid of the answer.

What if he was too broken to fix himself?

Was that why no one cared about him?

Not no one, the tiny rational part of his brain reminded him.

Your friends care.

Foster cares.

And almost like his desperation drew her to him, her soft, sweet voice whispered through his mind.

Please be safe, Keefe. Please be smart. And please come back as soon as you can.

Keefe let out a long, slow breath.

She still cares.

She even wanted him to come home—even though he ran away *again*.

Even after his gigantic, potentially humiliating confession.

It made him want to shout, *I'M A MESS, FOSTER— PLEASE COME SAVE ME!!!*

But she had enough pressure dumped on her shoulders and enough people waiting for her to save them.

He was going to have to save himself this time.

EIGHT

I'M NOT STALLING," KEEFE TOLD THE TREES and birds and anything else willing to listen to him. "I'm *not*."

He wasn't!

He'd *needed* to sleep in after such an exhausting day and weirdly emotional night.

And then he'd woken up starving, so of course he *needed* to devour the entire bag of Flamin' Hot Cheetos—and then *needed* to run around flailing until his mouth wasn't a fiery inferno of doom.

Those things were *hot*.

Also, bizarrely delicious—and he already wanted more.

But seriously, *HOT*.

And then he'd hiked to his father's precious lake because he *needed* to see if there was something special about it.

Spoiler alert: There wasn't.

Now he was still hiking, hoping the fresh air would clear his head because he *needed* to come up with a plan for how to be around people without freaking out or ending up trapped in another boating nightmare.

So, really, he wasn't stalling!

He was waiting for inspiration!

And, boy, was inspiration taking its sweet time to show up.

His current best idea was to plug his ears and walk around screaming, *LA LA LA LA LA LA LA I CAN'T HEAR YOU!*

Which, you know, wouldn't even work, since emotions weren't heard—they were felt. And he'd never figured out how to turn off his feelings.

"Yeah, but I'm a master at ignoring them," he reminded the birds hopping along the nearby branches.

The fact that he could spend time around Fitzphie without barfing or punching something totally proved it.

But this was a whole lot more complicated than the Great Foster Oblivion, or the triangle that started out as a square.

This was hundreds or thousands of feelings blasting him from every direction.

There *had* to be a way to tune them out, though.

Oooh, maybe he needed to pretend the emotions were one of his father's lectures!

He'd been tuning those out for years.

Though . . . they usually put him into a sleeplike trance, and he needed to be able to function.

Really, what he needed was a way to be distracted enough.

A level of awareness that fell somewhere between *wandering around talking to an Imaginary Sophie* and *FEELING ALL THE THINGS EVER.*

Would whistling work?

He tried—but who knew whistling for a long time would make his lips so sore?

After a minute or two, the only sound he could still squeak out was a pitiful wheeze.

And when he switched to humming, he ran out of melody.

Music wasn't really a thing in the Lost Cities, unless he counted the "natural melodies" Tammy Boy's family was so famous for—which he didn't. And he hadn't been a big fan of dwarven songs either. They were way too peppy.

He could try singing the screechy siren songs he'd heard in detention—but that would probably get him tackled.

"Oh! What if all I have to do is . . . ?"

He paused, waiting to see if his brain would finish the sentence.

"Ugh, I really thought that might work."

Maybe he was overthinking it.

Maybe he just needed to find something simple to focus on.

Like . . . counting his steps.

That seemed a little more promising—except he lost count every time he had to think about stuff like not crashing into trees. And when he *didn't* think about not crashing into trees, he tripped over a fallen branch and ended up with a face full of dirt and a missing shoe.

"No need to rub it in," he told a bird who was totally tweet-snickering at him.

He triple-knotted the laces so his shoe wouldn't slip off again—which of course meant he immediately realized there was a pebble in his shoe. Right under the ball of his foot, so he felt it with every step.

It's fine—it doesn't even hurt, he told himself when he couldn't get the laces untied.

But all he could think was *Pebble in my shoe.*

Pebble in my shoe.

Pebble in my shoe.

Pebble in my—

Wait.

"Could it really be that simple?"

He took a few steps—and then a few more.

Each time his brain felt the need to remind him that he still, in fact, had a pebble in his shoe—but he was also able to watch the path ahead for tripping hazards. And he could still hear the rustling wind and the fluttering birds.

"Huh," he said, wondering how long he should test it for.

It seemed really, really, really, really, really promising.

But he wouldn't know for sure until he was around a bunch of humans, and he was afraid to get his hopes up after Operation Foster Distraction.

"Okay, *now* I'm stalling," he admitted as he dug out his pathfinder and stared at the crystal—then stared and stared some more.

He couldn't decide if it would be smarter to go back to one of the places he'd already been or to try his luck somewhere new.

It might be helpful if he knew what to expect—but he could also end up on that horrible boat again.

But any new place could have even bigger problems.

"Seriously, stop overthinking it!" he told himself as he spun the crystal to a random facet and held the pathfinder up to the sunlight. "If this is going to work, it'll work wherever. And if it doesn't . . ."

He decided not to think through the end of that sentence.

It would only make it even harder to step into the light.

"Deep breath. Remember: If this works, I can use Daddy Dearest's money to buy some more Flamin' Hot Cheetos—plus some other food that won't scorch the taste buds off my tongue!"

His stomach growled in agreement, and he hitched the straps on his backpack higher up his shoulders.

"All right. Let's do this!"

He closed his eyes and stomped hard on the pebble as he stepped into the warm, rushing light.

NINE

*T*HIS IS ACTUALLY WORKING!!!!

Keefe wanted to twirl in a happy dance—but he'd only been there five minutes, so it was a little too early to celebrate.

Then again, five minutes was longer than he'd lasted in most of the other crowded places.

More importantly, he still felt like himself.

Well . . .

Mostly.

Emotions were definitely slamming against his senses— but every time he stepped down on the pebble, his brain would shift its attention to that point of discomfort. And the constant distraction kept him from getting too overloaded.

He was pretty sure he was going to have a giant blister, so it wasn't a perfect solution.

BUT.

He was walking down a busy human street, and he didn't have to tune everything out or run away because he was about to numb everybody!

So really, he just had one final test before he could call it a victory.

I can do this, he told himself. *It's safe. No words are pressing against my lips or burning the back of my throat.*

Actually, his mind was so blank, he had no idea what he should say.

Excuse me?

Where am I?

Is it always this cold and drizzly here?

Yes, my hair really is this awesome—thank you for noticing.

The fact that he was coming up with jokes felt like a really good sign—but he still stepped extra hard on the pebble and decided to go with the tiniest word he could think of.

He also kept his voice barely above a whisper as he said . . .

"Hi."

HE DID IT!

HE USED HIS VOICE AROUND HUMANS, AND NOTHING BAD HAPPENED!!

No one froze!

No one went into any trances!

In fact, no one was even paying any attention to him!

He wanted to laugh and cry and jump around and hug everyone and shout, *DID YOU HEAR THAT, MOM? I'M LEARNING HOW TO BEAT YOU!*

Instead, he turned to study the busy street.

Now that he knew it was safe to wander, he wanted snacks, and baked goods, and anything else with a funny name or with tiny elves drawn on the packaging.

Also: real food.

Preferably something warm, since the wind was picking up and the drizzle was turning into more of a light rain.

Oooh, maybe he could find one of those all-you-can-eat buffet things like he'd seen in the other city and just hang out there stuffing himself until the weather changed!

Sadly, though, there wasn't a buffet in sight.

No markets, either.

Just a ton of the boring, super-tall buildings humans loved to fill their cities with, even though they made the streets feel claustrophobic.

But the place was enormous, so he just needed to do a little exploring.

He made his way to the nearest cross street, trying to decide which direction to go.

The street leading toward the ocean seemed the most promising, since it was busier than the others. But it also meant that if he lost control, there was a chance he'd end up on another boat—or on the giant metal wheel thing he could see in the distance.

Won't happen. There's a pebble in your shoe, he reminded himself as he crossed the street and eased into the thickest part of the crowd. *You won't lose control.*

And he didn't.

Even as the crowd got louder and busier.

He crossed street after street and never lost focus for more than a few seconds.

Yes, he definitely *was* going to have a sasquatch-size blister when he took off his shoes—but the pain was worth it when he spotted a giant red sign that said PUBLIC MARKET CENTER.

"Now we're talking!"

He picked up his pace, trying not to look like he was running, even though he totally was.

But there was food!

He could smell it!

And it smelled . . .

. . . Sorta good?

It was hard to tell because the drizzle-soaked street had a dirty, musty odor, and the ocean air was much more pungent than he was used to—like rotting seaweed mixed with fish poop.

Or maybe it wasn't the ocean air after all.

"Are those . . . dead fish?" Keefe mumbled as he watched several gray floppy things fly across one of the market stalls.

"They sure are," a raspy voice told him, and Keefe whipped around so fast, he almost toppled over.

He hadn't expected anyone to answer him—much less a human girl with bright blue hair, a jewel pierced through her eyebrow, and tattoos winding up her pale neck.

Ro would've wanted to be her best friend.

"So is it everything you thought it would be?" she asked, pointing to the fish-tossing people. "Or are you wondering why this is on every Seattle Must-See list right after the Space Needle?"

"Uhhh . . ."

Keefe leaned on the pebble in his shoe while he searched for a better response.

He could tell his new Polyglot ability was doing its job and translating her words—but apparently that didn't mean the words would actually make sense.

Seattle?

Is that the name of the city?

And what is a Space Needle?

The girl smirked. "Okay, you look pretty lost, so let me help you out. Most of the tourist traps around here aren't worth it. Skip the first Starbucks—it's just a regular Starbucks with an extra-long line. The pig statues are just big gold pigs with people crowding around them. And the gum wall is just a bunch of chewed saliva stuck to a wall that people take dorky selfies in front of."

That last one actually sounded kind of awesome, if Keefe

was being honest—though he had no idea what a selfie was. But he had a much more important question.

"What about the food here?"

She shrugged. "It's fine. Kinda overpriced, but you gotta expect that. The famous chowder place is that way"—she pointed over his shoulder—"or there's—"

"Chowder?" Keefe interrupted. Clearly, his Polyglot ability was going to be zero help with anything cultural.

"Yeah, they have red and white—and not just clam. It's like . . . salmon chowder and scallop chowder and oyster chowder. Pretty much any seafood you want."

Keefe grimaced as another dead fish went flying by. "Never mind."

He'd forgotten humans ate meat—and as starving as he was, he didn't think he could do it.

She tilted her head to study him. "Vegan or vegetarian?"

He had a feeling that asking *What's a vegan?* would make him sound super clueless. So he went with "Vegetarian," hoping it meant what he thought it meant.

"Cool. Okay. That makes it easy, then. You need to go that way"—she pointed in a different direction—"and get yourself a giant, gooey mac and cheese. Trust me."

Keefe saw no reason not to.

She clearly knew what she was talking about—and even though he wasn't sure what "mac" was, she had him at "gooey cheese."

He verified the direction and headed that way, which might've been the best decision he'd ever made.

Well, second best, after becoming president of the Foster Fan Club.

The mac and cheese was melty and warm and the gooiest of the gooey.

He devoured every bite and really, really, really wanted to get another, but he probably needed to be careful with his money—at least until he found somewhere to sell his mom's jewelry.

It felt like he had a lot of cash, but it was all in different currencies, so it might not go as far as he needed.

He wasn't in the Lost Cities anymore, with a birth fund that covered everything he could possibly want or need.

"Gotta stick to a budget," he told himself—then pulled out his sketchbook, wrote the same words, and titled them *Lesson Two*.

He also added a Lesson Three: *Ask the locals*.

They knew the best places to go—and hopefully they wouldn't mind helping, since the girl had been the one to strike up the conversation with him.

He wished he'd done a better job of thanking her.

Or had at least gotten her name.

"Thanks, blue-haired girl," he mumbled as he drew a quick sketch of her face—making sure to capture her *I'm smarter than you* expression. "I owe you big-time."

He really did.

Now he finally had a plan—or the start of one, anyway.

He made a note of that, too.

Even drew a big box around it to make it feel more official.

Keep a pebble in your shoe.

Ask the locals.

Get to work.

TEN

"OH GOOD, ANOTHER STATUE," Keefe mumbled as he craned his neck to study the humongous bronze woman holding a wreath while standing next to a lion.

This was the third city he'd visited since leaving the drizzly streets of Seattle, and once again he had no idea where he was or how to find any of the things he needed.

And now he also wanted to know why humans seemed to be so obsessed with lions.

The first city he'd leaped to after he'd finished his mac-and-cheesy goodness had a giant statue of some sort of half-lion, half-fish creature spitting water into a glittering bay.

It also had some of the tallest, weirdest-shaped buildings he'd ever seen.

And he'd gotten to try something called kaya toast, which was definitely a snack he'd crave again.

But the only clothing shops he'd found were super fancy, and everything cost *way* more than the little bit of cash he had—and he didn't see anywhere he could try selling his mom's jewelry.

The whole living-on-a-budget thing was getting pretty annoying.

He one thousand percent didn't recommend it.

Especially since his next leap brought him somewhere even less helpful: a ruin high in the mountains, with nothing but fallen stones and a few curious llamas.

Even the locals didn't know why the city had been built or what had happened to the people who used to live there— which made Keefe wish he'd paid more attention in elvin history.

Elves tended to be connected to most of the weirdness in the ancient human world, so he was sure there had to be some sort of story there. But he'd only memorized the bare minimum from his textbooks so he could pass with a grade that would make his father's eye twitch. And this place didn't look familiar.

Someday he'd have to find out what happened—but right now, he had bigger mysteries to solve.

Like, seriously, where was he going to buy some better clothes?

Definitely not in this current city, which had a huge festival going on in front of the bronze lion-lady statue, with tents and booths and music and a huge crowd of people dancing and singing and clinking heavy-looking glasses.

There were so many different emotions pummeling his senses that he had to rub his foot back and forth, even when he was standing, to keep the pebble in his shoe constantly on his mind.

And the only outfits he saw for sale were a bunch of embroidered shorts with suspenders attached, paired with knee socks and funny little hats—and he doubted he could pull that off.

Actually, no, he totally could.

He would rock those shorts and knee socks like no one had ever rocked them before.

But.

He needed to stay focused.

He'd added a very important fourth step to his plan, and it was his new top priority:

Get back to London.

His mom had been going there for a reason, and it was time to find out what she'd dragged him into—even if he was more than a little terrified of the answers.

But getting there could turn out to be an obnoxiously slow process.

He'd counted the facets on his father's pathfinder, and there were one hundred forty-two—and with his luck, the London facet would end up being the last one he tried.

He'd only tested about a dozen facets so far—and given how exhausting it was to adjust to each new place, he didn't think he could handle more than five or six a day.

So the math didn't look good.

Unless . . .

Surely some of the other facets went to places that were *close* to London, right?

In fact, the architecture of some of the buildings around the festival reminded Keefe of the style he'd seen while he was there!

"Excuse me," he called to a woman working at a booth selling giant heart-shaped cookies dangling from strings.

"Yes, hello, which one?" she asked, gesturing to a display where the hearts were all decorated with little sayings like *I love you* and *Hug me* and *Little Sparrow*.

Keefe pointed to a cookie with a blue loopy border that said *My Snuggle Mouse.*

Why not?

Most of the crowd seemed to be wearing the hearts around their necks, so he might as well blend in.

Plus . . . cookie!

"Quick question," he said as he fished through his stack of money, trying to find the right currency. "How do I get to London?"

"London?" she repeated as she guided him to the right bills. "You mean . . . London, England?"

Keefe was pretty sure that was correct, so he went ahead and nodded.

She frowned. "But . . . we're in Munich."

"I know," he said—even though he didn't. He had no idea where he was—or even what language he was speaking at the moment. "But how long would it take to get to London from here?"

"Well . . . I don't really know." She told another customer browsing the cookies that she'd be with them in one minute. "Depends on if you fly or take the trains, I guess."

"You can *fly*? Please tell me it isn't like going on one of those boat things—but in the sky."

She laughed and took the cash he handed her. "Sounds like you might need to stay away from the tents for a little while."

Keefe had no idea what that meant, but he could tell she was getting tired of his questions. Plus, he was starting to see why it might seem strange to ask how to get to a place that was actually quite far away.

Traveling had to be a much bigger deal when you couldn't jump on the next beam of light.

So he thanked her for her help and slipped his new cookie necklace around his neck, focusing on the pebble in his shoe as he headed deeper into the festival.

He spotted someone selling giant, twisted, breadlike things

and figured that was a justifiable use of his budget.

After all, it was *bread as big as his head.*

Apparently, it was called a pretzel—at least according to the lady who sold him the pretzel-y goodness.

And he could smell lots of other delicious things he wanted to try.

But the emotions kept ramping up every time people spilled out of the various tents, and it was getting harder and harder to keep his focus on the pebble in his shoe.

He looked around for a deserted place to leap—and spotted something that could be the answer to all his problems.

"WAIT—WHERE DID YOU GET THAT?" he shouted as he rushed over to a gray-haired couple, making them both jump. "Sorry," he said, flashing his best *I-swear-I'm-not-a-creeper* smile. "Didn't mean to startle you. I was just wondering where you got that map."

He pointed to the folded paper in the woman's hands, which didn't just show all the streets in the city—it had cute little drawings of the various landmarks, along with handy labels telling what they were and footnotes sharing the history behind each place.

If he could find something like that with all the different human cities on it, it would be an absolute game changer. Then every time he leaped somewhere, he could match whatever weird statue or buildings he saw against the map, and he'd know exactly where he was—and if it was close to London.

"Our tour guide gave them to us when the bus dropped us off," the woman explained.

"But you can have mine," the guy added, pulling an identical map from his back pocket. "All the maps I need are up here."

He tapped his temple, and the woman laughed.

"*That's* why we get lost so often," she told Keefe as he took the map the man handed him. "So a word to the wise—don't be afraid to ask for directions."

"And always listen to your wife," the man added with a wink. "Or . . . whoever calls you their Snuggle Mouse."

He glanced back at the woman, and they exchanged such sweet, sappy smiles that Keefe wasn't sure if he wanted to hug them or beg them to share all their other life lessons.

Instead, he thanked them for their help and ducked out of the way so he could study his glorious new treasure.

"Perfect!" he said when he spotted his new destination.

He had no idea what a Hugendubel was, but the little drawing showed books—and where there were books, surely there would also be maps.

It took him longer than he was proud of to find his way there—and he might've stopped to try a vegan currywurst along the way because, wow, those smelled amazing and the sign made it clear they were totally meat-free. But he eventually made it to a store that would've made the Forklenator very proud of him.

Books everywhere!

All sorted into different categories and alphabetized.

He kind of wanted to stop at the FANTASY—ADVENTURE section and see if there were any pointy-eared elves on the covers—but he was too excited to waste any time.

"Excuse me," he said, stopping a guy he hoped worked there. "Do you know where I can find a map of the world?"

"Sounds like you need an atlas." He motioned for Keefe to follow him, and they wound through the stacks, over to a section where the books all looked very thick and boring.

He handed Keefe the thickest one, and Keefe flipped through the pages, which were filled with intricate maps covered in tiny lines and writing.

"Actually, I was hoping you'd have something more like this"—he showed him the map he'd been given and pointed to the illustrations—"but of the whole planet."

The guy frowned. "I don't think we have that."

"We might in the children's section," a woman nearby jumped in.

She motioned for Keefe to follow her over to the most colorful section of the store, where most of the books had kids doing adventurous things on the covers—and if Keefe hadn't been trying to stick to a budget, he totally would've grabbed one that showed a girl flying on an alicorn.

But then the woman handed him a book called *My Very First World Atlas*, and it was *perfect*.

The map on the cover was decorated with dozens of the

drawings he needed—plus a bunch of smiling children and cute animals.

"Is this a gift?" the woman asked as she rang up the sale.

"Nope. It's for me."

He could tell she was judging his taste in literature, but he didn't care as he handed over the money.

The first two pages were exactly what he needed.

As soon as he was outside the store, he pulled the pages free from the binding so he could keep them handy in his pocket and shoved the rest of the book—and his Snuggle Mouse cookie—into his backpack for safekeeping.

"Let's try this again," he said as he ducked down an alley and pulled out his pathfinder. "Look out, London. Here I come!"

ELEVEN

N OPE."

Keefe was getting very tired of saying that word.

He'd already used it when he reappeared near a tall red building with a bunch of different roofs stacked on top of each other—which his handy map told him was called the Chureito Pagoda in Japan.

It was a beautiful place, especially with the snowcapped mountain in the background.

But it was nowhere near London.

Neither was the row of enormous ancient trees called the Avenue of the Baobabs in Madagascar.

Or the super-fancy white-domed building surrounded by a bunch of towers called the Taj Mahal in India.

Or the Leaning Tower of Pisa in Italy, which really did look like it was about to fall over.

And now he was standing in a desert in front of what was apparently called the Grand Canyon—and the name was very fitting.

The canyon stretched on and on and *on*.

The sky was also the brightest shade of orange he'd ever seen, which made the canyon one of the most beautiful places he'd been—even counting the Lost Cities.

But he was still in the middle of nowhere.

Still far away from London, or anywhere he could sell jewelry or buy clothes.

And he was on his ninth leap of the day.

Or, wait.

Was it his tenth?

He'd totally lost track.

All he knew for sure was that he'd pushed himself to keep going, thinking his shiny new map would surely lead him where he wanted to go.

Instead, it'd been "nope" after "nope" after "nope."

And yeah, he was getting really good at finding awesome human foods to stuff his face with. But he was failing pretty epically at everything else.

So now his legs were wobbly, and his head felt foggy, and the blister from the pebble in his shoe was more like an open sore—and he was pretty sure he could only handle one more leap before his brain imploded.

Which meant he had a super-fun decision to make.

Spin the pathfinder again and hope the next facet *finally* brought him to London—or at least somewhere he could rent a room for the night without burning up all his remaining cash.

Or leap back to his father's stuffy little art cabin and spend another night there.

With the way his luck was going, the first option didn't seem like a smart decision.

But . . . he never wanted to see that boring lake ever again.

"I could camp out here," he reminded himself. "It won't be too cold. And there won't be any yetis prowling around."

But there'd be snakes.

And scorpions.

And probably a few jaculuses.

And the thought of waking up to another day of wasted leaps sounded even worse than cuddling all night with creepy-crawlies.

"It shouldn't be this hard," he grumbled, kicking the ground and sending pebbles flying over the edge of the canyon.

The words echoed back at him, and he cupped his hands around his mouth and shouted them again.

"IT SHOULDN'T BE THIS HARD!"

He had a map now—and a crystal that could take him around the world in the blink of an eye.

Why couldn't he find the one place he needed to go?

Because he was still missing the most important map.

The map of all the facets on his father's pathfinder.

He'd thought he could get by without it, but clearly, he'd been wrong.

Which did leave one other option for where he could leap to—but he'd rather get chased by yetis or do ten more rides on that miserable boat.

"Okay," he said, closing his eyes and taking a deep, calming breath before he forced himself to ask the question that always helped him make the right choice—even when he really didn't want to.

What would Foster do?

He needed to get that embroidered on a tunic or something.

Because Foster always did the smart thing.

Even if it was horrible.

Even if it would hurt.

Or give her nightmares.

She was brave and clever and dedicated like that.

And he wanted to be the same way.

So he dug through his backpack and fished out the crystal he almost hadn't packed but threw in just in case he needed to get back to the Lost Cities.

He refused to call it a home crystal.

It definitely didn't lead *home.*

"Please don't be there," he mumbled, not sure if he meant his father or Ro.

Actually, he could handle the angry ogre princess.

All he'd have to do is tell her about his little Foster confession, and she'd be so busy making kissy noises that she'd forget she wanted to pummel him for running away.

But Daddy Dearest was a whole other story.

Keefe wasn't sure he could look at him now that he'd seen his little artist retreat.

"Doesn't matter. He won't be there," he told himself as he held the crystal up to the fading sunset sky. "He'll be at the apartment in Atlantis he never invited me to—or some other secret house he has because he needed fifty different ways to escape his family."

And when he re-formed at the Shores of Solace, it was as dark and quiet as he'd hoped it would be.

The only sounds were the crashing waves and Keefe's shaky breaths.

Still, he decided to tiptoe as he made his way inside and headed straight for his father's private study, hoping the map to the pathfinder would be somewhere in the giant desk.

If not, he wasn't sure where else to look.

Maybe the nightstand in his father's bedroom?

Or it could be—

Keefe screamed and clutched his chest as the lights flicked on.

His father laughed from the doorway. "I had a feeling you'd be back."

TWELVE

NO NEED TO USE A COMMAND," Lord Cassius said, holding out his hands. "I'm not going to prevent you from doing whatever you're doing. In fact, I'm here to help."

"Help," Keefe snorted, surprised at how normal his voice sounded.

He hadn't even had to think about the pebble in his shoe to keep himself under control.

Then again, there weren't a whole lot of emotions hitting his senses at the moment.

He could really only feel one—and it wasn't an emotion he usually felt from his father.

"I don't need your help—or your concern," Keefe told him. "I'm doing just fine on my own."

"The fact that you're here would suggest otherwise," Lord Cassius noted. "Though it does appear you've gained some level of control over your new abilities if you can speak so freely."

Keefe definitely caught the plural there—but he knew his father was baiting him.

Daddy Dearest may have figured out that he'd manifested more than one ability, but there was no way he knew what he could do.

No one did.

Not even Keefe.

He went back to searching his father's desk, making sure to slam each drawer as hard as he could.

"Looking for this?" his father asked, holding up a slightly crumpled piece of paper.

It was hard to tell from a distance, but it looked like a drawing of a circle with lots of tiny lines and text.

"It's the map to my blue pathfinder," his father explained. "I met with Councillor Bronte this morning and convinced him to give me a copy—which was no easy feat, I can assure you. I had a feeling you might need it. Clearly, I was correct."

Keefe's jaw wanted to fall open—but he gritted his teeth and looked away.

"The words you're looking for," his father told him, "are 'thank you.'"

"Trust me, they aren't," Keefe snapped back. "Especially since you haven't said what you want yet."

"What I *want*?"

Keefe dragged a hand down his face. "Look, it's been a really long day. So can we skip the part where you pretend you're on my side and—"

"I *am* on your side, Keefe. In many, many ways. You think I don't want to stop whatever madness your mother is planning?"

"No, I think you want to be able to take credit for stopping her, and not have to actually do any of the work or take any risks or make any sacrifices."

"That would be nice," his father agreed.

There was a hint of humor in his tone and a tiny glint in his eyes.

"*Don't*," Keefe warned, curling his hands into fists. "You don't get to stand there and pretend to be charming and—"

"I *am* charming," his father insisted. "Where do you think you get it from?"

Keefe slammed his fist on the desk. "I SAID DON'T!"

His father sighed.

Keefe traced his finger across the top of the desk, trying to decide if he had enough energy to lunge for the pathfinder map and leap away.

"I have other things you're going to need," his father told

him, as if he knew exactly what Keefe was thinking. "I'm guessing you've already used up most of the money I keep at the cabin—don't try to deny it. I know you've been there. I can recognize my own clothes. Plus, I swear the pathfinder spins to that facet far more readily than others, given how many times I've used it—though I haven't been in a while. Not since I found out the truth about your mother."

"Is that supposed to make me feel sorry for you?" Keefe asked.

"Of course not. That's another thing we have in common, son. Neither of us is looking for pity." When Keefe didn't respond, he cleared his throat. "I'm assuming you have some questions. . . ."

"Not really. I mean, I guess I'm curious how you could spend decades painting the same boring lake over and over and still not be very good at it."

His father's jaw tensed, and waves of bristly outrage wafted through the room.

Keefe grinned.

So Daddy Dearest was sensitive about his little lake paintings. Good to know.

"I wasn't painting the lake," his father informed him as his outrage faded to haughtiness. "I was painting the *light*. Trying to capture its ever-changing essence."

Keefe rolled his eyes as dramatically as he could. "Is *that* why you're always destroying my sketches? They aren't pretentious enough? Guess if I dabbed a bunch of paint blobs on paper, I wouldn't be such a huge disappointment. Right, *Cass*?"

His father looked away, folding and refolding the map to his pathfinder, and the emotions in the room swirled into a mess Keefe couldn't begin to translate.

He leaned on the pebble in his shoe to tune them out.

"I realize this may be hard for you to understand," his father said quietly, "and that my methods have been far from perfect. But all I have ever done—or striven to do—is to help you accept that you must learn to conform if you want any chance of success in our world. The Lost Cities are not kind to those who refuse to follow the rules."

"And how is keeping a secret cabin in the human world *conforming*?" Keefe demanded.

"It's not. But it took me decades to acquire the trust and resources I needed in order to set up that retreat. Life is a very long game, and you have to play by the rules before you can break them. Prove you're someone worth trusting, so that no one watches you too closely. Earn a reputation for faithful obedience, and no one will expect anything less. But you've always jumped straight to rebellion, with no thought to how that affects people's perception—"

"Of *you*," Keefe finished for him. "That's what you're really worried about, right? Can't be Lord Perfectpants if you have an out-of-control son."

"I can't," his father agreed. "Though your mother did far

more to destroy my reputation than anything you've ever done."

"One of the few things I'd love to give her a high five for," Keefe mumbled.

His father closed his eyes, taking several long breaths before he said, "I'm not asking for your forgiveness, Keefe. Nor am I trying to earn it. I think we both know that would be a pointless endeavor. But I do need you to listen to me—for once in your life. I have far more experience with the Forbidden Cities than you do. I know how to play by their rules. And you're going to need my help if you want to remain there for any extended amount of time."

"Ahhhh, so *that's* what this is about! You're trying to keep me out of sight before the rumors start flying about your son's freaky new abilities!"

"I assure you, it's far too late for that." He met Keefe's stare. "There is plenty of speculation about what you can and can't do—and none of it is good."

"Great." Keefe kicked the side of his shoe, leaving a nice big scuff on the pristine white—which his father definitely noticed.

Keefe could tell he wanted to launch into one of his lectures about showing proper care and respect for his possessions.

Instead, he told him, "I'm not going to pretend you have an easy road ahead, Keefe. Or promise that things will go back to normal."

"*Normal*. Has my life ever been normal?"

"I used to think so. But . . . no." His gaze turned distant. "Like it or not, you're part of your mother's plan. So until you're ready to challenge her, it's best to ensure that she cannot find you."

"Oh, I'm ready."

"Are you? So you've mastered your new abilities?" He studied Keefe's face. "That's what I thought. Your control at the moment feels . . . tentative."

"It is," Keefe agreed. "So you should be careful about how angry you make me. One wrong word and . . ."

He left the threat hanging.

His father looked more curious than afraid. "Do you even know what the new abilities are?"

Keefe wished he could say, *Of course!*

But his father would know he was lying.

"The only thing I need to know is how to end her," Keefe reminded him. "And I have plenty of plans for that."

His father trailed his fingers through the air. "Interesting. I can feel your resolve all the way over here—which does suggest you might be ready to face that decision. But you're forgetting something."

"And I'm sure you're going to tell me what it is."

"You're forgetting that your mother will only show herself when the timing is right for *her*. How did that work out for you in Loamnore?"

Keefe went back to tracing the desktop with his finger. "Not my favorite day. But I survived."

"You did. But do you really think your mother is done with her little experiments?"

Keefe didn't have an answer for that.

He wanted to believe the whole almost-dying thing was the last of it.

But . . . could there be more?

His father's mood had shifted again, to a churning, bitter unease—as if he knew something he wasn't saying.

"I don't mean to scare you," his father said, stepping closer.

"I'm not scared!"

"We both know that's a lie." He placed his hand on Keefe's shoulder, and Keefe jerked away. "There's nothing wrong with fear, Keefe. It can be a powerful motivator. Look where it's led you. You've found the perfect place to hide while you adjust to your new abilities. And I can help you—"

"I DON'T NEED YOUR HELP!"

"That's a strange tantrum to throw when you're standing in my office, searching my desk for the map to my pathfinder while wearing my clothes, with my money in your pocket."

"Yeah, except you didn't have anything to do with any of that."

"Didn't I? Do you honestly think I leave my cabin unlocked so that any wandering hiker could make themselves at home?"

Keefe really, really, really wanted to argue.

But . . . he actually had been surprised the cabin had been unlocked.

And then he remembered the way the handle had stopped turning for a second before it clicked open.

"There's a fingerprint sensor built into the handle," his father explained. "And I programmed it to accept your prints."

"*Why?*"

"Hard to say." He turned away, staring out through the window at the moonlit ocean as his mood turned pensive—with a hint of nervousness trickling through. "I suppose I figured if you ever found your way there, it might be time for us to have some longer conversations. And I might as well open the door, so to speak."

The words were an invitation.

But Keefe was too tired to accept.

Too angry.

Too lost.

"Anyway," his father said, clearing his throat, "it worked out well. Now you have a safe place to hide out."

Keefe shook his head. "I'm never going back there."

"I had a feeling you were going to say that. And it's a mistake. You can resent me all you want and still take advantage of having a warm bed that no one can trace you to. Where will you sleep otherwise?"

"I'm still figuring that out."

"Right. And how many more leaps can you put yourself

through while trying to piece together a plan? You're already looking faded—"

"No, I'm not!"

"Have you looked in the mirror? If you turn any paler, you'll be verging on translucent. The shadows under your eyes also look like bruises. I'm guessing you've only gotten a few hours of restless sleep since you ran off—and then pushed yourself through at least a dozen leaps before you turned up here. And I know you're going to tell me you don't need my help. But why don't you see what I have to offer before you turn me down?"

Keefe crossed his arms and leaned against the desk. "Fine. Impress me."

"You say that sarcastically—but you *will* be impressed. After I convinced Bronte to give me *this*"—he handed Keefe the pathfinder map—"which you never would've gotten otherwise, I also went to see a friend who's a Technopath and had him make you this."

He reached into the pocket of his jeweled cape and pulled out a small blue booklet.

Keefe raised one eyebrow. "Is that all you've got?"

"Actually, no. But you don't know what this is, do you? It's called a passport, and it's a form of human identification—an incredibly vital one. The Forbidden Cities are split into hundreds of different countries, most with their own currency, language, culture, and government—and a passport allows you to gain access from one to the next. You may also be asked to show it from time to time, to prove that you belong."

He waved it under Keefe's nose, waiting for him to take it.

Keefe sighed. "I'm assuming you had to give me a fake name. Let me guess—I'm Kay Lordeson?"

"Actually, I figured you might struggle to respond to a new first name. So I only altered the last name. But I think you'll approve of what I selected."

"Only if it's Hunkyhair." Keefe flipped to the last page, which was shinier than all the others—and couldn't stop his jaw from falling open.

There was a photo of him, flashing his trademark smirk.

Next to the name: KEEFE IRWIN FOSTER.

THIRTEEN

UGH, YOU COULD'VE AT LEAST given me a new middle name," Keefe grumbled, choosing to ignore the much bigger weirdness he was staring at.

His father shook his head, and a haze of annoyance thickened the air. "I honestly don't understand why you have such a problem with 'Irwin.'"

"Seriously?"

"It's a family name. Your great-great-great-great-great-grandfather is Irwin Sencen."

"Yeah, well, have you ever looked at my initials? You named me K.I.S.!"

He made a few kissing sounds for emphasis.

His father's lips twitched ever so slightly—but the annoyance didn't fade. "I'll admit, I didn't notice that when I chose the name. But you turn absolutely everything else into a joke—why not this? In fact, given your fondness for flirting, I'd think you'd embrace it."

Keefe rolled his eyes. "Yeah, because everyone wants to kiss an *Irwin*."

"You're not an Irwin—you're a Keefe. But I'm done with this discussion. The new last name fixes the problem with your initials, doesn't it?"

Keefe studied the map to the pathfinder, deciding it was easier to ignore the question.

He had no idea what his father was trying to imply by naming him Foster—but he wasn't in the mood for it.

"You seem to think I'm mocking you," his father murmured. "Strange, since I chose the name to be inspiring. Your mother is trying to make you believe that shifting to her cause is inevitable. So I thought you might welcome a reminder that you've already chosen your side. No matter what your mother claims—or what you discover about your new abilities—you'll always have a say in your future."

The words shouldn't have meant much, coming from his father.

But Keefe's eyes teared up.

His father cleared his throat as Keefe tried to dry his tears with his sleeve. "You should know she came by yesterday.

Sophie—not your mother. She showed up a few hours after you left, demanding I give her the list of cities my pathfinder went to so she could try to find you."

Keefe's heart swelled like a supernova. "Did you give it to her?"

"Yes and no. She saw it in my memories. But she's decided to leave you be."

Just like that, the supernova burst.

His father shook his head. "Young love is so exhausting. No need to deny it. Your feelings are obvious. Well . . . to everyone except her."

Keefe could feel a hint of glee pulsing through the room—and was tempted to throw the passport at his father's head.

But he was probably going to need it.

And even though he knew he was going to hate himself later, he had to ask, "Why did she change her mind?"

"Because she, unlike you, occasionally listens to reason."

"Translation: You talked her out of it."

"To a point. Mostly, I assured her that you could handle yourself in the human world and helped her realize that she'd be better off using her time and energy to look into other things."

All of that was true.

It shouldn't make him sad.

But it did.

He definitely sounded sulky when he asked, "Any idea what she's working on?"

"I have my theories. But she was obnoxiously vague." His

father tilted his head to study him. "If you're worried about her safety, it seems the ogre princess is now serving as an additional bodyguard."

Keefe cringed.

He could only imagine what kinds of teasing must be happening. Especially if Ro read his note—which she obviously had, because she was super nosy like that.

Yet another reason he should be glad he'd be hiding in Humanland for a while.

But knowing Foster really wouldn't be coming after him felt . . .

Nope.

It was better not to dive into those emotions.

His father cleared his throat, and a strange tangle of discomfort and regret radiated from him as he said, "If it helps, she really did want to find you. I didn't have to be an Empath to see that."

Keefe tried to find a response.

Best he could come up with was to shove the passport and the pathfinder map into his backpack and mumble, "I should go."

"Not quite yet." His father retrieved a bundle of colorful bills from his cape pocket and handed it to Keefe. "I'm sure you need more cash—but try not to carry more than this when you're out. The Forbidden Cities have all manner of different thieves, so it's best to limit how much they can steal. That's why I also had my friend make you one of these."

He offered Keefe a small black rectangle with a string of numbers on the front, along with the name KEEFE I. FOSTER.

"It's called a credit card—and that one is particularly powerful. One quick tap on the right human machine, and any purchase will be covered—but don't use the one you took from my cabin. You may get asked to show ID when you use it, so you'll want the name on the card to match your passport."

Keefe squinted at the small chip set into the card. "Can anyone track this?"

"They shouldn't be able to—but if they did, it would only lead them back to Cass Lordeman. I've set up several human accounts over the years, and this is tied to those for the monthly payment."

Keefe stared at his father, wondering how many other secrets he was keeping.

"As I said, if you prove yourself trustworthy, no one watches you too closely," his father reminded him.

Keefe refused to be impressed.

After all, if Daddy Dearest had spent a little less time creating a fake life in Humanland, he could've occasionally tried being an actual father.

Who knew? He might've even figured out that his wife was an evil murderer running experiments on their son.

"Is that everything?" Keefe asked, trying to shove the cash and credit card into his pocket—but his handy world map was in the way.

"Not yet. You may have already noticed that humans are incredibly reliant on small gadgets they call smartphones—but those can be monitored by the various human governments, so I wouldn't recommend acquiring one. I've also made some general notes"—he dug through his cape pocket and retrieved a palm-size notebook—"on things like foods to try. Which to avoid. Common expressions and customs. Tips to find places to stay or where to find important information or how to use human transportation. I'm sure your instinct will be to ignore this the same way you ignore all my other advice. But you'll regret it if you do."

Keefe doubted that.

But he shoved the notebook into his backpack, along with his handy world map and the cash—then put the credit card in his pocket, since that seemed like something he might need to use fairly often. "*Now* can I go?"

"Almost. You probably noticed that I marked three of the facets on the pathfinder map. The first is the facet that takes you to the cabin—though I'm sure your photographic memory can already help you with that one. The second is the facet to London, since I'm assuming that's where you're heading next. And the third is—"

"What makes you think I'm heading to London?" Keefe interrupted.

"Because you're smarter than you like people to realize." He held Keefe's stare, daring him to deny it. "I doubt you'll find what you're looking for, but it's the right place to start, regardless. I wouldn't recommend staying very long—"

"I'm not planning on it," Keefe assured him.

It was clearly the most predictable place he could go, so the sooner he got out of there, the better.

"Good," his father told him. "The pathfinder map should help you follow any leads from there. But before you do any of that, you must visit the third facet I've marked and learn how to recognize surveillance."

"Surveillance?" Keefe repeated as his insides dropped with a sloshy thud.

"Yes. The Black Swan has the most extensive network. But the Council watches the Forbidden Cities as well. And I'm sure it's safe to assume the Neverseen are also monitoring as much as they can."

Keefe had to lean on the desk.

He knew Forkle had zillions of cameras—but he'd forgotten all about them.

How could he be so careless?

"Don't be so dramatic," his father told him—though it sounded more snippy than supportive. "I doubt you've appeared on as many recordings as you're fearing. There's no surveillance near my cabin—I've made sure of that. And for the rest of the facets, the observation points aren't always near the arrival points. Given how much you've been moving around, I'd wager they've only caught footage of you in one or two locations. You can correct that from here on out. It took me a while to figure out what to look for, but once I did, it was easy to keep my face turned away. It'll make more sense once you leap where I'm sending you. The trick is to watch for the sparkle."

"Watch for the sparkle," Keefe repeated, raising one eyebrow.

"As I said, it'll make more sense when you see it. It's a different kind of sparkle than any shimmer the humans create. It's meant to draw the eye there, to ensure they record everyone's faces. So once you can recognize it, you'll feel that pull and instinctively know to turn your head away."

Keefe dragged a hand down his face. "Seriously . . . who even are you?"

The father he knew didn't have human bank accounts or know how to dodge elvin surveillance.

He also barely acknowledged Keefe's existence most days— and when he did, it was only to lecture or criticize.

Keefe knew what to do with that father.

But this guy?

This . . . Cass Lordeman—lake painter extraordinaire and expert on the Forbidden Cities, who took the time to make him a human survival kit?

This guy made no sense.

"Okay, I have to ask," Keefe mumbled. "Why?"

"Why am I helping you?" his father clarified.

"That's part of it. But also . . . why humans? Why all the secrets? Just . . . why?"

The emotions in the room faded to a blur.

"Honestly, sometimes I wonder that myself," his father murmured. "The best answer I can find is that while humans have their share of problems, they're also incredible creatures—full of beauty and kindness and creativity. And they can be so much more open-minded than we are. I disagree with many of the Black Swan's decisions, but one thing they truly got right was having Sophie grow up believing she was human. The perspective she gained from the experience is truly invaluable—and while you cannot ever achieve the same effect, I hope you'll use your time in the Forbidden Cities to experience as much as you can. I realize you'll be focused on your mother and your abilities—but I hope you'll occasionally let yourself get distracted. Taste their foods. See their sights. Embrace their cultures. Let their world shape you. You'll be a better person by the end of it."

Keefe could tell his father meant every word—and it made him want to shout, *IF IT MAKES YOU A BETTER PERSON, WHY ARE YOU SUCH A JERK?*

But all he said was "Right. So . . . is that everything—or are you going to try to give me some art tips, too?"

His father's irritation surged. "I suppose I shouldn't have expected a thank-you—even though I deserve one. But despite your lack of gratitude, I *am* here for you. If you get into trouble, come find me. And if you run out of money—"

"I won't," Keefe jumped in. "I took some of mom's jewelry. As soon as I find somewhere to sell it, I'll be all set."

"Clever," his father admitted. "I'd recommend seeking out what's called a pawnshop. But be careful—those tend to not be in the safest neighborhoods. A young man carrying a bag of jewelry—or a bag of cash from selling that jewelry—would make an easy target. I'd also suggest breaking the pieces apart and selling them stone by stone. Jewels are much rarer in the Forbidden Cities, since they never learned dwarven mining techniques. So they will place a *very* high value on an entire piece of our jewelry, which would make things rather complicated, since humans rarely make payments of that size in cash."

"Noted," Keefe said, digging out the blue pathfinder.

"Actually, wait—I almost forgot." His father opened one of his desk drawers and removed a lumpy black pouch. "I gathered a few of our most vital elixirs, since I'd hate to have you at the mercy of human remedies. There's Fade Fuel in there. I suggest you drink some before leaping again."

Keefe was really getting sick of taking his father's help.

But . . . he should've thought to pack some medicine.

And he honestly wasn't sure he could handle another leap without it.

So he chugged the Fade Fuel—which felt like ice surging through his veins. And he decided to grab the bottle of Youth that was sitting on his father's desk, since he wouldn't get to have it for a while.

In fact, he was probably going to need a detox when he came back.

If he came back.

"You will," his father said, somehow guessing what he was thinking. "But wait until you're truly ready—and not just to challenge your mother. Wait until you're ready to face your new reality. Like it or not, you've changed, Keefe. It's time to find out who you are."

The words could've been inspiring. But since it was his father, they came out like an order—which made Keefe want to spin the pathfinder to any facet other than the one his father had marked.

But he needed to learn how to avoid the surveillance—especially before London.

"So you're finally learning to trust me," his father said smugly as Keefe spun the crystal to the facet he'd memorized from the map.

"I'm not doing this for you."

"I know. Remember to watch for the sparkle," he added as Keefe held the crystal up to the moonlight. "Oh, and one last thing."

It was the perfect moment to tell his son he'd miss him.

Or that he was proud of him.

If nothing else, he could tell him to be careful.

Instead, he smoothed his hair and told him, "Do yourself a favor. Before you leave the next place, make sure you try one of their churros."

FOURTEEN

WATCH FOR THE SPARKLE," Keefe grumbled, mimicking his father's snooty tone as he glared at the crowded courtyard. "How is this the best place to do that? There's sparkle everywhere!"

Twinkling lights in the trees.

Shimmering banners hanging from the lampposts.

And at least half the crowd was wearing something glittering or glowing.

It was pretty and all—but definitely not helpful for trying to find some sort of sparkly surveillance. Especially since it was also nighttime, and the lights illuminating all the paths seemed to amplify anything shiny.

Keefe closed his eyes and stepped on the pebble in his shoe to clear away the anticipation and frustration and exhaustion and excitement hammering his senses.

This was the biggest crowd he'd been in since he found a bit of control, and they seemed to be waiting for something to happen—but there was no sign telling him what it was.

At least the lake he was standing by looked more like a fountain, so if some sort of boat was involved, it would have to be pretty tiny.

In fact, everything about this place felt smaller than he would've expected.

Maybe he'd been spoiled by Eternalia and Lumenaria, but the pink-and-blue castle everyone kept taking pictures of almost seemed more like a mini replica.

So did the snow-covered mountain in the background.

Honestly, everything felt like a facade, built to create a very specific aesthetic, with spotlights on every tree and music playing from hidden speakers. The street even had all these weird tracks and grooves, as if the carriages and carts were stuck following the same path over and over.

But none of that was as bizarre as the people walking around in costumes with oversize animal heads.

Was one of them a giant mouse?

And was the mouse . . . famous?

He seemed to be, since people were lining up to take pictures with him.

There was also a life-size statue of him in the center of the courtyard, holding hands with some human dude.

In fact, the mouse was also on people's shirts—and Keefe had a feeling that some of their hats and headbands were meant to look like mouse ears.

Normally he would've loved that kind of randomness— probably would've even gotten himself a pair of sparkly ears.

But he was tired.

And his foot hurt.

And he was still weirded out by the lovely chat with Daddy Dearest.

And he had no idea where he was—and his handy map was buried in his backpack and—

"Wait . . . something about this feels familiar," Keefe mumbled, realizing Foster had mentioned a place like it before—or had it been Dex?

His brain was too tired and overloaded to find the exact memory. But he was pretty sure it was called something like Dizzneehaven or Dizzneeglen, and that Foster gave Dex a watch from there as one of her midterm gifts.

Keefe spun around and . . . yep!

There were stores selling jewelry and knickknacks and shirts and all kinds of other stuff—and one of the moms near him was holding a giant shopping bag that said DISNEYLAND.

"So this is where Foster went as a kid," he said, wondering if she'd worn a little crown like so many of the other girls in the crowd—or maybe a pair of sparkly wings.

He wanted to imagine her giggling with her sister and munching on a bucket of the popcorn stuff a nearby cart was selling, since it smelled salty and buttery and amazing.

But odds were she'd spent the whole time bombarded by thoughts she didn't know how to block while forcing a smile to hide her pounding headache. And as he stood there, pressing the pebble in his shoe into yet another blister, it made him wish he could use the Imparter that Grady gave him to hail her and say, *Every time I think I understand how brave and strong you are, I find even more proof that you're amazing.*

But that would be way too sappy.

Plus, he wasn't supposed to be hailing her.

He wasn't supposed to be hailing anyone.

He was *supposed* to be watching for "the sparkle."

Keefe scanned the scenery again, letting his eyes go out of focus in case that would help.

"Okay . . . I see blurry light. And blurry people. And blurry trees. And a blurry castle. And blurry lanterns. And . . ."

Keefe froze.

"Oh." He blinked a few times to make sure. "Huh. I guess I get it now."

One of the lanterns by the castle had a strange sort of flicker. Kind of like a soft, twinkling star was tucked inside the filigree.

His eye was drawn to it, even though he wasn't fully aware of it.

It felt like some deep part of his subconscious was whispering, *Look over there*—and Keefe listened to the voice, flashing a smirk that hopefully said *I'm onto you* as he faced the lantern dead on.

Then he turned his head away, memorizing how the sparkle looked in his peripheral vision so he'd be able to spot it without showing his face again.

"Okay, that's done," he said—then realized he should stop talking to himself.

A few of the people around him were starting to glance over their shoulders.

In fact, he should probably find somewhere safe to leap away, since someone now had a recording of him being there.

But . . . he wasn't sure where to go.

His next stop was supposed to be London—but he had to be quick when he got there, and he still didn't have a plan for how to find what he was looking for.

And maybe he was dreading that little part of his self-discovery journey and wouldn't mind stalling.

He also needed sleep—but he *really* didn't want to go back to his father's cabin.

Plus, the popcorn smell was making his stomach growl.

And it looked like there were lots of other amazing snacks he also needed to try.

But no churros, he told himself.

That would make his father way too happy.

Instead, he made his way over to a stand selling cups of swirled yellow fluff and ordered a float, which was cold and sweet and pineapple-y. And the guy in line behind him—a dad with two kids in long brown robes who kept referring to themselves as Jedi—told him that if he wasn't going to treat himself to a churro, he needed to at least try something called Mickey beignets.

It took Keefe much longer than it should have to track down the sugar-coated, mouse ear–shaped goodness—but they were worth the effort. Similar flavor to a butterblast, but sweeter and lighter, with a bonus dipping sauce.

And the more he wandered around the "park," as he heard people calling it, the more he couldn't help smiling—even with the pebble digging deeper and deeper into his foot.

Magic seemed to be a big theme in the land of Disney, and it was absolutely hilarious.

Magic wands.

Magic keys.

Not to mention an abundance of "magical" creatures.

Fairies that looked like tiny girls with sparkly wings. A bright blue genie attached to a gleaming golden lamp. And a red-haired, green-fish-tailed mermaid, just like he'd thought he'd seen before.

Plus a ton of talking animals with oversize eyes and cutesy

smiles—and a whole other galaxy full of Ewoks and Jawas and Wookiees.

It made him want to buy a bunch of silly souvenirs—especially the shiny pins that reminded him of the prizes in Prattles.

But as he tried to find a pin that said "Disney" to bring to the Dexinator, he realized he had no idea when he would give it to him.

Even if he did make it back to the Lost Cities, Keefe wasn't sure if Dex would want to see him.

After all, he was the guy who could ruin one of Dex's brothers' lives.

Yeah, he probably wasn't the reason that Rex hadn't manifested a special ability when the other triplets did—but he *could* get him labeled as Talentless way earlier than he should be.

And now Dex was going to have to spend years pretending he didn't know what was going to happen to his brother, which would totally change their relationship.

All because Rex touched Keefe's hand.

Keefe had hoped that leaving the Lost Cities would mean he could forget about that horrible, empty sensation he'd felt—and the enormous ramifications that came with it.

But it wasn't something he could run away from.

Like it or not, he'd manifested an ability that could change *everything*—and he couldn't tune it out with a pebble in his shoe.

That's why he needed to figure out what Mommy Creeptastic was planning—before she showed up again and used him to sort everyone to her liking.

Or worse . . .

Honestly, he couldn't begin to imagine all the awful ways she might use that power.

And even if he took her out of the equation, it still wasn't safe.

The Council could abuse his ability just as easily.

So could the Black Swan.

It was the type of power that *no one* should have—and even if he learned how to control it, he might still have to stay away to make sure no one ever found out what he was capable of.

He'd known that when he left, of course.

That's why he'd taken the time to write Foster that letter.

He'd been *very* aware that his goodbye could be forever.

But standing outside a land that was supposed to be a human vision of the future, he had to admit that some part of him kept hoping he'd find a way to erase all these new abilities and have things go back to the way they were.

Even now, his brain wanted to convince him everything would be okay.

But . . . as annoying as it was to admit . . . his father was right.

He'd changed.

It was time to start accepting that.

"I may never go home," he said out loud, trying to make it feel more real.

"Same, bro," said a guy holding a long, thin, cinnamon sugar–covered stick in each hand, before taking a bite of one. "I might just stay here eating churros forever."

Before Keefe could figure out a response, music swelled, and the sky erupted with sparkles and color and light—and the crowd's emotions all shifted to the same tingly awe.

It reminded Keefe of the Celestial Festival, only much noisier.

But each *BANG!* and *CRACKLE!* and *WHIZ!* brought a new explosion of light.

Some soared like shooting stars.

Some burst into huge sprays of colorful shimmer.

Some blasted into shapes like hearts or mouse ears.

And when the final blasts faded and the crowd applauded, Keefe had to admit . . .

Humanland was a pretty incredible place.

He was surrounded by families of all different shapes and sizes, and he could feel their love and joy and wonder radiating like a warm glow.

And then he realized . . .

None of them would care if he could predict whether someone was going to manifest a special ability.

None of them were ever going to manifest—or knew what it meant to be labeled Talentless.

His new ability—whatever it was—was pointless here.

He closed his eyes and let that sink in.

His new powers didn't matter in Humanland.

Yeah, he definitely missed his friends—and he'd never stop hoping that he'd find a way to go home. But in the meantime he'd ended up in a pretty awesome new world.

It wasn't perfect.

But . . . maybe it was perfect for him.

Maybe this was the closest to normal he'd ever find again.

So maybe he should let himself enjoy it a little more.

Eat one of those life-changing churros—who cared if his dad recommended them?

And he should treat himself to some pins and mouse ears, too.

He had a long, hard road ahead—and he'd start down that path very soon.

But first . . . a little more human "magic."

FIFTEEN

RIIIIIIIIIIIIIIIIIGHT," KEEFE MUMBLED as he watched the soft glow of dawn seep through the thick fog. "Forgot about the whole time-zone thing."

When he'd left Disneyland, it was still pretty early in the night. But according to the big fancy clock tower he'd reappeared in front of—what did Forkle call it? Huge Harry? Giant George? Big Ben?—the next day was already starting.

So much for grabbing a few hours of sleep.

He'd planned to find a room, crash there until morning, and hopefully come up with a better strategy than *wander around and see if I remember anything*—then get to work first thing and get out of there as fast as possible.

But the night was already over, so it looked like he'd be going straight to wandering.

And the city was way bigger than he remembered.

At least he'd finally made it, though.

London!

The land of disappointing biscuits!

Also the place where he'd lived some of his worst memories—and done some possibly horrible things his mom went to great lengths to make sure he couldn't remember.

So this was probably going to be a traumatic little adventure.

But . . . at least he could start piecing the mess together.

And, hey, maybe he'd also find some better desserts to console himself with.

There had to be a decent baked good around there somewhere, right?

First: He needed to get far away from the sparkly surveillance point he could feel trying to draw his attention.

The feed was probably being watched pretty closely, since London was such an obvious place for him to turn up. So Keefe tucked his chin and kept his face carefully angled away as he ducked down the nearest side street.

But that didn't make him any less jumpy.

Every shadow looked like a black-cloaked figure.

Every sound felt like an ambush.

And Mommy Dearest's voice kept echoing around in his head.

Embrace the change.

Embrace the change.

Embrace the change.

He'd been in London the first time she'd given him that lovely little life tip, and it had haunted him ever since.

He'd even thought he'd given in—embraced the change in Loamnore and become Mommy's little Legacy Boy with a bunch of freaky new abilities.

But as he turned down another street to make sure he wasn't being followed, he couldn't help wondering . . .

Had he given in?

Or was he still fighting?

Wasn't that why he was there—and what the pebble in his shoe was all about?

He wasn't sure.

But he liked thinking of it that way.

It made the blisters hurt a little less—and made running away feel more like a victory.

And yet, his annoying brain had to remind him that there'd been a second part to his mom's warning.

Embrace the change or it will *destroy you.*

"Sounds like a problem for Future Keefe," he said, shoving his hands into his pockets and changing direction again to avoid what might've been another sparkly surveillance point.

The soggy air sank straight through his sweater, making him wish he had a nice, heavy coat.

But every clothing store he passed was still closed.

"Time zones," he muttered.

At least the streets were nice and empty.

Just a few scattered people radiating a whole lot of grumpiness, so he assumed that meant they were on their way to jobs they hated—plus some joggers who seemed to be voluntarily running at the crack of dawn and weirdly enjoying themselves.

No one paid him any attention as he wandered around aimlessly, trying to keep his head down and his eyes open for anything that felt familiar.

Sooner or later he was going to recognize something.

And then he did—but only because he'd somehow managed to walk in a huge square.

"Okay, new plan," he said, crossing the street to head into a big green park with a lake in the center.

He couldn't feel any surveillance there, and the wide-open space would make it easy to see if anyone scary was approaching.

But most important: There were benches, and his feet were killing him.

He chose one facing the water and collapsed onto the weathered wood, wondering how he was going to find the willpower to get back up again—especially since he was realizing his whole "quick stop in London" plan wasn't going to work.

If he *really* wanted answers, he was going to need to be way more methodical.

Go street by street.

House by house.

It would probably take days or weeks—and that would definitely be a risk.

But.

Now that he was only a few streets away from where his mom asked him, *You wouldn't want to harm anyone else, would you?* he needed to know what she meant.

So he was going to have to find somewhere safe to hide out for as long as that took.

But first, he was going to rest his feet and update his sketchbook.

He'd already tucked the pathfinder map neatly between the pages and made notes about how to watch for the sparkle, and how he needed to make it one of his top goals to eat as many kinds of fried dough covered in sugar as possible.

But he added a new reminder: *Check the time zone before you leap somewhere.*

Also: *Alternate which shoe has the pebble,* even though that meant he'd end up with both feet throbbing.

He was pretty sure his blisters were starting to ooze, which probably meant the real note should be: *Find a better way to control my abilities*—but he'd already tried everything he could think of.

He closed the sketchbook and checked the elixirs his father had given him, hoping to find a numbing balm or healing poultice.

Sadly, there was only a single vial of pain reliever, along with a note that said, *If you need more than this, go get checked by Elwin.*

Keefe scowled, even though a tiny part of him knew that kinda made sense. "Fine. It'll be the Great Keefster Ooze Fest."

Not as fun as Foster's infamous Ooze Fest—but how could anything ever be?

He untied his shoes and swapped the pebble, letting out a huge sigh of relief when the pressure went back to just being annoying.

It'd take at least a couple of hours of walking before it would start hurting, and maybe he'd figure out where he was going to stay before then.

According to his father's notebook—which he'd skimmed back at Disneyland while eating his body weight in churros— he needed to find something called a hotel. But of course it didn't say where to find one, or what the protocols were for reserving a room.

It *did* tell him he should try to look respectable before going in, though—and then suggested combing his hair into a more subdued style and avoiding any use of the word "dude."

That's how all the little tips were.

A bit of half-useful advice, followed by a bunch of judgyness.

Daddy Dearest in full effect.

"Okay, if I were a hotel . . . ," Keefe said, squinting at the nearby buildings, "where would I be?"

He dug out his handy map, but all it showed in London was the clock tower and a square-shaped bridge by the river.

"I'm sure I'll find one as I wander," he mumbled, testing

the pressure of the pebble against his unblistered foot.

It didn't feel good.

"*Or* I can sit here and eat snacks and wait for someone to walk by who can help me!" he added, remembering his whole "ask the locals" plan—which sounded like a *much* better idea.

He propped up his feet and fished out the snack stash he'd bought before he left the land of Disney: one more churro, a bag of "sour balls," chocolate-covered marshmallows on a stick, and something everyone kept calling "the Grey Stuff."

Of course he started with the churro, taking a huge bite as he watched the ducks and wrens and pelicans by the lake.

But the churro went *plop* into his lap when he spotted a lone black swan gliding across the water.

He knew it was just a bird living its best life in London—but after all the sign of the swan stuff, he couldn't help wondering if it meant something.

And when the swan locked eyes with him, he felt like it was trying to tell him a secret.

Or, you know, it wanted some of his churro. . . .

He reached down, wondering if it'd be a bad idea to toss the swan a small piece, and then realized the churro had vanished.

"What the . . . ?" Keefe said as he checked the ground around him.

Then he spotted a blur of red fur with a long tail, leaving a trail of cinnamon and sugar as it darted across the grass.

"Hey! Get back here, you fluffy-tailed thief!"

He jumped up and chased after it—but the fox was too fast.

It disappeared into one of the flower beds, and Keefe could've sworn he heard it snickering.

"Don't think I won't come in there!" Keefe warned, even though it probably wouldn't be the best idea.

For all he knew, there was some weird human law about tromping on their flowers.

"They're sneaky little beasts, aren't they?" a voice asked behind him.

Keefe whipped around to find a very tall, dark-skinned, very athletic-looking man wearing jogging shorts and a thin sleeve-less top, despite the cold.

"I once had a fox snatch the other half of my cheese-and-pickle," he said. "At midday, no less! None of my mates believed me, so the next day I tried to trick it into taking my egg-mayo while I had my camera on. But it not only dodged my trap—it also stole my crisps!"

Keefe returned his smile, even though he was mostly think-ing, *Cheese-and-pickle?*

Sounded like the food in London was going to be . . . interesting.

"Where are you visiting from?" the man asked.

Keefe straightened up. "How did you—"

He pointed to Keefe's backpack, which Keefe had fool-ishly left unattended back at the bench. "Plus, you don't have a coat—or an umbrella. Classic tourist mistake this time of year."

"Ah." Keefe was tempted to point out that the guy didn't have those either, but he wasn't sure if that would seem rude.

One of his father's little tips had been *London is a very proper society. Don't be yourself.*

"Figured I'd do some shopping while I'm here," Keefe said instead, heading to grab his stuff. "But the stores are clo—"

"You all right?" the man asked when Keefe sucked in a sharp breath. "Didn't strain anything when you were running, did you?"

Keefe shook his head. "No. Just . . . dealing with some blisters."

His little sprint had pretty much destroyed both of his feet, and he couldn't stop himself from wincing with the next step.

"New shoes?" the man asked. "Been there. My first marathon, I decided to treat myself to some new trainers before the race. *Not* a brilliant idea. My toes were on fire after the first kilometer—and by the time I crossed the finish line, my socks were soaked with blood."

Keefe shuddered.

"Certainly not fun," the man agreed. "Though still better than when I did this."

He pointed to a scar running the length of his knee.

"Tore my ACL during a triathlon—then made it worse

finishing the race. But after all that training, it's hard to give up, isn't it?"

"Uh, sure . . ."

He laughed. "My surgeon looked at me the same way you are when I told him I kept going. So did my physio. But . . . I get in a zone when I'm racing. My brain tunes out everything except the next step, and the one after that. But sorry—I'll stop boring you with tales of my running injuries."

"No, it's fine," Keefe assured him. "I wish I could get my brain to focus like that." And since the guy seemed so chatty, he decided to add, "Actually, I don't suppose you know any good hotels around here?"

"I reckon I can think of a few. What are you looking for?"

Keefe thought for a second. "Which one has the softest beds and the best desserts?"

He laughed. "Is budget an issue?"

"Nope." Not now that he had his shiny credit card.

"Well, if you're okay spending a few quid and want a *proper* London experience, I know the perfect place." He rattled off a name and address and pointed the way. "They should also be able to get you some ice for those blisters. And hopefully they'll have a room ready. You look like you could use a bit of sleep."

"You have no idea," Keefe mumbled, dragging his fingers through his hair and realizing it was a lost cause.

"There's a lovely little coffee shop along the way," the man told him. "I realize I sound like a traitor to my country for not suggesting tea—but if you need a good strong jolt, it has to be coffee."

Keefe had no idea what coffee was. But a jolt sounded amazing.

"Thanks," he said. "Seriously." And for some reason he couldn't help adding, "This trip has been a little . . . overwhelming."

The man tilted his head to study him. "If it helps, I'd be happy to share the trick I use to get in the zone when I'm running—though I should warn you. My husband is a counseling psychologist. He's always going on about the value of visualization exercises—but when I told him what I came up with, he said it was total rubbish. Still teases me about it, actually—though I swear it works better than anything he's ever suggested. I suspect he's just bothered that he didn't think of it first."

He winked.

"At this point, I'm game for anything," Keefe assured him.

"Always a good way to be. And it's actually quite simple. Before I start a race, I close my eyes and imagine there's a switch in my brain that's connected to all the parts of my consciousness that pay attention to things like fear or nerves or discomfort—anything that could slow me down or stop me. Then I picture myself flicking the switch off. And if an injury switches it back on, I just flick it off again. Sounds a bit simplistic, I realize, but it makes a tremendous difference—for me, at least. Mind over matter, and all that."

"I'll give it a try," Keefe promised.

And he meant it.

In fact, as soon as he said goodbye and started heading toward the hotel, he imagined a switch in his brain tied to his throbbing blisters.

He waited until he could feel each connection—then pictured himself flicking off the switch.

"Whoa," he mumbled as he stepped down hard on the pebble.

The pain had dulled enough that he could basically tune it out—at least for a little while.

Which made him wonder . . .

Would the same trick work with his abilities?

He didn't see how it could—but he still squeezed his eyes tight and imagined a great big switch in his brain, tied to all his freaky new powers.

He waited until he could see each individual thread glowing with energy and feel his pulse radiating from the switch.

Then he imagined his stubborn will pushing and pushing and pushing against it.

But no matter how hard he tried, the switch wouldn't flip.

"That's what I figured."

Abilities couldn't be turned off once they'd been activated.

Everyone knew that.

And yet, as he sat in the coffee shop trying to choke down something called a flat white—which might've been the most bitter thing he'd ever tasted but was also making him feel VERY WIDE AWAKE—he couldn't help wondering if he'd tried switching off the wrong thing.

Maybe his empathy got rewired during his mom's little experiment, and that's why he'd become so ridiculously over-sensitive. So he closed his eyes and imagined traveling deep into his emotional center, searching for signs of any raw, exposed nerves.

His senses shivered and hummed, but he kept going and going until he slipped through a murky veil and landed in a cramped, fuzzy space.

Inside was a tangle of thin, glowing strands crackling with energy and flashing with colors.

His head spun and his skin tingled as the strands twisted and turned—trying to break free but only tangling tighter.

And he tried imagining a switch in the center.

But it wouldn't connect.

His brain wasn't wired that way.

So he reached in and slowly unraveled the tangle.

One by one.

Thread by thread.

And as he pulled the last strand free, he felt a soft *click*.

Then everything faded to gray.

SIXTEEN

THIS IS OFFICIALLY MY NEW HAPPY place," Keefe said as he sank into a giant pile of pillows and took a huge bite of some sort of fancy chocolate cake—which felt like a particularly bold statement, given the reason he was in London and his rather depressing history there.

But he was developing a special kind of love for this foggy city and all the people and foods and sights within it.

Didn't hurt that his day was turning out to be made of win.

Not only had the flat white given him so much energy that he probably could've run three of those marathon things back-to-back-to-back.

But that little visualization trick?

IT WORKED!!!

He had no idea *why*—and he wasn't going to try to figure it out, since that could make his brain be like, *You're right! This makes no sense. Let's go back to Misery Mode!*

All that mattered was that after he'd unraveled that last mental thread, the blaring emotions faded to a soft, steady hum—a sound he could easily tune out without needing anything to distract him.

So he'd dumped that horrible pebble out of his shoe and kicked it as far away as he could.

Then he turned down the busiest street to make sure nothing changed when he was around a bigger crowd—and thankfully, the emotions remained a harmless buzzing that his brain was more than happy to ignore.

It made him want to pump his fists and jump around shouting a bunch of particularly saucy taunts at Mommy Dearest and her little cloak-wearing buddies.

Sure, he still had his other weird abilities to deal with—but he was actually making some *real* progress.

It felt like he'd been holding and holding and holding his breath, and he'd finally had a chance to exhale.

Part of him wanted to sprint back to the park, find that jogger, and tackle-hug him across the grass—or at least get his name so he could write an epic ballad in his honor. But he'd have to settle for adding another grateful portrait in his sketchbook.

And he'd have to make sure to credit him for the *awesome* hotel recommendation.

The building looked a little plain from the outside—and the inside had that weird kind of human fanciness where all the furniture looked super rigid and uncomfortable, and everything was decorated with flowers.

But when he got to his room?

Whoa.

He'd asked for the nicest one they had available, figuring, *Why not? Daddy Dearest is paying for it.* And he'd ended up in a suite that felt like his own private apartment, with multiple bedrooms and huge windows overlooking a park.

The hotel also had a guy called a concierge whose job apparently was to help guests with anything they needed. So Keefe asked him if he knew anywhere he could sell some old family jewelry, and also where he could buy some new clothes.

Less than an hour later, he had a list of jewelry buyers waiting for his call and had been chauffeured to an enormous department store, where a girl introduced herself as his personal shopper and helped him buy an entire new wardrobe—everything from coats, shirts, and pants to pajamas and socks. It was a good thing he had his handy credit card—and that he remembered to bring his passport and sign *Keefe Foster*. He even treated himself to a Batman hoodie and a T-shirt that said IT'S ME. HI. I'M THE PROBLEM, IT'S ME.—which felt very fitting.

According to his shopper, it was a lyric from a song he needed to listen to.

She'd actually gasped when he'd asked, "What's a Swiftie?"

She'd also recommended a pub Keefe should try for lunch, and Keefe decided to order something called bubble and squeak—because how could he not? And even though it turned out to be a pile of potatoes and cabbage that neither bubbled nor squeaked while he ate it, he still gave it points for the funny name.

Now he was back in his suite, enjoying an abundance of room service, which was one of those *Where has this been all my life?* kind of things.

One quick call, and every dessert on their menu had been brought to his room on shiny silver platters.

Then he'd changed into the fluffy robe he'd found in the closet, set himself up on the sorta-comfy couch with every fluffy pillow he could find, and started soaking his blistered feet in a couple of ice buckets while gorging on fancy baked goods.

If that wasn't a happy place, he didn't know what was.

But the whole "getting control of one of his abilities" thing felt like it deserved a little celebration.

He didn't even mind that the water they brought him tasted like they'd either bottled puddle water—or someone's old foot-bath.

Or that Silveny and the twins had started bombarding him with transmissions again.

It was actually nice knowing they hadn't given up on him yet.

He found himself chanting along with them—*KEEFE! KEEFE! KEEFE!*—as he updated his sketchbook with a detailed portrait of the jogger and filled the page next to it with all his latest survival lessons:

Always ask for a suite.

Get used to being called Mr. Foster.

No amount of sugar will make coffee taste better—but it's still worth it.

Guard your snacks in the park.

Room service might be the greatest invention in human history.

Order tea instead of the horrible water.

Concierges are geniuses.

WEIRD VISUALIZATION EXERCISES CAN FIX ANYTHING!!!

He underlined that last one three times, then drew a bunch of stars around it. But it still didn't feel like he'd properly captured how huge the revelation was.

He added a few more flourishes before he realized the reason it still looked small was because he'd learned something *much* bigger—something he was honestly a little afraid to write down, in case seeing the words on paper would make them feel less possible.

But he was going to need the reminder.

So he took a deep breath and wrote four words he hadn't believed in a very long time:

I'm in control now.

Ever since his mom's hood blew back on Mount Everest and he realized who she *really* was, he'd felt like he was spinning, spinning, spinning.

Trapped in a huge, horrible whirlwind he couldn't escape and wasn't sure he could survive.

"But I'm in control now," he said out loud. "I stood in a crowded store and tuned out everyone's emotions without even thinking about it."

If he could do that, surely he could learn to manage the rest of his abilities.

He just needed to find the right visualization exercises— which might be a little tricky since he didn't really understand how the abilities worked.

But he'd figure it out.

Just like he was going to figure out what role he'd already played in his mom's little schemes.

"I'm in control now," he told himself, flipping to a new page in his sketchbook. "Anything that happened before was just . . ."

His voice trailed off.

He wanted to say "the past"—as if that would somehow let him off the hook.

But things in the past were still a part of him.

Erasing the memories didn't change what had happened.

Nothing would.

So he sat up a little straighter as he said, "Anything that

happened before is part of my story—but it doesn't have to define me."

He was in control now.

If he'd done something he regretted, he could make it right.

But how? that obnoxious, hard-to-please voice in the back of his head wondered.

He was trying to find out if he'd played a role in the deaths of two innocent people.

How could he ever make up for *that?*

Maybe he couldn't.

But . . .

He could at least set the record straight.

Make sure his mom didn't get away with whatever she'd done.

And who knew—maybe the truth wouldn't be as bad as he was fearing.

Only one way to know for sure . . .

He squared his shoulders and shook the tension out of his wrists before he slowly wrote:

Find out what happened to Ethan Benedict Wright II and his daughter, Eleanor.

Seeing their names made him want to barf up all the delicious desserts.

But he didn't look away.

Instead, he wrote the two questions he *had* to find the answers to:

Did my mom kill them?

Did I help?

A lump caught in his throat, and it took three tries to clear it away before he could mumble, "I guess the best place to start is with what I actually know."

He filled the rest of the page with everything he'd been able to figure out so far, listing each fact on a separate line.

Ethan and Eleanor lived in a house in London with a green door.

Mommy Dearest made me deliver a letter there when I was eleven—and then had the memory shattered.

The letter had a symbol on it: two crescents surrounding a star. No idea what it means. (Side note: I'm really sick of symbols!)

I was supposed to drop the letter off without being seen—but I must've handed the letter to Ethan because I remember what he looked like.

According to Fintan, my mom had been trying to recruit Ethan for one of her "side projects," and it didn't work out.

Sometime after I delivered the letter, Ethan—and his daughter— were killed.

The obituary called it an accident. Said they were hit by a bus.

But my mom was in London that night—barely an hour after it happened.

I don't believe in coincidences.

He decided not to include what Mr. Forkle had told him— that he'd checked through all the surveillance archives and found no record of Keefe being in London the week before the accident or the entire week after.

All that meant was that he hadn't been *seen*.

He needed to know if he'd been *involved*—and the best way to do that was to go to the scene of the accident and see if it triggered anything.

If it *did* . . .

Well . . .

At least he had his answer.

If it *didn't* . . . he still had more searching to do.

And while a big part of him wanted to say, *Cool, this is a good start!* and close the journal and get some rest . . .

He knew he wasn't going to be able to sleep until he stood at that intersection and found out if he recovered any memories.

Before he could change his mind, he got up, changed his clothes, called room service, and asked them to send up some coffee.

Then he called the concierge and said, "How do I get to the British Library?"

SEVENTEEN

S O THIS IS WHERE IT HAPPENED," KEEFE mumbled, staring at the busy intersection framed by enormous redbrick buildings.

Vehicles of all different shapes and sizes kept zooming by, one after the next after the next.

Add in the people crowding the sidewalks or rushing back and forth across the streets, and he could definitely see how someone could step off the curb at the wrong moment—or how a distracted driver might not see them until it was too late.

But just because it was *possible* didn't mean that's what happened.

His mom was smart enough to pick a plausible scenario to cover her crime.

In fact, that was kind of the Neverseen's specialty.

Like when they made everyone believe a tidal wave had crashed through the Havenfield caves and swept Foster and Dex out to sea.

Everyone was so convinced by the story—even without finding any bodies—that their families ended up holding plantings in the Wanderling Woods. Meanwhile, Foster and Dex had been kidnapped and were locked up in a human city getting interrogated.

Keefe's insides turned sour and squirmy—like he'd swallowed a bucket of rotten sludgers—when he remembered the way his mom had given him her handkerchief after he'd broken down at the plantings.

She'd even rested her hand on his shoulder and defended him when his dad lectured him about "making a spectacle."

Then she'd said, "I didn't realize you'd grown this close to either of them"—which was probably what inspired her to turn him into her personal tracking device after Foster and Dex escaped.

And then she—

Nope.

He could play *Which Mommy Memory Is the Worst?* later.

Right now he was trying to solve a murder.

He studied the intersection again, watching for any sparkle—but the only surveillance seemed to point toward the library.

That's probably why Forkle didn't have any recordings of the "accident"—which felt like more proof that his mom had to be behind it.

She would've chosen her location strategically—then lurked in the shadows waiting for Ethan and Eleanor to show up.

Or maybe she only planned for Ethan to be there, and Eleanor was an unexpected complication.

Either way, a ten-year-old girl ended up dead, along with her father.

And all his mom would've had to do was give them a quick little mental shove with her telekinesis.

Anyone watching would've assumed Ethan and Eleanor tripped in front of the bus.

Then again, Keefe had a feeling his mom would've let someone else do the creepy part.

She would've wanted to protect her sanity.

So maybe she sent Trix to knock them into the road with a gust of wind. Or ordered Gethen to do some freaky mind trick to distract them—or the driver. Or let Umber—

A huge red bus whizzed past, and Keefe stumbled back.

It was so much bigger than the buses he'd seen in other cities.

It even had a second story.

Getting hit by something like that . . .

He didn't want to picture it—but he closed his eyes and made himself visualize the scene.

There would've been screams. Tires screeching. Probably some sort of horrible THUD. People running away—or rushing to help. And the bodies . . .

He covered his mouth, but that didn't stop him from gagging as the gruesome images flooded his head.

But after a couple of deep breaths, he realized the images were horrible and ugly—but they were also missing a ton of details.

He couldn't see what Ethan and Eleanor were wearing, or how their hair was styled, or if they died in the middle of the road or right next to the sidewalk. He didn't even know what Eleanor looked like. He also couldn't make out any faces in the crowd or hear anything anyone was saying. And he couldn't see the time on the library's clock tower, or tell if any cars stopped to help, or any of the other things his photographic memory *would've* filled in if he'd actually witnessed that moment instead of just trying to imagine it.

"Nothing's triggering," he mumbled, taking another long look around and realizing that he wasn't feeling the right things either.

Emotions couldn't be erased the way memories could—so if he'd been there, he would've felt shocked and scared and horrified and overwhelmed and all kinds of other things that were so much stronger than the nervous dread coiled deep in the pit of his stomach, which he'd been feeling since he left his hotel.

"I wasn't here when it happened," he said, letting out a breath as the words sank in. "I couldn't have been."

Something would've triggered if he had.

A fragment of memory.

A wave of emotion.

"I wasn't here," he repeated, finally starting to believe it.

His knees wanted to collapse with relief—*BUT*.

That didn't mean he wasn't still involved with what happened.

He'd seen Ethan Benedict Wright II's face well enough to be able to draw a detailed portrait—and in the portrait, Ethan had been holding Mommy Dearest's letter.

So he definitely delivered it.

And what if the note had been a threat?

Or told Ethan to be in front of the British Library the day he died?

It made Keefe really, really, really, *really* wish he'd read that letter.

He honestly couldn't believe he hadn't.

Yeah, his mom had ordered him not to open the envelope—even threatened to send him to Exillium if he did. And yeah, she'd also assured him he wouldn't be able to understand the letter if he did try to read it because it was written in a human language.

But since when did he pay attention to stuff like that?

Unless he didn't . . .

He *could've* carefully opened the envelope, read his mom's letter—or tried to, at least—sealed it back up before he delivered it, and just didn't realize it because the memory had all kinds of damaged bits.

That sounded *way* more like him—and would also explain why his mom didn't just have the memory washed.

She'd had it *shattered*.

Maybe she knew he'd seen the letter and had to do everything in her power to make sure he'd never remember.

But he *had* remembered.

All he needed was one more teeny, tiny piece.

Less than a second's flash of the letter, and his photographic memory would help him record every detail.

Every word.

Every flourish.

Everything she hadn't wanted him to see.

And if it was written in a human language, he'd be able to read it now.

Being a Polyglot came in super handy.

But . . .

He was in the wrong place if he wanted to trigger that memory.

For *that*, he needed to find a way back to where he got dragged into this nightmare in the first place—and it wasn't going to be easy.

All he knew for sure was that the house was somewhere in London.

And it had a green door.

EIGHTEEN

I
T *MIGHT* HAVE A GREEN DOOR," KEEFE
corrected.

He wouldn't put it past his mom to make sure that
little detail changed, since it was one of the only things
she'd told him about how to find the place.

And if she *had* changed the color, then all he knew for sure
was that it was a house with a door—like every other house in
London.

Great.

He kicked a loose pebble into the street and cringed when a
car crunched it into itty-bitty pieces.

Don't think about it.

Don't think about it.

Do. Not. Think. About. It.

But his brain still went ahead and reminded him that Ethan and Eleanor had died that same way.

STOP!

He sucked in a breath to shut down his much-too-vivid imagination.

Focus on learning the truth.

That's what matters right now.

There had to be a way to find that house without having to check every door in the city.

Maybe he could remember something that would help him narrow the search.

He closed his eyes and replayed the shattered memory, focusing on the tiny details he might've overlooked—like how thick the envelope felt, which probably meant the letter had multiple pages. And how the cobalt-blue leaping crystal his mom gave him only had one facet.

She must've created it specifically to reach Ethan's house—which made him want to leap back to Candleshade and tear the place apart.

But that'd be a bigger waste of time than walking every street in London.

His mom would've destroyed that crystal the moment her little recruiting project failed.

Which made him wonder . . .

What exactly was she trying to recruit Ethan for?

And why Ethan Benedict Wright II?

Why him and not any of the zillions of other humans out there?

"Wait," Keefe said—then realized he should probably stop talking out loud when two old ladies raised their eyebrows expectantly.

He offered a sheepish smile and walked away—but only a few steps.

He didn't want to go any farther.

Because he happened to be standing outside of a giant library—and this might be one of those rare moments when "research" was actually a good idea.

Is it, though? he had to ask.

Ninety percent of the time, research was a phenomenal waste of effort.

But . . . he didn't have a lot of other options.

And who knew?

Maybe he'd get really lucky and Ethan's address would be on file somewhere.

Did humans have some sort of registry with a record of where everyone lived?

Probably not.

But he did remember Alvar telling him one time—back when he was bragging about all his little trips to the Forbidden Cities—that whenever he got stuck or lost or in over his head, human librarians were his heroes.

"*Fiiiiiiiiiiiiine,*" Keefe said, making the word a giant sigh as he turned to head toward the library.

But Forkle doesn't get to know about this.

If anyone asked, he was a genius who figured everything out by his own sheer brilliance.

He also definitely did *not* walk into the wrong building on his first try—though, in his defense, it seemed like a logical assumption to think that the library would be the big fancy building with the clock tower and all the decorative frills.

Nope!

That was actually a giant train station full of very stressed-looking people rushing around trying to find the right platform.

The library was the big, boring, squarish building across the street—which was honestly kind of fitting.

Keefe might've stood in the entrance a lot longer than he meant to, trying to figure out where to start.

It was a *lot* of books.

Like, a LOT, a lot.

So many, in fact, that it almost seemed easier to check every door in London.

But . . . Alvar said librarians were his heroes, so maybe Keefe could get a little help.

He made his way over to one of the desks, flashing his most charming smile—but he didn't need any charm.

It turned out librarians actually *enjoyed* research.

Keefe also needed to get way better at answering their questions.

The librarian looked at him like he had six heads when he said, "What's a Google?" and then admitted he didn't have any kind of phone.

But after a particularly awkward moment where he might've talked about the internet like it was an actual net, the librarian did a quick search and printed Keefe a small stack of obituaries.

The top article was the same one that Forkle had already shown him.

The two after that were so short, they were barely more than the names.

The fourth described Ethan Benedict Wright II as a "prominent astrophysicist"—which was at least some new information. But when Keefe asked the librarian for a book on astrophysics, they started listing off a bunch of titles that sounded like they might be the most boring books in the entire universe.

The fifth obituary had a short note about a burial happening at a specific cemetery—and Keefe made a note of the location. But he wasn't sure he could handle visiting their graves.

Not until he knew if he was responsible.

Especially after he checked the last obituary.

It didn't tell him anything new.

But . . . it had a photo.

Ethan Benedict Wright II looked exactly like Keefe had drawn him, with his wild hair, tweed jacket, and crooked bow tie. And he had his arm around an adorable little girl.

Her hair was a dark color—maybe brown, maybe red. It was hard to tell from the grainy black-and-white. And her cheeks had deep dimples from smiling the hugest grin ever.

Keefe probably should've been relieved that she didn't look familiar and that no memories were triggering.

Maybe that proved he really wasn't involved with what happened to them.

But seeing her made it a zillion times harder to let himself off the hook.

"Did you know them?" the librarian asked, and Keefe jumped so hard, he dropped the obituaries, sending the pages fluttering to the floor. "Sorry—didn't mean to startle."

"It's fine," Keefe said, scrubbing tears out of his eyes. "And no, I don't think I did."

Probably the wrong answer.

Keefe had a feeling the librarian was probably now wondering why someone would ask for the obituaries of people he didn't know—and start crying over them.

But it was too late to change his answer.

And he was too overwhelmed to find a way to cover.

So he just thanked the librarian for their help and turned to leave.

"Did you want me to have any of these astrophysics titles

brought out for you?" the librarian asked. "I can set you up with a pass to use one of the reading rooms."

But it would probably mean giving his name, and that seemed like a very bad idea.

Especially in London.

In fact, if he wanted to do any more research, he should probably leap somewhere else. Spread it out between a bunch of libraries, so no one would remember him or be able to ask too many questions.

But he wasn't leaving London, either.

Not after seeing that photo.

He owed Ethan and Eleanor answers—and he'd walk the entire city if he had to.

One door at a time.

One library at a time.

As long as it took.

It was the least he could do.

NINETEEN

DON'T EVEN THINK ABOUT IT!" Keefe warned the glowing eyes that were staring at him from the shadows of a nearby flower bed.

He'd stopped to rest on the same bench in the same park as he had a few days earlier, so he probably shouldn't be surprised that his little fox buddy was also there, trying to steal his lunch.

Or was it his dinner?

It'd been lunchtime in the city where he'd just spent several hours in a giant public library reading up on astrophysics— and trying not to face-plant into the books because, wow, were they boring.

But he'd taken the "slice" he'd bought himself back to

London, where the sun was now setting, so that probably meant he should count it as dinner.

All he knew for sure was that his piece of pizza was melty and cheesy and twice as big as his head—and time zones would never stop being confusing.

"Seriously, stop looking at me," Keefe told the eyes, which had widened in a way that made them look extra pathetic. "You can't have my pizza. Or my giant chocolate chip cookie. Or my bagel. Actually, wait—do foxes eat fish? I didn't realize that's what this lox stuff was."

He unwrapped his bagel and peeled off the thin pink strips, wondering if it was a bad idea to feed the furry little thief.

The eyes blinked, and Keefe was pretty sure he heard a tiny whimper.

"Ugh. Fiiiiiiiine—but this is all you're going to get from me!"

He tossed the lox toward the flower bed—but intentionally shorted his throw, letting it land about halfway between them.

Seemed only fair to make the little furry dude have to work for it.

"Stop being so paranoid," Keefe said when the fox paced in the shadows. "I'm not going to hurt you."

The fox wasn't convinced.

"Suit yourself. But I'm betting one of the birds over there is going to swoop in and grab your dinner any second now."

A bird let out a particularly loud screech, clearly agreeing with him.

The flowers rustled.

And even though Keefe knew exactly where to look, he barely saw the fox as it darted out, snatched the lox with its teeth, and fled to the shadows.

"Not bad," Keefe told him. "I should have you give me some tips on blending in."

He'd been to five other libraries now, in five different cities over the last five days—all from a list of the best libraries in the world that the concierge was awesome enough to make for him. And no matter how hard Keefe tried, he always ended up saying or doing something that drew way too much attention.

But how was he supposed to know what the Dewey decimal system was?

Or that the little clicky gadget they used for their computers was called a mouse?

And don't even get him started on the whole "meme"-"hashtag"-"emoji" stuff everyone was always talking about. Or how apparently it was a good thing to go "viral."

He'd also accidentally worn thick pants, long sleeves, and a heavy coat to the first city he visited, which turned out to be hot and humid and a place where everyone else was in shorts and tank tops. He ditched what he could and rolled up his sleeves, but by the time he'd trudged to the library, his skin was bright red, and he learned the hard way that sunlight was much, much stronger in the human world.

Apparently, they even had this whole UV index thing to help them prepare for it, along with air-quality alerts—which kinda made him want to stay inside and try not to breathe.

Instead, he used up one of the balms his dad gave him to treat his sunburn and drowned his sorrows in queso and sweet tea, like the librarian recommended.

He was seriously starting to regret teasing Foster for sometimes getting confused about elvin stuff—even though she looked so adorable when she blushed.

He never realized how hard it was to blend in when everything you knew didn't match.

And for added fun, every place he went was completely different.

Different clothes.

Different languages.

Different customs to keep up with.

He probably wouldn't have felt so overwhelmed if he were at least making some progress on his projects. But so far all he'd learned about astrophysics was that it was about studying the forces of the universe—and that humans got a ton of stuff wrong when it came to science.

And while Ethan Benedict Wright II had been called "prominent" in that obituary, Keefe had yet to find a single reference to his work.

Keefe also made time every day to wander more streets in London—crossing each one off on a map that his buddy, the concierge, gave him, to keep track of where he'd been.

So far nothing looked familiar—but that didn't mean as much as he would've liked it to, because the annoying thing about doors?

They were all pretty much the same.

Even with a photographic memory, it was hard to spot any differences between a wooden rectangle surrounded by bricks, and a wooden rectangle surrounded by bricks, and, oh wow—another wooden rectangle surrounded by bricks!

Color seemed to be the easiest way to tell them apart—but of course he couldn't rely on that. So he was stuck focusing on the only other significant detail: the thin metal mail slot he'd slipped the letter through.

But he couldn't remember the type of metal it was made of, or if there'd been any filigree or ornamentation.

Honestly, he couldn't actually remember delivering the letter—but he kept hoping that if he saw the mail slot again, his brain would suddenly be like, *YES! THAT'S IT!*

It wasn't much of a plan, but . . . he had to keep trying.

And at least he was getting to see some cool things and eat more awesome foods.

Like the giant shiny silver bean thing he'd walked by after visiting a library in a particularly windy city—where he also got to try a deep-dish style of pizza that was a completely different experience than the thin-crust version. Also the gooey, flaky butter tarts the third librarian told him he couldn't leave a pretty coastal city without trying, along with a giant box of fried dough balls called Timbits.

He'd even found the elusive Ding Dongs in the fourth city he visited—and they were . . .

Meh.

He was pretty sure the white stuff in the middle was some sort of glue—BUT!

They also led him to the greatest discovery he'd had on this little adventure so far—possibly the greatest discovery he'd ever made in his entire life.

HOW HAD FOSTER NEVER TOLD HIM THERE WERE HUMAN SNACKS CALLED RITZ CRACKERS?!

Sure, they were even drier and crumblier than those horrible digestive biscuit things.

BUT.

Fitz Vacker!

Ritz cracker!

There were Too. Many. Jokes!

He'd wanted to buy a box and bring it to Fitzy—maybe even pelt him with crackers—but he still wasn't sure when he'd be going home, and hauling it around in his overstuffed backpack would turn it into a Ritz-smush.

So he'd drawn the front of the box in his sketchbook—then drawn it again as "Fitz Vackers" with Fitz's grinning face on each of the crackers.

Then he'd filled the next page with all his other recent lessons and bits of wisdom.

Check the weather before leaping anywhere.

Always wear sunscreen.

New goal: Try every kind of pizza that exists.

It's way less shocking to say your phone "died" or that you "forgot it" than to say you don't have one.

The "bubbles" in bubble tea are actually slimy little balls—that are still kinda good if you don't mind having to chew your drink.

Some humans carry tiny dogs around in their handbags.

Never settle for someone's first offer.

The last note was inspired by the process of finally selling a piece of his mom's jewelry.

Keefe had taken his father's advice and started with a single stone—but he was pretty sure he didn't sell it for enough.

He'd gotten so good at tuning out human emotions that he hadn't considered it might've been useful to take a quick reading—until he'd already agreed to the amount.

Then the guy smiled the kind of smug, oily smile his father was a master of, and Keefe realized he should've countered.

But it didn't matter.

He had plenty of other jewelry to sell—and it was his mom's stuff anyway, so it wasn't like he cared about it.

He'd also still gotten enough cash to get him through a few weeks.

But next time, he'd negotiate better.

In fact, he felt the need to add one more very important lesson to his sketchbook.

Don't forget that you have special abilities.

Yeah, they were kind of a mess, and he was mostly trying to ignore them.

But they were still a huge advantage he should be using whenever they might be helpful.

It wasn't like that would be cheating, since he'd just be . . . being himself—which might be why it felt a little weird that he needed a reminder.

Almost like . . .

. . . he was starting to forget that he was an elf.

"Wow," he mumbled, glancing over to the fox, who was still watching him from the shadows. "Now who's being paranoid?"

How long had he been in Humanland? And he was already questioning his identity?

This caught-between-two-worlds thing was seriously messing with his head—and he couldn't help wondering if Foster had felt the same way.

But . . . of course she had.

She'd actually *thought* she was human—until Fitzy turned up and told her, *GUESS WHAT, YOU'RE AN ELF!*

Talk about an identity crisis.

And once again, he had to stop himself from grabbing Grady's Imparter and hailing her, this time to ask, *How did you deal with this? Please share all your secrets!*

But then he wouldn't be able to stop himself from telling her how much he wished she could be there with him, and how hard it was to ignore the alicorns constantly chanting, *KEEFE! KEEFE! KEEFE!*

And how he hoped his letter hadn't ruined everything because he couldn't stop thinking about her and—

He sat up taller, wondering if his brain was officially melting down, because he could've sworn—*sworn*—he'd just heard Foster's voice whispering around in his head.

But it couldn't be, could it?

He must've imagined it.

Still, he closed his eyes and concentrated and . . .

IT WAS HER!

I miss you, she'd transmitted. *It's better when you're around.*

For a second, Keefe couldn't breathe.

Then he needed to move—stand up—pace around the park, try to figure out if she'd somehow heard all the sappy things he'd just been imagining.

He didn't see how that could be possible.

But what were the odds that she'd been thinking about him—*missing* him—the exact same moment he'd been thinking about her?

And if that's really what happened . . . *What did that mean?*

Probably nothing.

But he couldn't help leaning back against a lantern and staring at the sky, where a full moon was peeking through a swirl of clouds, and imagining Foster back at Havenfield doing the same thing.

Maybe she had Wynn and Luna with her.

Maybe they were all calling for him together.

He'd probably never know.

But he told the moon and the stars, "I miss you too."

TWENTY

I COULD BE WATCHING A MOVIE RIGHT NOW," Keefe said through a very heavy sigh as he stared at the towering walls covered in brightly lit bookshelves.

It'd taken him longer than usual to find this particularly enormous library—partially because it was super far from the arrival point, but mostly because it turned out to be hidden inside something called a mall.

And a mall was apparently a bunch of places where Keefe would much rather spend the day, all crammed together into one space to taunt him.

Stores!

Restaurants!

Even some sort of aquarium.

Plus a big fancy movie theater—and one of the movies looked like it was about a character with superpowers.

So he *could* be watching a human dude run around in a skintight bodysuit pretending to save the world.

But no—he was stuck in the land of never-ending research and perpetually uncomfortable chairs.

Seriously, how did humans manage to make their cushions so hard and lumpy?

It almost seemed like it had to be intentional.

And why did they have so many books?

It was starting to feel excessive—especially since he rarely noticed anyone reading.

Every so often he'd pass someone in a café with a book in front of them, or spot kids in a park with their noses buried in a fantastical-looking story.

But ninety percent of the time, all he saw was people staring at their phones.

Even now, the library had these giant towers of illuminated bookshelves flanking a moving staircase—and what were people doing?

Taking pictures of the towers with their phones.

Keefe honestly wouldn't be surprised if a lot of the books were mostly there for decoration.

The librarian had even suggested he try using one of their tablets to do his research—which was basically just a bigger version of a phone.

And despite the librarian's assurance that the tablet was user-friendly, Keefe had to keep going back, saying, "Uh . . . I accidentally tapped one of the little square thingies, and now I can't find where I was searching."

So he was pretty sure the librarian hated him.

If not, it was only a matter of time, because he'd just clicked something that made the whole screen go black.

"Whoa, what did you do?" she asked with an expression that could've been boredom, frustration, or calmly plotting his destruction.

"No idea," Keefe admitted.

He tried to memorize the steps as she slowly fixed the problem—but he could tell he was definitely going to mess it up again.

Between the tiny buttons on the sides of the tablet and all the little app things, it was too much clicking and swiping and holding and tapping—and don't even get him started on the friendly robot voice who was supposed to answer his questions but mostly kept telling him, "I'm not sure I understand."

"I can't believe you've never used one of these," the librarian said as she handed the tablet back.

"Yeah, I know. I'm weird."

Keefe had found that acknowledging his oddness was often enough to make someone lose interest.

Sadly, though, the librarian still asked, "Where exactly are you from?"

Keefe was tempted to tell her, *Believe it or not, I'm an elf from a secret world hidden on this planet*, just to see what she'd say.

But with the suspicious way she was looking at him, she might believe him—or see it as proof that he'd lost his mind.

Either way, it was probably time to get out of there.

Or.

It kinda seemed like the perfect opportunity to put that whole "don't forget that you have special abilities" lesson to use and see if he was right about the librarian's mood.

So he told her, "I move around a lot," as he tried to concentrate on what she was feeling, and . . .

All he could sense was a dull, fuzzy hum.

Waving his hands back and forth to try to feel the emotions brushing his skin didn't help either—but it *did* make her eyebrows get all scrunched together and her lips curl into a frown.

Okay, probably time to go.

At least he was able to thank her for her help, hand the tablet back, grab his coat, and walk away without having to fight the urge to give any commands.

The library was also pretty crowded—and only got busier the more he moved toward the exit—but he didn't feel even slightly overwhelmed.

So, see?

Everything was still under control.

But . . . he didn't like how vague his empathy had felt.

Yeah, he'd been trying to train his brain to subconsciously tune out emotions—but when he actually *tried*, he should still be able to read everything clearly.

Had he overcorrected somehow?

Or . . .

The pit of his stomach started to churn like he'd eaten too many Flamin' Hot Cheetos when he remembered what happened to Empaths who let themselves feel too many intense emotions.

All the sensations would start to blur together, until they went . . .

"No way," he said under his breath, not letting himself finish the thought. "It couldn't happen that fast."

Then again, he'd spent days getting bombarded by an extreme amount of intense emotions. . . .

"Stop!" he told himself. "You're being paranoid again."

His empathy was just . . . different now.

He was still getting used to it—just like he'd needed to get used to it when he manifested the first time.

That's why Foxfire had twice-a-week special-ability sessions.

He'd been so focused on trying to rein the abilities in—or ignore them—that he'd forgotten he was also going to need to train them.

And the library seemed like a good place to get started, since it was crowded but not chaotic, and still fairly quiet.

He even spotted the perfect practice place: neat rows of

chairs, where a bunch of people had gathered—some by themselves, others in small groups.

They were all so busy reading or admiring the library or tapping on their phones that they wouldn't notice if he spent a few minutes staring at them.

In fact, none of them even looked up as Keefe made his way to an empty seat in the middle.

Okay, he thought, trying to remember his earliest empathy lessons. *Let's start with something easy.*

His first Mentor had been big on learning to read visual clues to help translate feelings. So Keefe had spent a bunch of time studying other prodigies' faces, trying to guess the emotions behind their expressions—and then taking a reading to see if he'd been right.

It was a cool exercise, honestly.

Got him really good at noticing tiny microexpressions.

The quick twitch of an eyebrow or the soft parting of the lips could say so much more than most people realized.

Let's see, he thought, focusing on the guy a couple of chairs over, who had bright blue bangs that probably would've made Tammy Boy jealous. His lips were pressed together with the slightest downward curve, and there were tiny lines across his forehead as he tapped the screen of his phone.

Keefe was pretty sure those were cues that the guy was feeling disappointed—but when he tried reading his emotions to verify, all he felt was the same vague hum he'd gotten from the librarian.

Totally fine, he told himself, even though his heart rate kicked up a notch. *I'm still warming up.*

He moved on to a group that should've been easier: three girls with wide eyes and bouncy feet, flipping through magazines about something called K-pop and practically oozing giddiness.

He closed his eyes, trying to stay calm when he picked up the same vague hum again.

Concentrate. They're obviously excited. Let yourself feel it.

His brain still didn't want to cooperate, but Keefe imagined his senses sweeping aside the dull noise—brushing it out of his way, so he could feel what was underneath and . . .

He picked up a faint, tingly crackle.

See? he thought, huffing out a huge breath. *It just takes practice.*

He tried not to think about how much harder he'd had to work to pick up that sensation.

Instead, he tried again—and was able to catch a wave of exhaustion from a mom wrestling with two very energetic kiddos a few rows over.

Then a tug of sadness from the girl behind him, who was reading the last few pages of a book.

The emotions definitely weren't as vivid as he was used to— but at least he was feeling each sensation a little faster.

And bonus: The other emotions in the room weren't starting to batter his senses.

So he wasn't undoing any of the progress he'd made with keeping the ability manageable.

Even when he pushed himself to reach farther and focused on a couple in the very first row of chairs.

There was such an obvious gap between them that they were either on a first date or about to break up—and Keefe needed several deep breaths before he was able to concentrate on their emotions.

At first all he picked up was prickly nervousness. But when he pushed his brain a little harder, he caught a whiff of warm delight.

Definitely a first date, then.

Probably with a second date to follow.

Even better—he'd read those feelings across a decent amount of space, so the training really was making a difference.

He'd have to add a lesson about that to his sketchbook.

One more, he decided, *just to really make sure I have the hang of this.*

He glanced over his shoulder and chose a guy in a dark coat sprawled across two chairs in the very last row.

His face was partially covered by the tablet he was reading, but . . .

Keefe froze, blinking hard to make sure his eyes weren't playing tricks on him.

The guy looked . . .

Familiar.

But it couldn't be him.

Not here.

Not anywhere, honestly.

Keefe had to be imagining it.

But he needed to be absolutely certain, so he waited a few breaths, trying to look very, very casual—ducking his chin below his shoulder as he turned his head enough to get a clear look.

Ice crackled through his veins, and his heart dropped into his stomach.

It wasn't a mistake.

The scars on the guy's face had lightened since the last time Keefe saw him—and he didn't look nearly so pale or bony.

But it was *him*.

Even though it was impossible.

There Keefe was, in the middle of a library, in the middle of a Forbidden City.

And so was Alvar.

TWENTY-ONE

RUN! KEEFE'S BRAIN SCREAMED.
GET OUT OF HERE IMMEDIATELY!
But he stayed put.
Not moving.

Barely breathing.

Trying to think.

Because even though most of his head kept insisting, *THE NEVERSEEN ARE HERE!!!* there was also a tiny, slightly more rational part that reminded him Alvar wasn't with the Neverseen anymore.

They'd kicked him out.

Blamed him for Umber's death and Ruy's ability getting damaged during the mutant-newborn troll attack at Everglen.

Left him to die from the injuries he'd sustained in that battle.

Which was why Alvar had looked like he only had a few days left to live when Keefe found him hiding in Candleshade—and that was back before everything Keefe endured in Loamnore.

So how could Alvar be sprawled across some chairs in a random human library, looking not only *not dead* but honestly not even close to death?

His eyes weren't hollow and sunken anymore, and his face didn't have that greenish, sweaty sheen.

Did that mean Alvar had been faking how sick he was when Foster convinced Keefe it was worth letting Alvar go in exchange for a tiny bit of information about his "legacy"?

Maybe.

But Keefe didn't see how Alvar could've pulled that off.

His body had been so frail, Keefe had been able to see his bones through his skin. And he'd had this horrible, raspy cough that sounded like a death rattle—and he was so weak, he kept flickering as he tried to vanish, like a fading candle.

Plus, Keefe had read Alvar's emotions, and underneath all the fury and arrogance had been a deep, nauseating dread.

Alvar had known his days were numbered.

He'd even given up trying to fight it.

So seriously, *how* was he still alive?

And what did he want? Because Keefe didn't see how they could both just happen to turn up in the same library in the same Forbidden City at the same time.

He didn't believe in coincidences.

And yet . . . so far, Alvar hadn't so much as glanced his way.

He hadn't looked at anyone.

Or talked to anyone.

Or done anything except tap on his tablet and read whatever was on the screen.

And when Keefe checked Alvar's emotions, all he felt was a cloud of calm boredom.

It almost made him want to launch over the chairs and tackle Alvar to the floor—maybe throw a few good punches while he was at it, since Alvar definitely deserved them.

But.

There was a teeny, tiny chance that Alvar somehow didn't know he was there—and if that was the case, Keefe had to play this smart.

He needed to find out what Alvar was doing in the Forbidden Cities—and stop anything horrible he might be planning.

So he slouched down, grabbed an abandoned book off the next chair to hide his face, and sat, and sat, and sat.

His back ached and his butt went numb and his eyes burned from trying not to blink—but he couldn't let his guard down.

Alvar would need less than a second to vanish.

And yet he just kept reading and reading and reading and—

Wait—he was getting up!

Keefe jumped to his feet—then realized he probably should've been more subtle.

He braced for Alvar to whip around, like, *Did you really think I didn't know you were there?*

Instead, Alvar made his way over to one of the librarians—leaving Keefe scrambling to grab his coat and catch up.

He hid behind a bookshelf and watched Alvar flash an almost charming smile while he returned the tablet—then zipped up his dark coat and headed out into the mall.

Keefe trailed behind, trying to blend in with the crowd and keep a safe distance.

He knew there was a decent chance Alvar was leading him to some sort of ambush—but that was a risk he had to take.

And it started feeling less and less likely the more he followed Alvar from store to store.

Weirdly enough, Alvar seemed to be . . . shopping.

First he ducked into a candy store and bought a small red bag of sweets—which honestly looked like the most boring candy in the entire shop. But he shoved that into his pocket and made his way to a store full of cute little things shaped like cute little animals.

Alvar admired several different plushies but ended up leaving without buying anything.

Meanwhile, Keefe lurked outside trying to wrap his head around the mental image of Alvar holding a pink fluffy bunny.

Like, seriously, what was happening?

How was this the same guy who betrayed his friends and family over and over and over?

The whole tackle-and-punch-him plan was starting to feel a *lot* more tempting—but Keefe gritted his teeth and kept his distance, watching Alvar browse a store selling clothes that were way too cool for him.

He must've agreed, because he didn't buy anything there, either.

Same with the store selling nothing but different-colored socks.

He did buy several small foil packets from a beauty store and tuck them into his coat pockets—and maybe that's what he'd been looking for, because he finally left the mall after that.

Wind blasted Keefe's cheeks as he followed Alvar outside, and he threw on his coat, wishing he'd worn one that was gray or black or beige—something that would blend in better than the blue he'd chosen. But it was too cold to go without it.

Or maybe the chills came from watching Alvar pull his black hood up to cover his head.

Alvar picked up his pace after that, weaving down the crowded sidewalk with a confidence that made it clear he'd walked that path before. Probably numerous times.

Did that mean he *lived* in this city?

It'd be a good place for Alvar to hide from all his enemies—but Keefe didn't see how that could be possible.

Then again, nothing about this made any sense.

Even the fact that Alvar was staying visible seemed super weird.

Unless Alvar WANTS to be followed . . .

The thought had barely finished forming when Keefe rounded the next corner—and realized Alvar had disappeared.

He raced forward, peeking in windows, wondering if Alvar had ducked into another store.

But he was gone.

And there was nowhere for Keefe to hide.

Just a few trees with brightly colored leaves and trunks that were way too slender for him to crouch behind.

So he shoved his hands in his pockets, both to cover how shaky he was and to reach for his pathfinder in case he needed to make a quick escape.

Then he searched the crowd—but all he found was humans.

Parents.

Kids.

Businessmen.

Tourists.

No sign of Alvar—until he felt an ominous prickle along the back of his neck.

It was the kind of warning he didn't have to be an Empath to translate, because everyone knew that unsettling feeling.

He's behind me.

Keefe tried to twist his lips into a smirk, but he was pretty sure it didn't reach his eyes as he spun around and . . . there was Alvar.

His face was hidden by the shadows of his hood, but Keefe could hear the smile in his familiar accented voice as he called out, "We probably shouldn't do this here."

TWENTY-TWO

YOU'RE RIGHT—WE NEED TO GO somewhere less crowded!" Keefe shouted, glancing at a mom walking past Alvar with her young son at her side.

She wouldn't get so close if she knew what Alvar was capable of.

Then again, Keefe wasn't sure if *he* knew what Alvar was capable of at the moment.

What he did know was: This wasn't the kind of conversation they could have on a busy street in Humanland.

People were already starting to stare.

"Got anywhere in mind?" Alvar asked.

Keefe almost said no, since he hadn't exactly planned on

needing a safe spot to meet with a traitor who was supposed to be dead—but he wanted to keep as much control of the situation as possible. So he glanced up and down the street and spotted a nearby alley that looked pretty empty.

"I have an idea," he said as he closed the distance between him and Alvar.

"Well then, by all means, lead the way!"

"You first." There was no chance Keefe was taking his eyes off Alvar for even a second.

Alvar snorted. "You realize I can't lead if I don't know where I'm going—which sums up about ninety percent of the problem with the Neverseen, don't you think?"

It did . . . but Keefe wasn't in the mood to agree—or to make sarcastic little jokes about a group that somehow kept winning, despite their unreliable leadership.

He pointed to the alley. "We're heading over there."

Alvar heaved a heavy sigh. "I was afraid you were going to say that. Wouldn't you rather try a nice quiet café? We could share some pancakes! They make both sweet and savory ones here—and the mung bean pancakes are amazing, even though they might sound a little strange."

"We're not getting pancakes!"

"Why not? Wouldn't that be way more fun than standing in a dark, filthy alley? Have you smelled an alley before?"

"I don't care!" Keefe dragged a hand down his face, trying to figure out Alvar's game.

Was he stalling?

Trying to buy time for backup to arrive?

Or maybe he—

Alvar clicked his tongue. "Wow, look who's gotten all paranoid and surly."

"That's what happens when you keep getting betrayed over and over," Keefe snapped back.

"I suppose that's true." A hint of bitterness crept into Alvar's tone, making him sound much more like he had the last time Keefe saw him, when he kept ranting about everyone who'd wronged him and how that justified his rebellion. "Ugh. Fine, we'll go to your stinky alley."

Keefe wasn't sure what convinced Alvar, but he didn't really care.

The alley was just a quick stop.

He spun the pathfinder in his pocket as he followed Alvar over, choosing a random facet that would hopefully take them somewhere quiet—and as soon as Alvar ducked into the shadows, Keefe grabbed his elbow, raised the crystal, and dragged them both into the beam of light.

Alvar screamed, "DON'T!" as the rushing warmth carried them away—but Keefe didn't care that he was basically taking him captive.

He was getting some answers, one way or another.

But he did at least wrap his concentration around Alvar, just in case the forced leap could cause him to fade.

And when they re-formed . . .

"Do you have any idea how dangerous that was?" Alvar asked, gasping for breath as he held up his hands to block the much-too-bright sunlight. "And for what? To drag me to a tiny island?"

"It's deserted, isn't it?" Keefe reminded him, relieved the random leap had finally brought him somewhere isolated.

The only signs of life were some coconut trees and a few crabs skittering across the white sand.

"It's also a million degrees and humid!" Alvar tossed back his hood, and Keefe took the opportunity to study his face.

His scars really did look better.

Most were just thin, pale lines.

And his cheeks were much fuller, and his dark hair wasn't so greasy.

He still didn't look like the guy he used to be, with fancy clothes and big muscles from working out all the time.

But he didn't look seriously ill anymore either—or like someone who'd almost drowned in a pod full of poisonous orange goo.

"Go ahead," Alvar said, sweeping his hair out of his eyes. "Ask me. I know you're dying to."

Keefe didn't bother pretending he wasn't sure what Alvar meant.

He met Alvar's slightly defiant stare and said, "How are you still alive?"

"Long story." Alvar laughed when Keefe's jaw went rigid. "Relax. I didn't say I wouldn't tell it. I just figured I should warn you in case you'd like to be smart and leap us out of here before the heat saps your concentration. It's not too late to go with my pancake idea. Did I mention the sweet ones are stuffed with brown sugar and cinnamon and nuts and—"

"Quit stalling," Keefe interrupted—even though those pancake things sounded pretty amazing.

He actually *was* starting to feel a little dizzy from the heat—but the privacy was worth a little sweat. He pulled off his coat and draped it over a nearby rock, then rolled up his sleeves as high as he could.

"Fine," Alvar said, taking off his coat and dropping it to the sand in a heap. "Have it your way. But I'm at least moving to the shade." He stumbled across the beach and settled into the slim shadow of one of the palm trees.

Keefe followed—not that the shade made much difference.

"The short version," Alvar said, fanning himself with a fallen palm frond, "since I'd like to get out of here as quickly as possible, is . . . human medicine saved me."

"Human medicine," Keefe repeated.

His mind raced through some of the stories Foster had told him about her various human hospital visits, and he couldn't help cringing.

"I figured that'd be your reaction," Alvar mumbled. "Elves love to think everything we do is better and smarter and safer than any of the other species. But the longer I'm around humans, the more value I see to their way of thinking."

"So . . . ," Keefe said when Alvar didn't continue, "you came to the Forbidden Cities because you wanted to meet with their doctors?"

"No, I came to the Forbidden Cities to die." Alvar let that sink in before he added, "After Sophie convinced you to let me go, I leaped to your dad's beach house, figuring I should warn him that you'd discovered our deal. I was also hoping he'd let me stay, since that leap pretty much destroyed me. I was too weak to stand, and my body wouldn't stop shaking. But he said he'd already helped me more than I deserved, and the best he'd do was give me a vial of Fade Fuel and make me a path to wherever I wanted to go next. I had five minutes to choose a place."

"Sounds like Daddy Dearest," Keefe mumbled, not sure why he was surprised that his father never bothered to mention any of this.

"Doesn't it? I knew I wasn't going to survive that leap," Alvar continued quietly. "Pretty sure your dad knew that too. And as I tried to pick where to go, I realized I didn't want to die in the Lost Cities. It wasn't like anyone was going to do a planting for me—"

"Your parents would," Keefe interrupted.

"Would they? Or would they *try*—and then back down if the Council forbid it, or if they got pressured into protecting the 'family name'?"

He spat the last words, and Keefe was sure Alvar was about to launch into some tirade about the Vacker legacy—and if he had to hear him pretend he knew what it was like to come from a horrible, evil family one more time, he might actually vomit.

"Think whatever you want," Alvar said, probably reading the disgust on Keefe's face. "It won't change the fact that my brother tried to kill me—and almost succeeded."

Keefe couldn't argue with that.

He also couldn't claim that Fitz wouldn't try to do it again.

But Alvar brought that on himself.

"We both know you're not a *victim*," Keefe told him. "You made your choices."

"I did," Alvar said, watching a wave crash against the shore. "And I stand behind most of them."

"*Most*," Keefe repeated.

Alvar shrugged. "Nobody's perfect."

Keefe couldn't tell if that was a joke.

He kept trying to get a read on Alvar—but Alvar's emotions felt like a whirlwind. Spinning and shifting and whisking away before he could even start to translate.

"*Anyway*," Alvar continued. "I thought about heading to a Neutral Territory and just . . . disappearing. But it felt like there should be *some* record of my passing—even if it was only an unsolved human file about a nameless body found on the street. Some tiny bit of proof that I'd existed."

"So you were feeling sorry for yourself," Keefe noted.

"Try being moments away from dying and see if you don't do exactly the same thing."

He waited for Keefe to argue, but Keefe had definitely had a bit of an internal pity party in Loamnore—even if he'd tried to pretend he wasn't scared.

"Exactly," Alvar said, annoyingly guessing what he was thinking again. "So I asked your dad to choose a random facet on his blue pathfinder, and he agreed. I didn't care which place I went as long as it was a Forbidden City. Then I crawled into the light thinking that would be the end of me— and I don't remember much after that. Just a few scattered pieces." He closed his eyes. "I can see an old guy with a bald head, leaning over me, saying something I couldn't understand. And a bright room with a really uncomfortable bed. And my arms"—he held them up and ran his hands across the skin—"I remember seeing all these needles and tubes and beeping things attached to them. And I remember thinking maybe I'd made a big mistake leaving my life in the hands of humans. Maybe I was going to be poked and prodded and scanned for days and days and days. But then . . . the pain started to fade. My head cleared. My strength came back. The people coming to check on me started smiling as they made notes. I couldn't understand their language, but I could tell I wasn't dying anymore. I left the hospital a few days later, and I've been on my own ever since. Mostly I hide out in the library trying to learn the language. Their tablets have an app with these handy little tutorials. And that's it—that's my big survival story. Satisfied?"

"Uh, not really."

"Shocking."

"Oh, come on—you left out all the details, like what the doctors did—"

"I don't know what they did," Alvar cut in. "I told you, I don't understand the language."

"Then how have you found clothes and money and food and—"

"It hasn't been easy," Alvar admitted, dragging his toe through the sand. "I knew *some* stuff about the Forbidden Cities from all the trips I made for my dad. So I knew I needed to sneak out of that hospital the first chance I got. I also had a ring with me that I was able to sell. The rest has just been trial and error—plus occasional kindness from strangers. That's the thing about humans—most are pretty generous and helpful. Especially for a guy recovering from an injury"—he pointed to his scars—"who doesn't speak the language and lost his memory."

"You lost your memory," Keefe repeated, raising one eyebrow.

"No. But that's the kind of story that earns a lot of sympathy. It's also a convenient way to get out of having to answer a bunch of questions."

"And it's probably pretty easy to pull off since you've faked memory loss before," Keefe muttered.

"That wasn't fake! It just . . . wasn't permanent."

"No, it was a ploy, so we'd let our guards down and you could betray us at exactly the right moment."

"And it worked out super well for me, didn't it?" Alvar countered.

"Oh boo-hoo—I feel so sorry for you."

"You're not supposed to!" Alvar blew out a long breath, swiping his hair out of his eyes again. "I don't want your sympathy, Keefe. I don't want anything. You're the one who started following me—"

"Yeah, so I could make sure you weren't . . ."

"What?" Alvar asked when Keefe didn't know how to finish that sentence. "What exactly did you think I was doing in that library? Gathering intel so I can form my own human army?"

Honestly, Keefe wouldn't put it past him.

But that wouldn't be a very realistic plan.

"Or maybe you thought I was there for *you*," Alvar said slowly. "That's it, isn't it?"

"Uh, you wouldn't be the first person who tried to capture me or kill me," Keefe reminded him. "Or use me to get to my friends."

"No, I wouldn't. But again—*you* followed *me*. And do you really think I didn't see you first? I spotted you the moment you walked into that library and started annoying the librarian."

"So you were watching me," Keefe noted.

"Yeah, at first. I wanted to make sure my brother didn't send you. Or my father. Or anyone else who'd try to drag me back to the Lost Cities and lock me up in some miserable underground prison—or Exile's creepy little somnatorium. But then I realized you were totally oblivious to my existence, and I figured I'd keep it that way."

"So why didn't you leave?" Keefe asked.

"Well, for one thing, it was kind of fun seeing how terrible you are with basic human technology. But mostly, I wanted to make sure I was right about why you were there."

"Regretting that now?"

"Kind of." Alvar swiped the sweat off his forehead. "I'll admit, I didn't expect to end up on a sweltering little speck of sand in the middle of the ocean. But I guess I should've known you'd overreact. So tell me this, Keefe. What's *your* next move? Since I think we both know you're not going to drag me back to the Lost Cities."

"And how do *we* know that?"

"Because you're clearly on the run. Human clothes. No bodyguard. No registry pendant. None of your friends with you—especially Sophie. I'm assuming you're hiding from your mom, probably so she won't know you manifested another ability—and I'm not talking about the fact that you're clearly a Polyglot now. I'm sure that comes in very handy—but it isn't worth fleeing your world to keep hidden. So you must be a triple threat: Empath, Polyglot, and something else. . . ."

He raised his eyebrows at Keefe, daring him to deny it.

Keefe tried to come up with a joke to cover, but his mind went blank.

"Don't worry—I'm not going to ask you what it is. Honestly, I don't care. I'm done with all of that. I'm done with the Lost Cities. I have absolutely zero desire to ever go back again. I realize, given my past behavior, that you're going to find that hard to believe. But truly, all I want to do is spend whatever time I have left in a world where the people cared enough to save me. So why don't you take me back to where you found me and let me get on with my incredibly ordinary existence? I haven't caused any problems for anyone since I've been there, have I?"

"Doesn't mean you won't."

"No, I suppose it doesn't." Alvar stared at the ocean for several long breaths before he said, "I get it. You're never going to trust me. And that's fine. I don't need you to. I just need you to realize I'm not a threat. So I'm going to share something I was planning to keep to myself because it leaves me pretty vulnerable, and hope it at least proves you don't have to worry about me." His gaze shifted to Keefe, and he took one more deep breath before he said, "I can't light leap anymore. Maybe it was the human medicine, or how close I came to dying—I don't know. But my concentration isn't even close to strong enough. Why do you think I screamed when you dragged me into the light? If you hadn't shielded me with your concentration, I would've faded away long before we reappeared. That's why

I'm standing here"—he waved his arms around the island—"drenched in sweat and covered in scratchy sand, instead of snatching your crystal and heading home for pancakes. And if you leave me here . . . I'll be stuck living off coconuts." He shuddered. "I'm really hoping you won't do that. Just like I'm hoping you'll use your concentration to bring me back to the city where you found me—and if you do, that's where I'll stay. I can't go anywhere else."

"You could use human forms of travel," Keefe argued.

"Which wouldn't get me anywhere near the Lost Cities," Alvar reminded him. "Those also require things I don't have. My resources are limited—and that's fine. I like where I am. I like being insignificant. No pressure. No past. No legacy."

Keefe flinched at the last word.

"Still fighting it, then," Alvar noted. "Good. I meant what I said at Candleshade. You'll never be what your mom wants—and the more you focus on that, the better chance you'll have of stopping her."

Keefe closed his eyes, trying to keep any emotion off his face.

But he was sure Alvar could see it.

And even though Alvar probably wasn't the right person to ask this question, he had to know. "Do you actually think I can stop her?"

"I *think*," Alvar said, dragging out the word, "that you're stubborn enough to do pretty much anything you want. You also have some superpowerful friends to back you up. So you've got a really good shot. *But*."

"Ugh—there's always a 'but,'" Keefe grumbled.

"Annoying, isn't it? *But* your mom's been planning this stuff for a really, really, really long time. It may seem like she's making it up as she goes along because the Neverseen are so divided and disorganized and always changing up who's in charge. But sometimes I think she did that on purpose."

"Did what? Let herself get overthrown? Ended up in an ogre prison?"

"Probably not the ogre thing," Alvar admitted. "But your mom *loves* being underestimated—and it's actually a smart strategy. Let your opponents think they know what to expect— then hit them with something they'll never see coming. So whatever you've pieced together about her plan, I guarantee there's way more to it."

"And I'm assuming you won't share what you know," Keefe said, not bothering to phrase it as a question.

Alvar sighed and kicked the sand. "Honestly, Keefe, I wish I had something worth sharing. I could use a good bargaining chip right now. But I spent way too much energy on my own agenda during my days with the Neverseen. So the best I can offer you is another piece of advice: Whatever you're doing right now with your little trip to the Forbidden Cities— whatever plans you're making—do it for your future. Don't get so caught up in exposing the past that you forget there's a whole lifetime ahead of you. Otherwise you'll end up like me, on borrowed time in a borrowed world—and I'm not trying to make you feel sorry for me. I like my life right now. That's why I'm standing here, trying to figure out how to convince you to take me back. I'm assuming I haven't won you over yet?"

"Nope," Keefe agreed, even though he wasn't sure what else he was going to do with Alvar.

If he dragged him back to the Lost Cities, he'd probably get stuck there too.

But if he let him go and something happened . . .

He turned to pace.

"Guess I'll just stand here and sweat," Alvar said after Keefe passed him a couple of times. "And hope the fact that I'm not tackling you earns me some points."

"Is that seriously supposed to make me trust you?" Keefe asked.

Alvar shrugged. "Why not? It's true. I'm not restrained. And I'm not as weak as you might think. If I wanted to take you down, you'd be pinned with a face full of sand right now. You also never searched me for weapons—and even though I don't have any, you didn't know that until I just said it. So I feel like all of that proves you must trust me at least a little."

Or it proved Keefe still had a *lot* to learn when it came to dealing with his enemies.

He *should've* checked Alvar for weapons the second he got near him.

And he should've shredded some palm fronds or ripped up his coat and used it to bind Alvar's hands and feet.

It probably *did* prove something that Alvar hadn't taken advantage of either of those mistakes—but Keefe still wasn't sure where that left him.

"Okay," he said after a few more minutes of pacing. "I'm pretty sure we both only have two options. *One*"—he held up one finger—"I can leave you on this island and check back in a couple of weeks. If you're still here, it probably means you aren't lying about the not-being-able-to-light-leap thing—"

"Uh, you're an Empath," Alvar cut in. "You can tell if I'm lying right now."

That was true.

But Alvar had fooled him before.

And Keefe still couldn't get a reading on him.

Maybe he was still getting used to his abilities.

Or maybe Alvar was too all over the place.

Either way . . .

"I think a test is smarter," Keefe told him. "Stay here. Prove you're not lying. Then maybe I'll take you where you want to go."

"And if I *am* lying and I leap away?" Alvar countered.

"Then you're going to do that anyway, and at least I won't have to kick myself for trusting you *again*."

Alvar reached up to rub his temples. "It's amazing how you can almost make this sound like it's a good, logical plan."

"I never said it was *good*. I said I only see two options."

"And option number *two* is?"

Keefe held up a second finger. "*Or* I bring you with me when I leave here, so I can keep an eye on you."

"And what? I'm your prisoner?"

"Yes and no. I'm not going to tie you up—but I do expect you to be on your best behavior—and if you try anything, I'll have no problem leaping you to the top of a mountain or the middle of a desert and leaving you there."

"*How* is that better than taking me back to my city and being free of me?"

"It's not. But I'd still know I didn't just take you at your word—and I *also* didn't assume the worst and punish you before you did anything. Either way, I'm giving you an opportunity to prove yourself."

He didn't want to be like Fitz, refusing to give Alvar another chance.

He also had a feeling that if Foster was there, she'd make Alvar the same offer.

Actually, no, she'd probably come up with a way smarter plan.

She was *way* better at this stuff.

But he was on his own, and this was the best his exhausted brain could come up with.

Maybe he'd regret it later, but . . . he'd just be taking Alvar back to London.

There wasn't much Alvar could do there except maybe mess up his hotel room.

"So . . . ," he said, meeting Alvar's stare. "Which option will it be?"

Alvar sighed. "It's not really a choice, is it? Stay stranded on a deserted island or let you drag me around the planet? Guess I have to go with option B—*but*. If I'm a good little elf and stay out of trouble, I want some assurance that you'll eventually take me back to my city. That whole 'maybe' thing isn't good enough."

The fact that Alvar chose *that* as his stipulation said a lot about his priorities.

It might even mean he really was just a guy trying to live some kind of ordinary existence.

Only one way to find out.

Keefe shrugged. "Fine. Do we have a deal?"

"I guess—but I hope you know what you're doing," Alvar warned.

"So do I." Keefe retrieved his coat and dug his pathfinder out of the pocket. "Ready?"

Alvar picked up his coat too. "I take it we're going somewhere cold."

Keefe nodded, and Alvar sighed and shook the sand off his coat before slipping it on. "Remember, I'm counting on your concentration—and you better take me somewhere with pancakes," he said as Keefe grabbed his shoulder and dragged them both into the rushing warmth.

TWENTY-THREE

"YOU JUST MADE A HUGE MISTAKE," Alvar warned as he took a giant bite of cake. "You never should've shown me how easy this room service thing is."

"It's pretty awesome, right?" Keefe asked, even though he was only half paying attention to the conversation.

Mostly he was trying to process the fact that Alvar was sitting on the couch in his suite stuffing his face with desserts, wearing the other fluffy white robe from the closet and a pair of padded hotel slippers. Especially since the day had started out so normal . . .

He'd had breakfast in the park.

Shared his croissant with his little fox buddy.

Then he'd wandered a few more London streets searching for the elusive might-not-be-green door—and hadn't found it, of course—before he'd headed to the next library on his list for more research.

Somehow it'd all escalated from there, and now . . .

He had Alvar Vacker staying with him.

If Fitz knew . . .

Well, it wouldn't be good.

Punches would definitely be thrown.

Add that to the list of reasons Keefe's brain kept asking, *WHAT WERE YOU THINKING, BRINGING ALVAR BACK TO YOUR HOTEL LIKE A LOST LITTLE ALICORN?*

But where else was he supposed to take him?

He'd brought him to London to keep an eye on him, so . . . apparently, they were roommates—or flatmates, as he kept hearing people call it.

"Seriously," Alvar said before slurping down some tea. "It's like living with a Conjurer—but better, because your stuff gets delivered by people in fancy suits, calling you 'sir.' Though one of them called *you* 'Mr. Foster.' Don't think I didn't notice that."

Yep, Keefe was definitely going to regret this.

He slumped into one of the chairs.

"Fine, we can save your girl troubles for a later conversation," Alvar told him. "I'm sure we'll have plenty of opportunities, since we'll be spending so much time together. Should I call you 'roomie'?"

Keefe resisted the urge to scream into a pillow.

He knew what Alvar was doing.

It was the same thing he would do in his situation: *annoy, annoy, annoy.*

Try to wear the other person down to get his way.

But if Keefe could handle Ro's never-ending teasing—and her abundant supply of horrifying ogre bacteria—he could handle Alvar Vacker.

"Yeah, I'm definitely going to need more desserts," Alvar said as he finished his last bite of cake. "And bonus: I can order it myself! It's nice being able to speak the language again. Never understood why my dad chose to make us learn English before our little Forbidden City searches, but it hasn't been very helpful—until now." He browsed the room service menu. "I might need one of each."

"Get whatever you want," Keefe told him.

"I was planning on it." He got up and placed a huge order before he plopped back down on the couch. "Okay, I have to ask. *How* are you paying for all this?" He waved his arms around the fancy room—then froze. "Wait. You didn't tap into your birth fund, did you? You know that can be tracked and—"

"I didn't tap into my birth fund," Keefe assured him. "There's no way anyone can trace any of this."

"You're sure?" Alvar pressed. "Because if the Council's going to come barging in—"

"They won't," Keefe insisted.

And he was tempted to leave it at that and keep Alvar guessing—but that would probably lead to a very long night of questions.

So he told him, "I did what you did. I sold some jewelry."

Alvar studied the room again. "Must've been a *lot* of jewelry."

"It was. I grabbed all my mom's favorite pieces before I left. Figured she owed me. And since she liked showing off, all her jewelry has big, flashy gemstones—which I guess are super rare for humans and worth way more than I expected."

It was true enough.

He definitely *could've* paid for the suite with jewelry money—and if he admitted the room was being charged to his father, it'd make it sound like he couldn't survive on his own.

"Okay, but you must also have some sort of human ID, right?" Alvar said, propping up his feet on the table. "And that's where the whole 'Mr. Foster' thing came from?"

Keefe reluctantly nodded.

Alvar whistled. "How'd you pull *that* off? Actually, never mind, since I'm sure you're not going to tell me—*but* if I pass all your little tests, think you could help me get one? It'd make life *so* much easier."

"I'm sure it would."

"Come on—I said '*if* I pass.' And I also said 'tests,' plural. I'll do anything you want me to do to prove I'm just a boring guy up to nothing worth mentioning. I won't even ask why there's a map of London on that table"—he pointed across the room—"where you've been crossing off the streets one by one, which kinda looks creepy, if I'm honest. Or why there's another map underneath it of the whole planet, where you've been making all kinds of little notes—which I didn't bother reading because I truly don't care what you've been doing. Does that count for something?"

"Nope," Keefe said, standing up.

He had no idea what time it was, but he was ready to crash into bed—and maybe bury his head under a pillow and hope when he woke up, all of this would turn out to be a bad dream.

"Okaaaaaaaay, what if I promise not to read all those journals you forgot to hide?" Alvar asked, pointing to four notebooks— one brown, one green, one silver, and one gold—which were sticking out of the backpack Keefe had brought with him. "I'm betting they're full of lots of embarrassing things."

Some of them were.

Especially the gold one.

Keefe had spent months filling those journals with detailed drawings of his memories, hoping he'd either trigger something his mom erased or at least isolate a blank spot. But so far, he hadn't had much luck.

There was also an even more personal notebook at the bottom of his backpack, where he'd taken Foster's advice and tried writing down his thoughts as he studied the memories, in case that helped him notice stuff he'd missed before.

He kept meaning to get back to that project, but he'd gotten sidetracked by recording all his human lessons.

"Noticed *that* little sketchbook too," Alvar said when Keefe's eyes darted to the one he'd taken from his father's cabin. "Interesting titles you considered. I managed to resist reading it so far—but if that doesn't score me any points, I might have to stay up late tonight learning all about your adventures."

Keefe sighed and gathered up all his maps and journals and sketchbooks—plus the list of libraries he'd been working from and the notebook his father gave him full of human tips—and carried them over to the safe he'd been shown when he first toured the room.

A few beeps and buttons later and his secrets were securely locked away.

Alvar laughed. "You realize I can probably guess your code, right?"

"I *highly* doubt that."

"Okay, then how about this? If I guess it in three tries or less, you have to get me a human ID."

"No deal," Keefe said, even though he was pretty sure Alvar wouldn't be able to guess it. "I'm heading to bed. Good night."

"Boo, you're no fun! And a word to the wise, by the way. If you went with one-two-three-four, everyone will try that first. So if you're keeping any cash in there—or any jewelry you haven't sold—you should probably change it. Same goes for anything like one-one-one-one."

"You're not going to trick me into telling you," Keefe informed him—while making a mental note to switch the code as soon as Alvar fell asleep.

"It's two-four-six-eight, isn't it?" Alvar asked as Keefe turned to head to his room.

It actually was, unfortunately—but Keefe wasn't about to admit it.

"You made up a little rhyme, too, didn't you?" Alvar pressed. "To help you remember. Something like 'Two-four-six-eight, to get the stuff inside my safe!'"

"'Safe' doesn't even rhyme with 'eight,'" Keefe argued.

"Eh, it's close enough. I'm sure your rhyme is way better, though. Come on, admit it! I'm right about the code, aren't I?"

Keefe dragged a hand down his face, glad Alvar wasn't a Telepath and couldn't hear him mentally chanting, *Two-four-six-eight, the code I picked is really great!* "I know what you're doing, Alvar—and it's not going to work."

"What? I'm just trying to have a little fun with my roomie."

"No, you're not."

"Actually, I am. I mean, yeah, it'd be great if I could convince you to get me an ID and take me home and maybe tell me how you pulled off the Great Gulon Incident while we're at it, because I've always been super curious about that. *But.* I've also been alone for a while now, between the human city and the lovely little prison the Council made for me—and no, once again, I'm not trying to make you feel sorry for me. I just . . . I forgot what it's like to joke around with somebody."

So had Keefe, honestly.

But . . .

This wasn't a new BFF he was hanging out with.

This was *Alvar Vacker.*

"Good night," Keefe told him again.

Alvar sighed. "Yeah, good night." He let Keefe get halfway to his bedroom before he called out, "I meant the other thing I said at Candleshade, by the way. I've always liked you, Keefe— way more than my own little brother."

A flicker of warmth ignited in Keefe's chest.

But he snuffed it out.

"That's just because you and Fitzy have *issues,*" he called back.

"We do," Alvar agreed. "I won't be sad if I never see him again. *But.* That isn't why I like you. You're . . . real. And you don't take yourself too seriously. You've been through more than pretty much anyone, and yet you can still joke around about it. So I want to make sure you know something."

He paused, probably hoping Keefe would turn back—but Keefe kept on walking.

Right before he closed his bedroom door, though—and locked it—he heard Alvar say, "You're one of the good guys, Keefe. Never forget that."

TWENTY-FOUR

GOING SOMEWHERE?" ALVAR ASKED, making Keefe jump so hard, he crashed into a table and knocked over a lamp.

"Vanishers," Keefe grumbled, rubbing his leg as he turned on the lamp to make sure it wasn't broken.

Alvar squinted at the bright light. "Uh, I wasn't invisible. You just didn't see me because you were too busy sneaking around in the dark."

"Yeah, well, excuse me for trying to let you sleep," Keefe muttered. "Why are you awake already? It's not even sunrise."

"It's not," Alvar agreed. "So the better question is, why are *you* awake? Since I can't help but notice that you have your shoes and coat on and you were heading for the door. Got a secret meeting you didn't want me to know about?"

Keefe rolled his eyes. "I just like to start my day with a walk in the park."

That's what he'd decided to call his quest to find the right door in London.

Alvar pointed to the window, which was streaked with streams of water. "It's pouring rain."

"Yeah, it does that a lot here. That's why I have a raincoat and an umbrella."

"Uh-huh." Alvar tilted his head to study him. "Fine—don't tell me what you're up to. I'll just assume you have a secret human girlfriend."

Keefe sighed and rubbed his temples.

This was going to be a very long day.

"Sounds like I'll need my own raincoat and umbrella," Alvar added. "Also some shirts and pants and socks and pajamas and boots, since *someone* brought me here without any of my stuff. And this"—he gestured to his outfit, which was the same one he'd been wearing the day before—"is all sandy and sweaty, thanks to your little island detour. So unless you want to take me home, I need to do some shopping. I also don't have a toothbrush, or a comb, or any hair gel, or—"

"Fine, I'll leave you some cash," Keefe cut in, heading over to the safe and keying in the new code he'd switched to as soon as Alvar had gone to bed. "The concierge can help you find some nearby stores."

Alvar frowned as Keefe pulled out several of the larger bills from his cash stash. "Uhhh, it kinda sounds like you're not planning on coming with me on my little shopping trip. Just like you were about to leave me here all by myself—which is strange, since I thought you'd taken on the role of my very own personal babysitter."

Keefe had thought the same thing when he'd brought Alvar to London.

But he'd been up all night trying to figure out how that would work.

Alvar would ask way too many questions if Keefe brought him along while he searched for the house with the green door. And taking Alvar to different libraries would be much too risky. Plus, he didn't want Alvar to know what he was researching.

So . . . either he was going to have to cancel all his plans and waste a ton of days watching Alvar's every move.

Or . . . he was going to have to leave Alvar alone and hope it didn't backfire.

It took him six or seven hundred rounds of pacing across his bedroom before he realized . . .

This was supposed to be a *test*.

A chance for Alvar to prove he wasn't a threat.

If he never let him out of his sight, all that would prove was that Alvar stayed out of trouble when he knew he'd get caught—and what Keefe really needed to know was what would happen if Alvar was left to his own devices.

The only way to do that was to actually leave him alone.

Risky?

Yep.

Terrifying?

Totally.

But . . .

He'd also taken Alvar away from the place he clearly wanted to be and limited his resources—surely that meant he couldn't cause too much trouble . . . right?

Keefe sure hoped so, because he held out the cash and told Alvar, "I'm assuming you can handle shopping by yourself."

"I definitely can," Alvar agreed. "But if you trust me enough to leave me all alone, why not just take me home and be done with me?"

"I *don't* trust you," Keefe corrected. "That's why I'm giving you this chance to start proving that I should."

"Okaaaaaaaaaaaaaaay," Alvar said as he slowly reached for the money. "Why do I feel like I'm missing a trap?"

"Only if you're planning on going back on the things you said yesterday. If you really are just a normal guy trying to live a normal life in the Forbidden Cities, then . . . go buy some new clothes. Get some lunch. Check out a museum or take a walk in the park. Then be *here*, waiting for me when I get back—and don't pester me with questions about things you supposedly don't care about."

"And if I *don't* do those things?" Alvar asked—just like Keefe knew he would. "You know, just . . . out of curiosity."

Keefe held Alvar's stare. "Then I have some very powerful new ways of hunting you down and making anything you've already been through seem like nothing more than a sweet little snuggle."

He'd chosen the threat carefully, hoping Alvar would assume he'd manifested some horrifying new tracking ability.

Didn't matter if it was true.

That was one perk of being his mom's mysterious Legacy Boy.

Everyone was ready to believe the worst about him.

"Well then," Alvar said, slipping the money into his pocket. "It looks like I have some shopping to do. And it sounds like your morning 'walk in the park' is going to stretch well into the afternoon. So is there any particular time I should be back? I hear this hotel has a lovely high tea with an abundance of pastries. Should I make us a reservation?"

Keefe shook his head and handed Alvar his extra room key. "I'll be back after dinner."

He left before he could change his mind—and tried not to spend the day imagining worst-case scenarios.

But his brain was more stuck on the why.

Why was he willing to give Alvar yet another chance after all the times he'd betrayed him?

Fitz would never understand it.

Foster . . . might.

But Keefe needed to understand it himself.

Was it just because there'd been a point in time when he'd thought of Alvar as the big brother he'd never had?

Maybe.

But . . . it felt like there was more to it than that.

And as he spent the day wandering soggy streets looking for a door that a tiny part of him didn't want to find, and then reading more books on astrophysics, trying to figure out why his mom would've cared about the subject, he had to admit . . . it wasn't really about Alvar.

It was about redemption.

If Alvar could find a way back to some sort of normal after all the horrible things he'd said and done and thought, then . . .

Maybe he could too.

No matter what memories he recovered.

Or horrible things he'd done—or was expected to do.

Maybe he wouldn't have to let any of that define him.

So he had no idea what to expect when he finally made his way back to his hotel.

But he was hoping for the best.

And when he opened the door to his suite . . .

Alvar was there.

Wearing a new pair of silk pajamas, surrounded by room-service trays and shopping bags, watching some sort of baking show on television.

He raised his cup of tea and flashed a smug grin as he told Keefe, "Welcome back, roomie. Surprised to see me?"

TWENTY-FIVE

ACK—WHAT IS *THAT*?" KEEFE ASKED, stumbling back a step when he found Alvar once again stretched out on the sitting-room couch, this time with a slimy paper thing suctioned to his face.

"It's called a sheet mask," Alvar told him—or that's what Keefe thought he said.

It was hard to hear him through the mask's little cutout for his mouth.

"Trust me—they're life-changing," Alvar assured him, tossing Keefe a foil packet, which Keefe was pretty sure was one of the things he'd watched Alvar buy from that mall's beauty store a few weeks earlier. "Try it."

"Yeah, hard pass," Keefe said, tossing the packet back to Alvar.

The mask looked way too much like something Elwin might use to melt off his skin.

Alvar shrugged. "Your loss. It's the best way to get rid of those bags you've got going on under your eyes. Well, other than sleep—but you seem to have a bit too much on your mind for that."

Talk about an understatement.

Not only was Keefe's head still regularly bombarded with an alicorn chorus of *KEEFE! KEEFE! KEEFE!* But the days were also starting to drag on, with way too much work and way too little progress.

He'd now crossed off more than three-quarters of the streets in London without any sign of the door he was looking for. And he was nearing the end of his list of the best libraries and still had zero idea what Ethan Benedict Wright II had been researching, or why Mommy Dearest would've chosen to recruit him over any other astrophysicist.

The only slightly interesting thing he'd found was a brief article that mentioned the "groundbreaking work of Dr. Ethan Benedict Wright II in the search for alternative energy sources."

Sadly, it didn't give any specifics about his research—but it was his title that caught Keefe's attention.

Dr. Ethan Benedict Wright II.

That matched the way all the other astrophysicists were always referred to in their endless articles.

Dr. This and *Dr. That* and *Dr. Wow That's Super Boring* and *Dr. Who Cares?*

And yet, all of Ethan Benedict Wright II's obituaries had left off his title.

Did that mean he'd lost it somehow?

Keefe wasn't sure if that was possible—or why that would happen if it was.

But it seemed like it might mean something.

Or maybe he was so desperate for a clue that he was adding significance to a simple typo.

"Uh, hello?" Alvar said, reminding Keefe he was standing there, zoning out. "I asked if you wanted to grab some lunch before you disappear on yet another mystery errand. I'm on a quest to find something called Welsh rarebit. No idea what it is, but I hear melty cheese is involved, and that's good enough for me."

Keefe shook his head.

"Aw, come on! A quick lunch won't prove you trust me or anything."

The weird thing was, Keefe didn't even completely hate the idea of a little extra Alvar time.

But the library he was heading to would only be open for a few more hours.

Alvar sighed. "You know . . . the old Keefe wouldn't have been able to pass up a Welsh rarebit quest. And he wouldn't have been in London this long without tracking down a piece of banoffee pie and some sticky toffee pudding. He also wouldn't be able to pass a store selling tiny stuffed elves without buying one—"

"Wait—what store?" Keefe interrupted. "Have you been *following* me?"

He'd thought he'd gotten pretty good at remembering to glance at his reflection in shop windows to see if anyone looked like they were trailing him.

But Alvar could vanish. . . .

"Ugh, no, I haven't been following you," Alvar assured him. "I've got way better things to do with my day! But the shop is on the way to the park, so I'm assuming you've been passing it every morning—unless you're *not* going on all those early walks like you keep claiming."

Keefe shrugged. "Stores aren't open at that time of day, so I haven't paid attention."

"Uh-huh." Alvar sat up and peeled off his sheet mask, which left enough shiny goop on his skin to make Keefe shudder. "I know what you're doing."

"Do you, now?"

"Yep. I saw your little London map with the streets crossed off—remember? And the list of libraries you tried to hide—as if they were a dangerous secret you needed to protect. 'Oh no, Alvar might follow me there and try to read some books!'"

Keefe rolled his eyes. "What's your point?"

"My *point*," Alvar said as he massaged the goop into his

cheeks, "is, I know why you're hiding out in London—and it's not for the Welsh rarebit. Or the chips and curry. Or the scones with clotted cream. It's not even for the fancy suite and the room service, since I'm sure you could find a place like this in any of the bigger Forbidden Cities." He balled up his sheet mask and tossed it toward the trash can across the room—pumping his fist when it swished into the bin. "And it's not to try to get a handle on all your new abilities—even though that's what you *should* be doing. Nope, you're staying in London because you're looking into that guy you delivered a letter to. What was his name? Evan Benedectine something?"

Keefe lunged for Alvar. "If you know something—"

"Whoa—I don't," Alvar promised as he leaped over the back of the couch to escape. "Well . . . I don't know what you think I know."

"And what's *that*?" Keefe demanded, chasing Alvar to the other side of the room. "Tell me right now—or I'm going to bust out the packets of bacteria I stole from Ro's stash and make you start oozing different kinds of goop from every part of your body."

"Wow," Alvar said, bending over and gasping for breath. "I knew you were getting desperate, but I didn't realize you were to the threatening-with-ogre-bacteria point—otherwise I would've barricaded you in your room before I brought this up."

"I'm going to give you to the count of three," Keefe warned. "One . . ."

"Okay, okay, stop counting!" Alvar collapsed into a chair. "Just give me a second to catch my breath. I'm not good with all this physical exertion stuff. Remember how I was basically dead not that long ago?"

"One minute," Keefe told him, mentally counting to sixty before he crossed his arms and told Alvar, "All right—now start talking."

Alvar rolled his eyes. "Fine. But just to be very clear right from the start: I don't have the answers you're looking for. I don't know who the guy was, or why your mom wrote a letter to him, or what the letter said, or what happened to him after that. Take a reading if you don't believe me."

He offered Keefe his hand.

But the emotions in the room were already a loud buzzing in the back of Keefe's head.

He'd never be able to make sense of them.

Alvar frowned. "Is something wrong with your empathy? I've noticed you don't really use it much these days."

"DON'T TRY TO CHANGE THE SUBJECT!" Keefe shouted. *"TELL ME WHAT YOU KNOW ABOUT ETHAN BENEDICT WRIGHT II!"*

"Is that his name?" Alvar asked. "Boy, is that a mouthful. They have weird names in this country—have you noticed that? I met a Basil the other day. And a Fergus. And a—"

"I'm going to get the bacteria," Keefe said, turning toward his bedroom.

"Ugh—I was just trying to lighten the mood! You know, the old Keefe was incapable of having a conversation without cracking a ton of jokes. I miss that guy."

So did Keefe, honestly.

He hadn't realized how serious he'd gotten.

But between almost dying, and the scary new abilities, and not being able to talk for so many days, and running away, and losing contact with everyone he cared about, and spending so much time alone, he'd definitely retreated into his head.

He wasn't sure how to come back out of this new hardened shell—but he could worry about that later.

"You're changing the subject again," he reminded Alvar.

"Caught that, huh? Yeah, I was trying to give you a little more time to calm down, since what I'm about to tell you is good news, actually. But I'm sure you're still going to freak out."

Keefe sank into the nearest chair. "I'm really getting sick of all the stalling."

Alvar sighed. "Okay. Just . . . try to think before you react, okay?" He waited for Keefe to nod before he told him, "The day you delivered the letter, your mom seemed frazzled, right?"

"Frazzled?" Keefe repeated.

"Yeah, scrambling a bit. Sending you on the errand out of the blue. Telling you to hurry. That kind of thing?"

Keefe nodded slowly.

Alvar nodded too. "That's because she never planned on

sending you. She only did because the person she was counting on to make the delivery canceled last minute."

Keefe sat up a little taller. "How do you know that?"

Alvar closed his eyes, bracing for impact as he said, "Because *I* was supposed to deliver the letter."

TWENTY-SIX

Y OU."

Keefe wasn't sure if the word was an accusation or a revelation—or something in between.

"*You* were supposed to deliver the letter?"

Alvar nodded. "I was always their handy errand boy, since they didn't have to worry that I'd be seen."

"Except you *were* seen, once," Keefe reminded him. "You were the Boy Who Disappeared."

That'd been one of Alvar's most infamous mistakes.

The Neverseen *almost* found Foster when she was still a little girl without any powers—except Alvar got confused by her eye color and reported back that she was human.

He also let her see him as he leaped away, which freaked her out so much, she tripped and fell and hit her head—and when Forkle scanned her memories trying to figure out what happened, he realized she'd almost been discovered. That's why he triggered her telepathy early and left her bombarded by human thoughts for so many unnecessary years.

"Brant never forgave me for that," Alvar murmured. "Neither did Fintan. Though, for what it's worth . . . I'm glad I messed it up. I don't know what would've happened if I'd realized what Sophie was—"

"Uh, I do," Keefe cut in. "They would've snatched her and tried to kill her, like they did after Fitz found her, remember? And, hey, didn't you help plan her kidnapping?"

"I did."

There was no pride in his tone.

In fact, he actually sounded like he meant it when he said, "I'm not going to pretend I regret everything I did for the Neverseen—and I can't change it anyway. But there's definitely stuff I wish I could take back. That's the thing about almost dying. It makes it really easy to spot your mistakes. So I know a waste of time when I see it—and that's what you're doing, Keefe. That's why I wanted you to know that you were never supposed to have been the one to deliver that letter."

"Why does that matter?" Keefe asked. "Actually, wait—I have a better question: Why couldn't *you* deliver it?"

Alvar's lips twitched with a hint of a smile. "Ironically enough . . . I couldn't get out of a family thing."

"A *family* thing."

"Yep. Your mom let me know she needed me that afternoon, and I told her I'd be there. But when I tried to leave, I found out my parents had a big Vacker family picnic planned. I tried making excuses, but my mom wouldn't take no for an answer, and it would've been too suspicious if I'd left. So I let your mom know I wouldn't be able to make the delivery until that night. And she said it couldn't wait. I found out later that she decided to send you, since your registry feed wasn't being watched and it was easy to have your memory erased."

"Shattered," Keefe corrected. "She had the memory shattered."

"Yeah, well . . . double lives are hard," Alvar mumbled. "You know the truth will come out eventually. But you also know it's going to be a mess. So you do whatever you can to avoid it as long as possible."

Keefe snorted. "Seriously, dude, I'm not going to feel sorry for you."

"I wasn't asking you to—and if you're making this about me, you're missing the point. The point is: You *have* to stop punishing yourself—"

"Punishing myself?"

"Yep. You're spending hours every day in libraries—and we

all know how you feel about research. And you're basically walking every street in London, trying to find that house again—"

"Do you know where it is?" Keefe cut in. "Did my mom tell you anything about where you'd be going?"

"All she told me was that she wanted me to deliver a letter to a human city. I'm sure she would've given me a few more details if I'd done the delivery, but since I didn't, I only know what I pieced together later—that it was in London, and the guy had a weird name I can never remember. I told you, I don't have the answers you're looking for. But I swear, Keefe: *You don't need them.* You've built this up in your head into this huge conspiracy that you were an integral part of, and you can't let yourself rest until you try to make it right. But you weren't an integral part! You were a last-minute fill-in."

Keefe closed his eyes, wanting to feel the relief Alvar clearly thought the words would bring him.

But . . .

"I still delivered the letter. And that letter could still be the reason the guy—and his daughter—are dead. In fact, maybe that's why my mom was in such a hurry to have the letter delivered."

"Even if that's true, it has nothing to do with you. You were eleven years old, and your mom came to you out of the blue with this weird demand. I'm sure she even made a few threats to scare you—"

"She did. But we both know I never cared about getting

in trouble. I should've thrown the letter back in her face—or ripped it open the second I was out of sight and read her secret message. In fact . . ."

He hesitated, not sure if he was about to share too much.

But . . . his plan wasn't exactly groundbreaking.

"I'm starting to wonder if I *did* read the letter," Keefe admitted. "And maybe that's why my mom shattered the memory. She knew I knew her secret and had to protect it. And if I'm right—and if I can find a way to trigger what I saw . . ."

"That's a whole lot of 'if's and 'maybe's, Keefe."

"Of course it is! I never get any giant clues that spell it all out clearly. I get itty-bitty fragments to piece together—"

"And that's why you lose," Alvar jumped in. "Because you spend all your time piecing together bits of the past, instead of trying to think ahead to the future. Glare at me all you want—you know I'm right. Think about it. Let's walk a few steps forward. Let's say you did read that letter, and somehow find a way to trigger the memory. Do you really think the letter is going to tell you anything about what your mom is planning?"

"Maybe. If I knew why she wanted to recruit this guy, that might tell me something."

"I guess," Alvar conceded. "But I doubt it. And I think deep down, you doubt it too. But you're still wandering the streets of London trying to trigger the memory because what you're *really* hoping is that the letter *won't* tell you anything. You're hoping it'll be some quick little note like, 'Hi, Evan—or is it

Ethan? Either way, hi, Human Guy. You still haven't gotten back to me about my generous offer. Would love for us to work together. Call me! *X-O-X-O*, Gisela.'"

"*X-O-X-O?*" Keefe asked.

"It's a human thing. It means, like, hugs and kisses or something."

Keefe snorted. "My mom would never—"

"I know. It was a joke, okay? Remember those? You used to be a master at them. Before you started punishing yourself."

"I told you, I'm not—"

"You are, though. And you're hoping that triggering the memory will finally give you permission to stop. But you don't need it, because you're forgetting the most important thing. You were eleven years old, Keefe—"

"You already said that."

"I know. But it's worth repeating. And that wasn't my point. That was just the buildup. So can you let me get through it without interrupting?"

"Seriously, if this little speech is your way of annoying me into taking you back to your city, it's almost working," Keefe muttered.

"Good to know. But that's not actually what I'm after right now—and I'm going to get through this next part even if I have to tackle you to the floor and cover your mouth with both hands."

"I'd like to see you try."

"I'm sure you would. Honestly, I would too, just to see how much strength I've really gotten back. But how about, instead, you just listen to me for *one* minute?" He waited for Keefe to nod before he said, "You were eleven years old, and regardless of what happened in London—whether you read the letter, or didn't read the letter, or came up with some brilliant plan to rise up against the Neverseen—none of that mattered, because when you got back to Candleshade, your mom was waiting for you with a Washer, who smashed your memories of that day into itty-bitty pieces. Nothing you could've done would've changed that. So let yourself off the hook. You couldn't have stopped whatever happened to the human guy and his daughter."

"Then how come my mom told me, 'You wouldn't want to harm anyone *else*, would you?' when she ambushed me in London?"

"Well, I'm not your mom, so I can only speculate here, but . . . I'm betting it's because she knew how hard those words would hit you. The one thing she never planned for is how stubborn you are—and she'll say or do *anything* to turn you into the obedient little wonder child she's been counting on. So don't let her get in your head. Seriously, Keefe, you only need to know two things about that day: Your mom was five steps ahead of you—and you were just her fill-in errand boy."

"You keep saying that, like I don't also have a *legacy*," Keefe reminded him.

"Actually, I keep saying it so you'll start focusing on your *legacy* instead of your brief stint as an errand boy. You want to spend all your time and energy on something? Figure out your new abilities instead of hiding from them."

"I'm not—"

"Yes, you are. Something changed with your empathy, right? That's why you don't like using it anymore? And then there's another ability—and not the fake tracking power you threatened me with—"

"How do you know it's fake?"

"Well, for one thing, you're not a very good liar. But even if you were, you've made it super clear that you're trying to keep the new ability secret. So why would you tell me exactly what it is—even as a threat?"

Keefe looked away, wishing Alvar hadn't made such a valid point.

"Look. I'm not going to pretend I know what it's like to find out you're part of an experiment—but I *do* know what it's like to live through something that completely changes you."

"That's not the same thing. You got trapped in a troll pod because you helped unleash a bunch of bloodthirsty newborns. I got strapped to a magsidian throne and had an ethertine crown shoved on my head and . . ."

"And . . . ?" Alvar prompted. "Have you ever talked about what happened? What it felt like? What your mom did?"

"Uh, I'm definitely not going to talk about it with you. We're not friends—"

"We could be—and don't worry, I'm not suggesting we get matching sweaters and call ourselves besties. All I'm saying is . . . we could occasionally grab lunch. And if you ever need to talk, or need help figuring out your new abilities—"

Keefe jumped to his feet. "Is that what this is about?"

"Uhhhh, you lost me."

"This whole big speech—sharing that you were supposed to deliver the letter—that's all just to get me to tell you what I can do now, right? Wow—how did I not see that? Let me guess, you figured my mom's probably dying for an update on how I'm doing, and you think if you give her one—"

"Okay, whoa—this is a whole other kind of paranoia. What? You think I can just hop on the Tube and meet up with your mom for tea? Or grab the phone and ring her up?"

Keefe didn't have an answer.

"I told you—I'm done with all that. I get why it might be hard to believe—but I mean it, Keefe. All I want is to go back to the city you took me from and disappear again. The only reason I'm offering to help is because I'm stuck here, and . . . I can tell you need it. You're all alone in this right now, and that's brutal. But if you want to keep struggling by yourself and making the same mistakes, be my guest."

He plopped onto the couch and flicked on the TV, switching to a show about a guy traveling around the universe in some sort of blue box.

Keefe knew he should get up, leap to the library like he'd

been planning, and read as much as he could before they closed.

But he found himself asking, "How would you help me with my abilities?"

"*Well—*"

"Nope—never mind," Keefe cut in. "It's never going to work."

"Because you don't trust me," Alvar guessed.

"Pretty much, yeah."

"And here I thought you'd brought me to this place to give me a chance to prove myself."

"Yeah, to prove you deserve to live a boring life in Humanland instead of rotting in an underground prison. Not to learn crucial stuff even I shouldn't know."

"Okay," Alvar said slowly, "well . . . is there anything I can do to earn your trust?"

"You can tell me everything you know about the Neverseen's plans."

"Wow, should've seen that one coming. And I already told you—if I had some big bargaining chip, I would've used it by now."

"Yeah, but you worked with them for years. Do you seriously expect me to believe you don't know *anything*?"

Alvar sighed. "I don't know anything good—"

"Wait, so you *have* been holding secrets back? After all the speeches about how you're done with that life—"

"I *am* done with it! The only reason I didn't share this last tiny thing is because you're going to say it's ridiculous."

"Try me!"

"Ugh, fine." He tore his fingers through his hair a little harder than necessary before he mumbled, "Stellarlune . . . apparently has something to do with . . . rocks."

Keefe blinked. "Rocks."

"See why I didn't tell you?"

"Yeah—but I'm hoping you're not talking about a pile of pebbles."

"I might be. I have no idea. All I know is that I heard your mom muttering under her breath one night about how she needed 'the rocks' for the next step."

"So . . . you mean the ethertine and magsidian she used on me in Loamnore."

"Maybe? But didn't you say those were a throne and a crown? It sounded more like she meant *rock*-rocks."

Keefe snorted. "Okay, you're right, that definitely wasn't impressive."

"Agreed! But do you at least trust me now?"

"Not really, no."

Alvar gritted his teeth.

"Oh, come on, you knew 'rocks' wasn't going to do it!"

"I did. But sadly, that's all I've got."

"Well then, I guess we're done here."

Keefe stood up.

"Wait!" Alvar chewed his lip for a second before he said, "I do actually have one more secret—but it's personal."

"Then why would I care?"

"Same reason you wanted to know how I was still alive."

Keefe studied him for a beat. "And you're willing to share this 'personal' secret?"

"I might be. I don't know."

"Wow, you're really that desperate to know about my abilities?"

"Nope. I seriously don't care what you can do, Keefe. And I'm not trying to redeem myself either—not that I think help-ing you would do that. I just . . . I know you've been given a rough deal. And I've always liked you. And I don't know if you can do this on your own—and even if you can, I don't think you should have to. And I'm here, so . . ." He shrugged. "But you didn't say whether sharing my secret would even help."

"It depends on what the secret is."

"I suppose that's fair. I could tell you I got so scared that I peed my pants during a few Neverseen missions—and that might make you laugh, but it probably wouldn't be enough to make you really open up. Right?"

"Pretty much."

"Great. So . . . it sounds like I'm going to have to share the secret either way, and hope it turns out to be enough to sway you."

"It does seem that way," Keefe agreed.

Alvar went back to chewing his lip, watching the guy in the blue box fly across the TV screen, before he said, "Fine—but this leaves me super vulnerable, so it'd be awesome if you didn't share it with anyone. I realize that's a big ask, so if nothing else . . . whenever you see my brother again, don't tell him, okay?"

Keefe wasn't willing to make that kind of promise.

Best he could give him was "Maybe."

Alvar fidgeted with his sleeves for a second before he closed his eyes and blurted out, "Fine. You already know I'm still alive, so . . . why not? Light leaping isn't the only thing I can't do anymore. I can't do *anything* elf-y. No telekinesis. No levitation. No breath control or body temperature control or appetite suppression. No skills. And . . . no ability."

Keefe froze. "You mean . . ."

Alvar nodded. "I'm not a Vanisher anymore. I'm as good as Talentless."

TWENTY-SEVEN

BUT I SAW YOU VANISH!" KEEFE ARGUED. "Right before I dragged you to that deserted island. I was following you, and then you disappeared, and I thought I lost you—until you reappeared behind me."

Alvar shook his head. "That wasn't vanishing. I just wanted to make it clear I knew you were following me. And I knew that block had an easy way to loop back without being seen."

"Okay, but what about . . . ?"

Keefe tried to think of any other times he'd seen Alvar vanish while he'd been in London, but his brain came up blank.

And now that he was thinking about it, Vanishers often

blinked in and out of sight when they walked—without even trying—and Alvar hadn't done that.

Not even once.

"Wow. That's . . . huge," Keefe mumbled, sinking back into a chair.

"Tell me about it. I never realized how much I relied on the ability until it was gone. Sneaking out of the hospital was an *adventure*. And I'm still getting used to being seen all the time. I liked it way better when I could disappear if I tripped, or stained my clothes, or did something embarrassing, or—"

"Wanted to eavesdrop on your dad or brother and then report back to your Neverseen buddies," Keefe finished for him.

"It did come in handy for that," Alvar agreed with a shrug. "So . . . maybe it's better that I don't have to worry about anyone tracking me down and trying to force me into spying on someone, or running a secret errand."

"Would you do it, if they did?" Keefe asked.

"Well, it's kind of pointless to speculate, but . . . I guess it would depend on how they tried to force me. I'm not great with physical punishments."

He traced his fingers along his fading scars, and Keefe couldn't help shuddering.

"It's funny. I always thought I was so much braver than I turned out to be," Alvar murmured. "I thought I could endure *anything*—though I guess I technically have."

He flashed a sad smile at Keefe.

When Keefe didn't return it, he said, "You still don't believe me, do you? You think I'm lying about losing my ability."

"I don't know. I thought abilities couldn't be switched off once they've been triggered."

"Yeah, that's what I thought too. But that's under normal circumstances—and I think we can both agree that nothing I've been through could ever be called 'normal.'"

No, it couldn't.

"So . . . do you think it was the troll goo or the human medicine that did it?" Keefe had to ask.

"Hard to say. I could still vanish after I escaped the hive—but I was weirdly flickery. Could've been because I was weak. Or it could've been the poison slowly working through my system. All I know for sure is that when I woke up in the hospital, the ability was gone."

"So it could've been a side effect of the human medicine," Keefe noted.

Alvar tilted his head to study him. "If you're thinking about trying to figure out what they gave me and taking a dose yourself—"

"I wasn't thinking about that."

"You sure?"

Keefe looked away.

He didn't *want* to take that kind of risk—but would it really be that different than the times Foster let the Black Swan reset her abilities?

In fact, that had been *way* more dangerous, since Foster knew she was allergic to the limbium they'd give her.

"Bad idea," Alvar told him. "Seriously, Keefe. For one thing, I haven't really talked about how painful the treatment was, or how many needles they stabbed through my skin, or—"

"Okay, I get it," Keefe cut in, wishing he didn't have that mental image in his brain.

Still . . . maybe it would at least be worth finding out the names of the medicines.

Dex could probably hack into the hospital and find Alvar's records.

He wouldn't even have to tell Dex it was Alvar, since the records were probably under something like Guy Found on the Street with Amnesia.

And Elwin and Kesler might be able to tweak the medicine's formulas. Turn them into a simple elixir he could just chug and see what happens.

"It was probably the troll poison," Alvar reminded him. "But even if it wasn't, you're not thinking about all the side effects. I know we tend to put way more emphasis on abilities over skills—but my skills saved my life. If it wasn't for my breath control and my body temperature control, I never would've walked out of that pod. And all those skills are gone now. I'm also pretty sure you'd lose *all* your abilities. Think about that. You wouldn't be a Polyglot anymore, which has been pretty useful for you, hasn't it? And I know you've been struggling with your empathy, but—"

"I'm not *struggling*."

Alvar raised one eyebrow.

"I'm *not*." Keefe waved his hand through the air. "Let's see. I'm feeling . . . Wow, that's a lot of envy. I mean, I get it—everyone wants my hair, but . . ."

Alvar laughed. "Finally! A joke! Does that also mean you don't need contact to take a reading anymore?"

It was an interesting question.

Before Loamnore, the only person Keefe could read from a distance was Foster.

So maybe the fact that all he could sense at the moment was a loud, blurry hum of indiscernible emotions meant his empathy was going back to normal.

But . . .

He didn't *feel* normal.

Especially since he was pretty sure he knew what would happen if he moved closer to Alvar and tried taking a reading.

The second their skin touched, he'd get that same horrible empty feeling he'd had with Kesler and Rex.

And then he'd know for sure that he could feel when someone was Talentless.

"Care to clue me in on whatever just made you turn so pale?" Alvar asked gently. "I'm guessing it's about the other mysterious ability you refuse to mention."

Keefe shook his head. "I *can't* talk about it. With anyone. Ever."

And he definitely couldn't talk about it with someone who'd already betrayed him multiple times.

"Okaaaaaaay," Alvar said slowly. "Maybe we can talk about it without *talking* about it."

"What does that even mean?"

"It means you don't have to get specific to share what's so upsetting. Like . . . is it painful? Or is it hard to control? Does it make you feel vulnerable? Or are you worried you might hurt someone?"

Keefe shook his head. "The only thing I can tell you is, *I hate it.*"

Which actually felt really awesome to admit.

"I hate it!" he repeated, louder that time. Then he cupped his hands around his mouth and screamed, "I HATE IT! It's the worst ability anyone has ever had in the history of the Lost Cities! So yeah, I *am* wondering if there's a way to get rid of it. Even if I have to get stabbed by a bunch of needles or end up with no skills or Talentless—it'd be worth it to be free of this miserable thing that's only going to cause a giant mess!"

The outburst left him gasping for breath, but Keefe was glad he'd said it—even if Alvar was staring at him like he was a hungry gorgodon who'd just escaped his cage.

"Sorry," Keefe mumbled.

"Don't be. It's okay to be angry. I definitely would be if I were you. But—"

Keefe rolled his eyes. "Another 'but.' I swear, you're starting to sound worse than the Forklenator."

"I know—and trust me, I'm not used to being the boring, responsible one in the conversation. *BUT*. I do think you might be forgetting a few things. First . . . manifesting is scary. Phasers get stuck in the floor. Frosters get trapped in balls of ice—"

"This is a little different."

"I'm sure it is. *BUT*. This ability you hate? It's a part of you. And it's always been a part of you. It may not feel that way because manifesting it almost killed you. But it still came from you—"

"No, it came from *her*. And from my awful father. And that's only because they drank some creepy, unnatural concoctions before I was born, trying to make me into their little Legacy Boy."

"You're right. But they had no idea what would actually result from their experiment. That's one of the things your mom complained about more than anything else—how little control she had over what would happen."

Keefe snorted. "Join the club."

"But that's the thing. *You* have the control. Right here. Right now. These abilities—even the one you hate? They're *yours*. And you can train them and refine them until they work the way you want them to—and then use them to do anything you want. If you want to hide—hide. I totally get the appeal of hanging out in Humanland forever. Or if you want to go back and fight—fight. I know you're probably going to tell me

I wouldn't say that if I knew what you're dealing with. But I know *you*. You're Keefe Sencen. You've got this. You just have to decide what you want to do."

It would've been a great little pep talk, if it hadn't been coming from someone who'd been way too loyal to the enemy.

"I think," Keefe said after what felt like an eternity, "I need some air."

He couldn't sit in that room anymore.

It felt too small—too close to someone he shouldn't be trusting.

And his secrets felt much too huge.

"I'll be here when you get back," Alvar told him, and Keefe was sure Alvar would be.

He just wasn't sure if that was a good thing.

Maybe it was time to take Alvar back to his city—before Keefe broke down and told him everything.

Or Alvar figured it out on his own.

But then . . . Keefe would be alone again.

"Whoa, it's bright," he mumbled as he stepped outside.

He'd forgotten it was still daylight.

Barely past lunchtime—which felt super weird.

How had so many revelations happened that quickly?

And where did he go from here?

He stared at the street, trying to decide which way to turn.

Was he going to stick with his current plan and keep trying to find out what happened to Ethan Benedict Wright II?

If so, he still had enough time to head to that library.

Or . . . was he going to admit that whatever he might learn probably wasn't important enough for him to dedicate so much energy to it?

And if he did shift his focus . . . was he ready to deal with his abilities?

Keefe wanted to say no.

Wanted to stick with the safer routine and keep reading boring books on astrophysics or searching London for the house with the green door.

He even started to turn down the road that would take him to the next batch of streets to cross off.

But then he caught a glimpse of the store Alvar mentioned—the one with the little stuffed elf plushies in the window. And he couldn't believe how many times he'd walked past it without noticing.

What else had he missed?

He made his way over and studied the tiny elf faces, with their pointy ears and silly hats and red-and-green stripy outfits.

His favorite was a little elf dude with messy blond hair and tiny bells on his shoes.

"Foster would love that."

Keefe said it out loud, letting himself admit it.

It made it easier to make the bigger confession.

He wanted to see her again.

He didn't want to end up alone like Alvar.

And as much as he was enjoying his time in Humanland . . .

He wanted to go back to the Lost Cities.

But . . . the only way he'd ever be able to do that was if he either did something drastic and tried to get rid of his abilities . . .

Or . . . if he learned how to control them.

Kinda seemed like he should give that second option a try, long before he started doing anything dangerous.

"I can do this," he said as he stepped into the store—not caring that the clerk gave him a weird look.

He was Keefe Sencen.

And he wasn't ready to give up.

So he bought Foster the tiny stuffed elf and tucked it safely in his backpack when he made it back to his hotel room.

Someday he *would* give it to her.

But he had some serious work to do first.

TWENTY-EIGHT

"CAN'T SLEEP?" ALVAR ASKED WHEN he found Keefe awake in the middle of the night, sitting by one of the larger windows with his knees curled into his chest.

Keefe nodded, watching drops of rain trickle down the foggy glass.

He knew switching his focus was the right decision.

But his brain kept shouting, *YOU CAN'T STOP NOW—YOU STILL HAVE MORE STREETS AND LIBRARIES TO CHECK!*

It felt like he was giving up on Ethan and Eleanor—especially since he didn't even have a plan for training his abilities.

And he'd tried coming up with one, but . . .

How was he supposed to train an ability that only worked when there was physical contact, but *also* keep the ability completely secret?

He'd tried brainstorming in his sketchbook but ended up just drawing a bunch of fancy question marks.

And he'd tried asking himself what Foster would do, and ended up spending much longer than he was proud of wondering how awkward it was going to be to see her after leaving that letter.

He'd even tried imagining that he was a Foxfire Mentor who needed to create a lesson plan for his challenging new prodigy, and mostly just felt sorry for everything he'd put his previous Mentors through.

He couldn't even come up with a good name for the ability.

Was he a Talenterator?

An Abilitypath?

Both of those sounded like a disease.

"Hey, I have an idea," Alvar said, clapping his hands to snap Keefe out of his downward mental spiral. "Let's get out of London!"

"Let me guess," Keefe told him. "You want me to take you back to where I found you?"

If Alvar had said yes, Keefe would've been willing to do it.

But Alvar said, "Eh, there's plenty of time for that. I was thinking more like a day trip. Preferably somewhere sunny."

"A day trip," Keefe repeated.

"Why not? Why stay in rainy London when you could light leap us anywhere we want! I hear France has these amazing, superthin pancakes called crepes. Or Denmark has these little round pancakes called aebleskiver. Or Colombia has fluffy arepas. Or—"

"Okay, what is it with you and pancakes?" Keefe had to ask. "And what'd you do, look up a list of the best pancakes in the human world?"

"Um, that's exactly what I did—because pancakes are *amazing*. And in case you haven't noticed, I've also had a lot of free time on my hands. You've been leaping all around the planet, and I've been stuck in the same city, where it's mostly been raining. So what do you say? Want to head to China to try their jianbing? Or go to India and try their dosas? Or . . . if pancakes aren't your thing, I also have a list of the best places for melty cheese. Or crusty bread. Or different flavors of ice cream. I also really want to track down something called a Tim Tam. I guess they make them in Australia—and hey, people also speak English there, so I'd actually be able to understand what everyone's saying, like I can here. Let's do that!"

"You want to go to Australia," Keefe clarified.

"You make it sound like I'm suggesting we move there. All I'm saying is . . . let's go grab some breakfast. Maybe soak up a little sunshine. I was talking to this sweet newlywed couple in the pub a few days ago who were visiting from Australia, and they said it's warm there this time of year." He pointed to the foggy, wet window. "I miss warm. And apparently Australia also has these small, fluffy pancakes called pikelets, and I definitely need to try them. So let's go!"

"You realize it's probably too late there for breakfast, right?" Keefe asked.

"Oh. Right. The human time-zone thing. Well . . . we'll get lunch, then! Or dinner. Who cares what time it is—let's get you a change of scenery. Maybe all we'll end up doing is eating some awesome food, wandering a bit, and heading back. But *maybe* you'll clear your head and come up with some fresh ideas. Sounds like a win-win either way."

When Keefe still hesitated, Alvar added, "Come on, this is totally the kind of idea you'd normally come up with yourself."

It actually *did* seem like something he'd try to talk his friends into if they were there.

And it definitely sounded better than watching the rain trail down the dark window, waiting for the sun to rise.

But . . . was he seriously going globe-hopping with Alvar Vacker?

Apparently he was, because a few minutes later they'd both changed to shorts and T-shirts, Alvar had grabbed on to Keefe's shoulder, and Keefe had leaped them to a sunny city by the ocean where people were smiling and telling them, "G'day."

"Now *this* is what I'm talking about!" Alvar said, stretching out his bare arms and doing a little spin. "I'm so sick of coats.

Honestly, that was one of the hardest things about being in the Neverseen. Those cloaks were miserable. Remember how itchy the fabric was?"

Keefe did.

But he was pretty sure his brain would explode if he had to reminisce about his brief time trying to infiltrate the Neverseen with the guy who'd once tried to recruit him for real.

"So . . . where to?" Alvar asked.

Keefe shrugged. "You tell me. This was your idea."

"Fine. Then I say we walk that way"—he pointed toward a park—"and see if we can find someone to ask for restaurant suggestions."

It didn't take long.

People seemed extra friendly in Australia—and they all unanimously recommended a nearby café that served breakfast all day.

"Admit it," Alvar said as the waitress set a giant plate of pikelets in front of him, covered in berries and drizzled with honey. "I'm a genius."

"I wouldn't go *that* far." Keefe poked at the green gloop smeared across his bread.

"Hey—I told you to skip the avocado toast. Human produce can never hold up when you're used to the gnomish stuff."

"Will you keep your voice down?" Keefe whisper-hissed, glancing over his shoulder to see if any of the other diners were listening to them. "You can't talk about gnomes here!"

"Why not? This place has a dessert on their menu called a fairy floss burrito."

Okay, maybe that was a valid point.

Keefe was *really* getting tired of Alvar having those.

"Come on, try a pikelet instead," Alvar said, sliding his plate toward Keefe. "You know you want to."

Keefe was tempted to deny it, but . . .

He grabbed his fork and cut himself a huge bite—then immediately scooped up another because, wow, those things were good.

"See?" Alvar said. "I told you I'm a genius. And we're definitely ordering one of those fairy burrito things before we leave."

"They're *very* sweet," the waitress warned as she came by to refill their waters—which sadly didn't taste any better in Australia. "If you're thinking about dessert, you should try our pavlova. The meringue melts like a cloud."

"Sounds perfect—we'll take two," Alvar told her. "And a fairy burrito on the side."

She laughed. "Big sugar rush coming up."

A few minutes later she brought them two fluffy white crackly blobs topped with fresh fruit and cream—and a bright pink, fuzzy-looking tube with a rainbow swirl in the center and a dusting of glitter and sprinkles.

"What's the verdict?" she asked after they'd tried bites of everything.

"You were right," Alvar told her. "The fairy burrito is way too sweet."

"Yeah, even my kiddos can only handle a few bites," she agreed, "but they still insist on ordering it because of the sparkles."

"Sparkles can be pretty hard to resist," Keefe said, wishing Ro was there to roll her eyes at him.

He wondered if she was still hanging around with Foster in Sparkle Town—as she liked to call the Lost Cities—or if she'd gone back to Ravagog.

"You okay?" the waitress asked, studying him with eyes that were a brighter blue than most elves'. "Something wrong with the pavlova?"

"No, it's amazing," Keefe assured her, taking another bite to prove it. "It really is like eating a cloud."

It might be the best dessert he'd had in Humanland—which was a *bold* statement.

The waitress smiled. "It's what we're famous for. Let me know if I can get you anything else."

"Actually," Alvar said as she turned to walk away, "maybe you can help us figure out where to go after we're done here. I'm trying to find something to cheer up my sulky friend—"

"I'm not sulky!" Keefe insisted.

"He totally is," Alvar argued. "And I'm hoping you might have a few good suggestions."

"Well," the waitress said slowly, "there's obviously all the really touristy stuff like the Opera House or the Manly Ferry—"

"No boats," Keefe jumped in. "*That* would make me sulky—and hurl pavlova all over my shoes."

"We definitely don't want that." She reached up and twirled the end of her dark ponytail. "How do you feel about cute animals?"

"Does anyone *not* like cute animals?" Keefe asked.

"If they don't, I hope they never sit at one of my tables," she said. "So I'd recommend heading to either the zoo or the wild-life park. The zoo's bigger, but I personally prefer the wildlife park. It's way more hands-on. In fact, my wife and I go at least once a month to check up on our koala buddies. It's only open for a few more hours, but it's not too far from here, so if you head over soon, you should have time to see all the critters."

"Sounds perfect!" Alvar said. "How do we get there?"

She seemed surprised that they didn't have phones to help them with directions but was nice enough to write some instructions down on a napkin.

"Oh, and if you're really looking for a laugh, make sure you ask someone to show you the drop bears," she added with a huge grin. "It's something everyone visiting here needs to experience at least once. Oh, and you'll need these."

She reached into the pocket of her apron and handed them a couple of yellow packets.

"Vegemite?" Alvar said, reading the name off the label. "I've heard about this stuff."

"Some love it, some hate it," she told him. "But it's necessary for the drop bears."

"You seriously want to go to a human animal preserve?" Keefe whispered when the waitress walked away.

"Why not? Apparently they have drop bears—and I've never heard of a drop bear, have you?"

"No, but it's probably just a weird name for a regular bear. And don't you think a human wildlife sanctuary is going to be pretty small and pathetic compared to our Sanctuary?"

"Wow, look who's suddenly Mr. Snobby Elf!"

Keefe glanced around again, but thankfully everyone was still ignoring them.

"I'm not being *snobby*," he insisted. "Humans just aren't exactly known for being the greatest at protecting animals. That's why we had to build our Sanctuary, remember?"

Alvar snorted. "Wow, you just managed to sound even snobbier."

"Oh please, I'm not saying humans aren't great at tons of other stuff. Their music is amazing."

"Right? And I love how they have it playing in the background everywhere. I never realized how weirdly quiet the Lost Cities are until I got here. And you know what else I love?"

"The pancakes?" Keefe guessed.

"I mean, *obviously*. And their desserts." Alvar scarfed another big bite before he added, "But I was thinking about their cans of whipped cream. Have you seen those? They have these little nozzles on the top that you can use to squirt it right into your mouth. I got one a few days ago and devoured the whole thing in, like, an hour—though, side note: I definitely do *not* recommend trying the canned cheese version. Whatever that orange stuff was, it *wasn't* cheese."

Keefe couldn't help laughing. "So this is what you've been doing while I've been gone?"

"I told you, I've had a *lot* of time on my hands."

"I guess." Keefe finished the last bite of his pavlova. "Did you try any coffee yet?"

"I did. Tastes *horrible*, but where was that stuff when I had to sit through elvin history sessions? And have you noticed how much art they have everywhere? The street art's my favorite. It's wild knowing someone was just like, 'Forget the rules, I need to make art *right here, right now!*' One of the coolest pieces I've seen is this painting on the side of a building near our hotel. It's not big or fancy or anything. Just two hands making a heart, like this"—he curved each of his hands into a *c* and then pressed them together—"and underneath, it says, 'You are loved.' Like someone knew people might need to see that message."

Keefe whistled. "Wow. I never realized you were so . . . sentimental."

It was hard to reconcile that with the bitter, furious guy Alvar had been when Keefe had found him hiding at Candleshade.

"Another side effect of almost dying," Alvar said quietly.

"Makes you realize life's too short to waste on anger and hate. Better to focus on things that make you happy. Like pancakes. And . . . friends."

He glanced at Keefe—and then quickly looked away, poking at what remained of the fairy floss burrito.

Keefe dragged his fork through the wilted cream from his pavlova.

He wasn't sure if he could ever see Alvar as a friend after everything he'd done.

But he also wasn't *totally* opposed to the idea.

"You know what else I love about humans?" Keefe asked, deciding it was probably better to stick to a safer subject. "Those teeny, tiny hot sauce bottles they give you with your room service."

"Yeah, I've totally kept a couple of them!" Alvar admitted.

Keefe laughed. "Same."

"Let's see . . . what else?" Alvar studied the room. "Oh, you know what I've noticed? Seems like there's no matchmaking in this world—and *that's* awesome."

Keefe frowned. "I thought you were all about matchmaking. Didn't you pick up your first list, like, the second it was available?"

"I did. And I dated pretty much everyone on it. But it felt so . . . forced. That's why I never picked up any other lists. It's like, 'Here are the people you're genetically compatible with. Go fall in love with one of them so you can have a baby with a powerful special ability.'"

"Ugh, when you put it like that, I'm glad I haven't registered."

Alvar smirked. "I think we both know why *you* haven't registered."

Keefe hated his cheeks for flushing.

"Don't worry, I'm not going to make you talk about it," Alvar promised. "But I will say this: Go with your heart, okay? No lists. Just love. It makes it so much more real. You can *see* the difference." He nudged his chin toward the other tables, which were filled with a huge variety of smiling couples and families. "And did you notice? The waitress said she has a wife."

"That's true," Keefe realized. "And now that I think about it, I actually met a guy in London who talked about his husband."

"Yeah, it's really cool."

"It is," Keefe agreed, glancing at the waitress, who was laughing so hard at something another customer had said that pink spots were dotting her pale cheeks. "Do you think the Council will ever get rid of matchmaking?"

"They should. It's hurt a lot of people and caused a *lot* of problems."

"It has."

Brant joined the Neverseen because he'd been ruled a bad match for Jolie.

And Dex had dealt with drama his whole life because his parents were a bad match.

"But change is slow in the Lost Cities," Alvar said quietly.

"And I'm done trying to make it happen. That's why I'm sticking with humans from here on out—even if their wildlife sanctuaries turn out to be disappointing."

"Uh, didn't you call me snobby for saying that?" Keefe asked.

"I said 'if.' Only one way to find out which one of us is right." Alvar tucked the Vegemite packets into his pocket and asked the waitress to bring over the check. "Come on, let's go see some drop bears!"

TWENTY-NINE

WELL, YOU WERE RIGHT. The elvin Sanctuary is way better," Alvar told Keefe as they studied the map they'd been handed when they bought their tickets to the wildlife park.

The place definitely looked a little weathered.

And it smelled very strongly of animals.

"But it's hard to compete with something built by dwarves inside a hollowed-out mountain range, with a rainbow sky and dinosaurs and unicorns running around," Keefe reminded him. "And, hey, at least those koalas over there look supercute."

"They do," Alvar agreed. "I'm also a big fan of kangaroos."

"And quokkas!" Keefe made sure they went to that exhibit first, because who didn't want to watch a bunch of smiling marsupials hopping around?

It almost made him wish he had a phone so he could use the camera to take a bunch of pictures.

Instead, he made a mental note to draw some in his sketchbook later—and maybe the echidnas, too, since he'd never seen one before and they kind of looked like spiky gulons.

The wombats were also particularly adorable, all blinky and sleepy in the sunshine.

And the emus had the zoomies and kept running around and around and around.

The different habitats and enclosures were a bit more cramped than the pastures at Havenfield or the Sanctuary—and some of the creatures looked like they might prefer to not have a bunch of people staring at them all the time.

But.

It was cool to see that humans really were trying to protect and preserve all these different species.

The elves loved to make it seem like humans were ruining the planet with their pollution and hunting and habitat destruction—and each exhibit definitely acknowledged that.

But the main message at the wildlife park was: *We need to do better.*

Humans may not have a Timeline to Extinction, and they might not be afraid that if a creature went extinct, the planet would be irreparably damaged. But it did seem like they cared about animals and were trying to protect as many as they could.

Which made Keefe wish the Human Assistance Program hadn't been dissolved.

If they all worked together, there probably wouldn't be any more endangered species.

"Hmm. This place is closing soon, and I still haven't found those drop-bear things the waitress mentioned," Alvar said, checking the map again. "I'm really curious to see if the humans know something we don't."

"Me too," Keefe agreed. "But didn't she say we'd have to ask someone about them?"

"That's right! Excuse me," Alvar called out to a very tan, very blond guy standing by the penguin exhibit wearing a khaki shirt and dark pants, like all the other employees. "We're trying to find the drop bears—any chance you can help us?"

The guy laughed and headed over. "Drop bears, huh? Who told you about those?"

"Our waitress," Keefe said. "I guess she comes here a lot, and she said it's something everyone needs to experience at least once."

"She gave us these," Alvar added, digging the Vegemite packets out of his pocket.

The employee laughed again. "Vegemite does come in handy. Did she tell you to put it behind your ears?"

"Why?" Keefe asked as Alvar ripped open one of the packets and dipped his finger into the dark goop. "Are the drop bears drawn to the smell?"

"Nope. They can't stand it—but that's a good thing. You want to make sure they keep their distance."

"What are they?" Alvar asked, dabbing some Vegemite on his earlobes. "I've never heard of them."

"Yeah, you wouldn't have, unless you're a local," the guy explained. "Think of a koala, but bigger—and with enormous fangs. So they draw you in with their cuteness—and then WHAM! They drop out of the tree and tear you to pieces. That's why we keep them off the map. Can't have them around any little kids, you know? But you two look pretty tough—think you can handle a drop-bear encounter?"

"Absolutely!" Alvar said, even though Keefe had been about to give a very different answer. He laughed when he saw Keefe's scowl. "Please tell me you're not afraid of drop bears."

Keefe leaned in and whispered, "Uh, humans don't train animals to be vegetarians like we do."

Alvar glanced at the employee. "Is it safe?"

"As safe as anything can ever be," he said—which wasn't very reassuring. "Just make sure you smear on plenty of Vegemite, and you'll be good."

"How come you're not putting any on?" Keefe asked as he reluctantly dabbed some behind his ears—and tried not to gag from the smell.

"I had a cheese-and-Vegemite scroll for lunch, so I'm good. They can smell it on my breath."

"Wow, you eat this stuff?" Alvar asked.

"Oh yeah—it's delicious!"

Alvar sniffed the packet. "Think I'll take your word for it."

"Your loss."

He led them to a section of the wildlife park with a few trees, and Keefe noticed there wasn't a fence to keep the drop bears contained—which seemed a little odd.

"They usually hide out in there," the guy whispered, pointing to the tallest tree with the thickest foliage. "Try to keep your voices down, so they don't know we're coming."

He ducked into a crouch and shuffled forward, waving his arm for them to follow.

Alvar shrugged and copied the guy's movements, and Keefe did the same—even though he could feel the little hairs on the back of his neck rising with every rustle and crackle of the leaves.

"Up there." He pointed toward the top of the tree. "Can you see them?"

Keefe and Alvar both shook their heads.

"We'll have to get a bit closer, then. Shhhhhhhh." He pressed his finger to his lips as he led them directly under the tree and pointed right above them. "See them now?"

Alvar frowned. "Maybe?"

Keefe squinted. "I don't think I—AAAAAHHHHHHHH-HHHHHHHHHHHHHHHHH!"

Something plopped onto his head, and his brain screamed, *DROP BEAR ATTACK!* as he thrashed and flailed.

"Hang on!" the guy told him, reaching for Keefe's hair. "Try to hold still."

"BUT THERE'S A DROP BEAR ON MY HEAD!"

Keefe's knees collapsed, and his vision dimmed, and he locked his jaw as the panic took over.

He couldn't move—couldn't breathe—couldn't . . .

"Got it!" the guy said. "Crisis averted. And don't worry, it wasn't a drop bear. It was just this little dude."

He held out his hand, and it took a few seconds for Keefe's eyes to focus.

"THAT'S WORSE THAN A DROP BEAR!" he shouted, and scrambled away from the enormous spider.

"Nah, he's harmless," the guy promised, wiggling his fingers to make the spider do a creepy little spider dance. "Then again, so are the drop bears."

"Then why did you say you have to keep kids away from them?" Keefe argued.

The guy laughed. "Yeah . . . so . . . funny story. Drop bears aren't actually real. They're just a joke we play on tourists sometimes—though we don't get to do it very often anymore, since the internet has tipped everyone off. It's usually more of a bushwalk prank—but since you asked about drop bears, I couldn't resist."

Keefe's hands curled into fists, but he wasn't sure if he

was angry or embarrassed or just trying to stop shaking. "Let me guess—the Vegemite was to lure the spider?"

"Nah, this little dude wasn't part of the prank." The guy stroked the spider's hairy legs before he helped it crawl back into the tree. "I was about to scream, 'Get down!' and cover my head—and that was going to be the whole gag. The spider was just a funny coincidence."

"Lucky me," Keefe grumbled, tearing his fingers through every inch of his hair.

He swore he could still feel something crawling around up there.

Maybe it had a friend. . . .

"The real question," Alvar said as Keefe swatted his head and swiped at his clothes, "is, did you pee your pants?"

"Of course not!"

Alvar laughed. "You sure? I wouldn't judge you if you did."

"I didn't! And you're also lucky I didn't give any . . ."

Keefe's voice trailed off as he realized he'd been about to mention his ability—and the employee was still standing there listening.

"How about I go get you two some coffee from the café?" he asked. "My treat, since you were such good sports about the whole drop-bear thing."

"I'm always down for coffee," Alvar told him. "And maybe some sort of wipes, since this Vegemite stuff is *super* sticky."

"You got it. I'll meet you at the exit since we're getting ready to close."

"He's lucky I'm not an Inflictor," Keefe grumbled after the guy wandered off.

Alvar grinned. "That probably would've been a little hard to explain."

"Yeah." Keefe swiped at his clothes again, but he couldn't shake that creepy-crawly sensation.

He'd probably be having nightmares about giant spiders and falling drop bears for a while, but . . .

He was also pretty proud of himself.

A few weeks ago, if he'd gotten that scared, he would've unleashed a command and frozen everybody—and yeah, he'd locked his jaw to be safe. But he hadn't actually needed to.

He'd been completely, one hundred percent in control.

So maybe all he needed to do was find the right visualization exercise, and he'd have that same level of control over the rest of his abilities.

Just because he hadn't been able to come up with one so far didn't mean the right exercise didn't exist.

"You look like you've had an epiphany," Alvar said as they collected their free coffees and exited the wildlife park.

"Yeah, I'm never letting you plan our day trips ever again," Keefe told him, scrubbing his ears with the wipes—but he still smelled like Vegemite.

Alvar laughed. "See, all I'm hearing is, you're game for more adventures."

Keefe wasn't so sure about that.

"Come on, you know you can't wait to tell your friends all about the day you tamed the mighty drop bear."

Keefe grinned, imagining Foster's face as she listened to him tell the story.

He wouldn't even leave out the embarrassing parts since her smile was worth the humiliation.

Though . . . he probably shouldn't mention that Alvar was with him—at least not right away.

That was the kind of reveal he'd need to prepare her for.

"I'm not even mad that I didn't find any Tim Tams today," Alvar said, dragging Keefe out of his mushy daydream. "It'll give us an excuse to come back—and then we can eat more pavlovas!"

Once again, the best Keefe was willing to give him was a maybe.

But he did clink his cup against Alvar's cup after Alvar raised his coffee and said, "To Lord Spiderhair!"

And it was the best coffee he'd had so far.

"Ready to go?" Keefe asked, tossing his empty cup and offering Alvar his hand.

"Back to London?" Alvar clarified.

Keefe nodded.

Alvar grinned. "Come on, roomie. Let's order more desserts and watch some British TV."

He grabbed Keefe's hand, and a flickery blast of warmth erupted between their palms as the light whisked them away.

"What was that?" Keefe asked as they re-formed in front of the familiar clock tower—in the middle of a London downpour.

"No idea," Alvar mumbled, shielding his face from the rain with one hand and steadying himself on a nearby lamppost. "I . . . think I must've faded a little. I feel super dizzy."

He took a few shaky steps, and Keefe gasped.

"What?" Alvar asked.

"Do that again."

"Do what?"

"Walk."

Keefe needed to make sure the rain wasn't messing with his vision.

"Uh . . . okay." Alvar wobbled a few steps forward, and Keefe's jaw fell slack as he watched Alvar blink in and out of sight.

"What's wrong?" Alvar asked, swiping water out of his eyes.

Keefe shook his head, not sure if he was stunned—or furious.

All he knew for certain was: "You can vanish!"

THIRTY

WHAT DO YOU MEAN, *I CAN vanish?*" Alvar asked, sweeping back his drenched hair.

"Oh please—drop the act!" Keefe turned and stomped away, wishing he'd brought a coat or an umbrella or—

"What act?" Alvar called after him. "I seriously have no idea . . . Whoa, *what is happening?*"

Keefe glanced over his shoulder and found Alvar staring at his feet as he hopped back and forth, watching them disappear and reappear with each leap.

"Do you realize what this means?" Alvar breathed.

"Yeah, you're a liar!" Keefe snapped back. "And I'm a loser for falling for it again."

Alvar fumbled to steady himself against another lamppost and shook his head. "No. It means we know what your new ability does."

The words were a bolt of lightning—bold and bright and terrifying—and Keefe froze, suddenly aware that they weren't alone.

The rain had left the street fairly empty—but there were still a few people around. And they were all staring at him and Alvar with nervous, confused expressions. As if they'd seen Alvar's little hopping move and were trying to convince themselves that their eyes were just playing tricks on them.

Alvar must've had the same realization because he said, "Not here. But I need your help," he added as Keefe turned away. "I wasn't kidding about feeling dizzy—and those little hops I just did made it way worse. Pretty sure if I try to walk right now, I'll collapse."

Keefe wanted to tell Alvar that was his own problem to deal with.

Then turn and flee.

Never look back.

Never find out if Alvar had betrayed him again.

Or worse, if he'd figured out Keefe's biggest secret.

But when he met Alvar's eyes, he saw genuine fear and desperation.

And . . . hadn't Keefe been looking for answers?

Was he really going to run away now that he was so close to finding some?

Keefe sighed and trudged back over, letting Alvar drape an arm around his shoulders—but he made sure to avoid any contact between their skin, hoping that would be enough to prevent any other weird stuff from happening.

"Thanks," Alvar said as they wobbled toward the hotel.

Keefe shrugged—not missing the fact that Alvar's flickering had stopped.

Maybe that meant the jolt of heat they'd shared—whatever it was—had run its course and burned itself out.

Or maybe Alvar had just remembered that he was supposed to be hiding his ability.

Keefe waited to ask until they'd made it through the lobby, up the elevator, and were safely back in the suite.

Then he dumped Alvar on the couch and told him, "Okay—prove you haven't been lying to me."

"*How?*" Alvar asked. "I have zero control over what's happening!"

"Then how come you've suddenly stopped vanishing?"

"Uh, probably the same reason I started again in the first place! Though, I wonder . . ."

He closed his eyes, squeezing them so tight, his face got all scrunched.

Nothing happened for a few seconds.

Then his body flickered in and out of sight.

"Yep. You definitely did something to me," he told Keefe.

"Or you've been pretending you lost your ability, and now you're just trying to cover it!"

"Why would I do that? It's not like it earned me all kinds of trust! Plus, I can't help noticing that you don't seem at *all* shocked by the idea that you might have an effect on someone's abilities."

He raised his eyebrows, daring Keefe to deny it.

"That's what I thought. So let's stop wasting time accusing me of lying and start trying to figure out what happened. Because this is big, Keefe. I mean . . . look at this."

He held up his hands, showing how his fingers were still flickering ever so slightly.

Keefe looked away. "Is that how it was when you first manifested?"

"No, this is completely different. The ability was unwieldy at first—but I also felt strong and energized and powerful. Right now . . . I don't know how to describe it." He sank back into the couch cushions and rubbed his temples. "My head is spinning, and everything feels blurry, and I can't stop shaking."

Keefe was shaking too—but that might've had something to do with his cold, damp clothes.

He went to his room and changed—and brought Alvar a robe.

"Thanks," Alvar mumbled as he peeled off his drenched

shirt, revealing a bunch more scars that hadn't healed as well as the ones on his face. "You know what's weird?" he asked as he slid his arms through the robe's thick white sleeves and wrapped it around his chest. "I actually liked not having an ability. I know that probably seems hard to believe—and it definitely took a little getting used to. But it kinda felt like proof that I belonged in the human world—and made it *way* easier to blend in."

"And you're sure it's back for good?" Keefe had to ask.

"I . . . think so. It's just super weak. Or maybe *I'm* weak—it's hard to tell."

He closed his eyes and vanished for a few seconds, looking pale and sweaty when he reappeared. "That's as long as I can hold it—and, wow, that made me dizzy."

"I think you need to sleep," Keefe said as Alvar rested his head between his knees.

"Maybe. But we both know *that's* not going to happen."

"Probably not." Keefe sank onto one of the chairs and stared at the rain-speckled window. "Want me to order some room service? Maybe eating would give you some extra energy."

Alvar closed his eyes. "Worth a try."

Keefe ordered a few random things and brought Alvar a glass of water while they waited for the food to arrive.

Alvar took a couple of sips and studied his hands. "It's the strangest thing. It's like . . . there's a pool deep inside me. Maybe it's something we all have. Some sort of . . . inner reserve of energy that fuels our abilities. All I know is, it dried up while I was dying. I felt it drain away—and I got used to the parched feeling. Stopped trying to draw from there. Kind of forgot it ever existed. But now . . . whatever that warmth was— it crashed through me like an earthquake. And it cracked open that pool, releasing a fresh trickle of energy that must've been hidden underneath. But it's not enough to fill the well. It's basically just enough to make me super aware of the emptiness. Does that make any sense?"

"Not really," Keefe told him, even though it kind of did. "Is that your way of asking me to try and heal you completely?"

He realized how that sounded a second too late.

"So that *is* your ability, then?" Alvar asked. "You heal other abilities?"

"How would I know? It's not like there are a lot of people needing to be healed."

"Ruy needs it," Alvar reminded him. "And don't look at me like that—I'm not saying you should heal him. I'm just trying to figure out why your mom would've thought it'd be worth everything she put herself through—and everything she put you through—to turn you into a Healer."

"Don't go giving it a name!" Keefe snapped—even though that sounded way better than anything he'd come up with. "You're making it sound like it's normal."

"Trust me, Keefe—I know exactly how *not* normal all of this is! I'm also pretty sure there's a lot more you're not saying. And since I'm sitting here, trying not to pass out because of what your ability did to me, I'm going to try to piece it together, whether you want me to or not."

"Whatever," Keefe told him, wishing he didn't sound so afraid.

But Alvar hadn't followed the logic yet—hadn't realized that Keefe could tell if someone was going to be Talentless.

And the more he questioned things, the more likely he was to piece that together.

"I think the healing is more of . . . a side effect," Keefe said, deciding his best option was to keep Alvar focused on the less terrifying aspects of his ability. "I think I'm more like . . . an Ability Triggerer—and I know the name needs work."

"It does. But are you saying you've triggered other special abilities?"

"I'm saying I *might* have. It was hard to tell. Everything was super chaotic, because we were trying to deal with the changes to my empathy—and yeah, you were right, my empathy's different now. And no, I'm not going to tell you how," he added, wondering how many other secrets he was going to spill before this conversation was over. "I'd been testing all these different things that were supposed to give me better control. But they weren't working, and I was getting super overwhelmed, and . . . all I know for sure is that I got this weird feeling when I made contact with someone who hadn't manifested—almost like I was picking up a tiny hint of their unmanifested ability.

I didn't know that's what it was at the time. I couldn't even tell if they'd touched my skin or just my clothes or what had happened. But the next day . . . they manifested, and when I heard what their ability was, the thing I'd felt suddenly made sense."

"Made sense *how*?" Alvar pressed. "Come on, Keefe—you have to give me at least a few specifics if we're going to figure this out."

Keefe chewed his lip, trying to decide which of the triplets would be safest to reference.

The blast of cold he'd felt from Lex seemed like too generic of a sensation, since lots of people felt cold sometimes. So he went with Bex's ability and told Alvar, "It's a little hard to describe, but their hand felt . . . squishy."

"Squishy," Alvar repeated.

"Yeah, like the bones weren't totally solid anymore."

"And I'm assuming this person later manifested as a Phaser?" Alvar asked.

Keefe nodded, impressed that Alvar had pieced that together. "But they manifested the next day, not immediately after. So the whole thing could have totally been a coincidence."

"I thought you didn't believe in coincidences."

"I don't like to—but apparently it was a coincidence that you happened to be in that library the same time I was."

"True," Alvar said, staring at the ceiling. "Of all the gin joints in all the towns in all the world . . ."

"What does that mean?"

"It's a line from an old human movie. A pretty famous one, since I've seen it a bunch of places."

"Okay, but . . . why are you quoting it?"

"Just thinking about the odds of us finding each other and all this happening—though I guess the odds were pretty good, since you've been leaping around the world visiting libraries, and I was going to a library every day trying to learn a new language. Sooner or later we were bound to run into each other. But . . . I was *fine* where I was at. It wasn't perfect—but I'd found my path. I was happy. I was steady. I was slowly piecing together a whole new life—a whole new future. And then you turn up and . . . now I'm *this*." He gestured to himself.

"Yeah, I'm still not sure what you're trying to tell me."

Alvar buried his face in his hands. "I was happy, Keefe. I didn't care that I was Talentless. I would've stayed that way for the rest of my days without giving it a second thought. But now you cracked open that pool, and . . . I don't know if I can stand it. Now I feel hollow and cold and . . . wrong. But I also know that if I ask—even if I get down on my knees and beg—you're not going to want to grab my hand again and see if you can pry that crack open wider to unearth more energy. And you're definitely not going to want to try to find some other way to fix me. So . . . I'm probably going to be stuck drowning in this emptiness. And I get it—you don't trust me. But—"

"Don't put this on me!"

"It *is* on you," Alvar argued. "You have all the power here,

Keefe. Every single drop of it. You could reach out and heal me right now—"

"You don't know that! I could just as easily do something that overwhelms you or undoes whatever the human medicine did and sends you back to the hospital!"

"Is that what happened to the people whose abilities you might have triggered?"

"What do you mean, 'people'?" Keefe asked.

"Come on, I caught your slip. You said you didn't know if they'd touched your skin, but then you said you'd specifically touched their squishy hand. So I'm assuming that means there were at least two people affected. Maybe more. Did they get sick or hurt afterward? Is that why you ran away?"

It probably would've been smarter to agree and make Alvar believe the ability was deadly.

But it was clearly hard enough to keep all the what-ifs and maybes and complicated details straight without adding a bunch of lies to the story.

So Keefe told him, "They were healthy and hadn't come super close to dying. I mean . . . look at you. You can't even stand up right now, and you only touched my hand for a couple of seconds. And it hit you the moment we made contact. Basically instantly."

"But maybe that's a good thing! You said the others didn't feel anything until the next day, right? And I'm assuming you triggered them pretty much right after you manifested. So the fact that I felt the change almost immediately could mean your abilities have had enough time to settle in and start working the way they're supposed to be."

Keefe snorted a dark laugh. "Pretty sure that's *not* it."

"How do you know?"

"Because it's never that easy! Nothing ever just fixes itself with a little time—especially for me! It gets harder and harder and harder, trying to wear me down so I'll surrender, or 'embrace the change' or whatever."

He hadn't meant to start shouting—but his words echoed around the room.

Alvar cleared his throat. "I realize I'll never understand what you've been through, Keefe. And given the role your mom has played in your life, you're probably right to be *concerned* about your potential. I'm sure there's a risk. I'm sure there could be side effects or consequences. But . . . I'm okay with that."

"You want your ability back *that* badly?"

"'Want' is the wrong word. But . . . this emptiness . . ." He wrapped his arms around his waist and squeezed as hard as he could. "I *need* the ability to fill it."

Keefe buried his face in his hands.

"You're also forgetting something," Alvar added after a very long, very awkward silence. "I can help you find the answers you've been looking for. How will you ever know what this ability does unless you use it? And here I am: the perfect test subject."

"How convenient for you."

Alvar snorted. "*Nothing* about this is convenient. For either of us. But you already admitted that you have no idea how this ability works—and how are you ever going to control it if you don't figure that out? So test it on me and get the answers you need. Wouldn't that be worth it?"

No.

Yes.

Keefe wasn't sure what to say.

He *did* need answers.

And . . . Alvar also seemed to be in pain.

Because of him.

"*If* I considered this," Keefe said after his brain had gone round and round and round about fifty gazillion times, "and I'm not saying I am. But *if* I did . . . I'd have three conditions."

"Whatever they are, I'm sure I could live with them."

Keefe was sure Alvar could too.

The bigger challenge would be believing him.

"Number one," he said, clearing his throat when his voice squeaked a little. "You can't tell anyone about any of this—"

"Who would I tell?" Alvar interrupted.

"We both know there are *lots* of people you could tell if you want to. You could tell my mom, or the Council, or the Neverseen, or Ruy—"

"The key word in that sentence is 'want,'" Alvar jumped in. "You think I *want* to help the people who sentenced me to prison? Or who left me for dead?"

"For the right price, you might," Keefe argued.

Alvar shook his head. "No price would be worth seeing any of them ever again. I keep telling you I'm done with that world. I don't know how to make you believe me. So how about we think logically instead? Heal me or not, I already know your secret—and you're not a Washer. So either way, you're going to have to trust me. Wouldn't it be easier to trust someone you *helped*? Instead of someone who you dragged out of their life and then left half-healed because you were afraid to do more?"

"Why does that sound like a threat?" Keefe asked.

"It's not. It's just reality. Like it or not, we're in this together. So what's your second condition?"

Keefe wasn't sure that Alvar had actually satisfied the first one. But he still told him, "I'm only going to try to heal you once. If it doesn't work—or it doesn't do as much as you're hoping—that's your problem."

"That's fair," Alvar agreed. "And the third condition?"

Keefe stood and stepped closer, holding Alvar's stare as he said, "You tell me everything. Everything you feel. Everything that changes. Everything that stays the same. I'd be doing this for answers, so I need to know—"

"Everything," Alvar finished for him. "Got it. I'll share the good, the bad, and the ugh-I-really-wish-I-didn't-have-to-know-that. And then some. Does that mean we have a deal?"

Does it?

Keefe couldn't tell.

But Alvar did have a point about his first condition.

They were in this together—and had been since the moment Keefe chose to get up and follow Alvar out of that library.

He could've let him walk away.

And now here they were.

"Okay." Keefe tried to look way more confident than he felt when he said, "Fine—then I have one more condition. We do this right now, before I change my mind."

Alvar smiled, looking equal parts nervous and victorious as he said, "Sounds like we have a deal."

THIRTY-ONE

THIS IS A BAD IDEA," KEEFE MUMBLED, not sure if he'd meant to say that out loud.

But it didn't matter.

It was true.

And Alvar agreed.

"But we're still going to do it, right?" he asked Keefe.

Keefe nodded slowly.

Good or bad.

Right or wrong.

This was happening.

It had to.

For better or worse, he was getting some answers.

"Are you ready?" he asked, even though it was a pointless question.

There was no way either of them could ever be ready for this.

Alvar nodded anyway and told him, "Let's do it."

And Keefe tried to look confident as he reached for Alvar's hand—tried to tell himself it wasn't going to be a big deal.

But he paused right before their fingers made contact.

"Not too late to change your mind," he warned. "I can't guarantee—"

"I know," Alvar interrupted. "But . . . I trust you."

"You shouldn't. It's not like my mom gave me an instruction manual for this ability. And I've had zero training. I still don't even know what the ability is—"

"I get it," Alvar assured him. "There are a lot of unknowns. So let's start getting some answers, okay?"

He held Keefe's stare as he closed the last sliver of distance between them and grabbed hold of Keefe's hand.

They both gasped as heat seared through their skin.

And once again, the warmth felt flickery.

But it was also steadier.

Like a pulse.

A lifeline.

A connection forged between them.

And Keefe could feel his power pouring down that thread, sinking farther and farther and farther, until it reached that parched pool that Alvar had told him about.

Then it felt like fire hitting sand.

Crystallizing the darkness.

Turning it cool.

Clear.

A sea of crackled glass.

Strong, but still fragile.

And very, very empty.

Desperate for energy.

Keefe tried to fill it.

He sent every drop he could scrape together, until his head was spinning and his hands were shaking and his ears were ringing.

But it wasn't enough.

He wasn't enough.

He was just a failed experiment—unless he embraced the change. . . .

The words were like a beacon, shining through the dark.

Lighting a path that twisted and tangled and wound down and down and down into his core.

Keefe followed the glow.

Turning colder and colder.

His teeth chattered, and his body shivered, and everything slowly went numb.

And when the last of his senses faded and everything was dull and bland and colorless . . . *there.*

A frozen pool of energy.

Iced over.

Waiting for him to reach for it.

To call for it.

To embrace it.

NO!

Keefe wasn't sure where the voice came from—but he knew it was some primal part of himself that had fought through all the doubt and fear and insults and criticism and mind games that had been thrown at him his entire life.

A stubborn survivor, refusing to let him give up.

And that same voice whispered through the darkness, *You have no idea how much power you have.*

Warmth flared in Keefe's core with the words, like rising steam.

He reached for it, floating up, up, up.

Until he drifted into an endless chasm, where a thick, pulsing energy bubbled and churned.

It was a daunting amount of heat.

Indescribable.

Overwhelming.

But also exhilarating.

Keefe knew the energy was *his.*

And it always had been—long before the shadows and light tore him apart and tried to rebuild him.

This was power he'd somehow saved for a fight he'd always known was coming.

Boiling beneath the surface.

Waiting and waiting and waiting.

All he had to do was call for it—draw on it.

The moment he did, the heat swelled into a wave.

Rising higher and higher and higher.

Growing stronger and stronger and stronger.

Until it was flooding through his skin.

More and more and more.

Too much, he realized as his strength slowly drained out of him.

It took the last of his willpower to yank his hand free, severing any connections with an icy jolt that sent him tumbling backward as Alvar coughed and gasped and wheezed.

Keefe crashed to the floor, unable to lift his head—unable to respond as Alvar called out, "Are you okay?"

All he could do was sink into the darkness and let his consciousness drift away.

THIRTY-TWO

YOU'RE ALIVE!" ALVAR CHEERED as Keefe slowly opened his eyes.

"Uh, were you afraid I wasn't?" Keefe asked, wincing as the much-too-bright light slammed into his already-pounding brain.

"Not really. I mean, you've been out cold for a few hours—but I wasn't ready to drag you to a hospital or anything. Your breathing was steady, and you'd stopped shivering, so I figured you mostly needed to rest. But I stayed by your side just in case, and when you started stirring a few minutes ago, I thought it'd be fun to add a sense of drama to your big awakening. Sooooooo"—he raised his hands like a *v* for victory and shouted—"LORD SPIDERHAIR LIVES!"

Keefe didn't have enough energy to smile.

He scraped his tongue against the roof of his mouth, trying to make it feel less sticky and gross, and realized his spit tasted super sour. Kind of like . . .

"Wait—did I throw up?" he asked.

"A little," Alvar admitted. "Well . . . I guess it was a lot. But I was able to drag you to the toilet in time, so it wasn't a big deal."

That explained why his stomach felt like it was currently inside out.

And why the light was so much brighter than he'd been expecting.

And why the floor felt particularly cold and hard.

He must still be in the bathroom.

What it *didn't* explain was why he'd passed out and vomited in the first place.

He tried to sit up, but his head clearly wasn't ready for that, and he would've thudded back to the floor if Alvar hadn't swooped in and caught him.

"I'm assuming the healing at least went okay," Keefe said as Alvar helped him lean against the wall. "Otherwise you wouldn't have been strong enough to haul me in here."

"You're welcome for that, by the way," Alvar told him, "since there was a fifty-fifty chance you were going to throw up on me. Thankfully you didn't—but I still deserve credit for risking the vomit. And yeah, I'm doing good. I was a little shaky at first, and the ability is kind of unruly, so I'm going to have to train myself to use it all over again. But you can definitely call the healing a success. Any idea why it was so much tougher for you?"

Keefe shook his head, trying to replay his memories of the healing, but they felt a little hazy and scrambled. "It might help if you tell me what you remember. Maybe I can piece it together if I know how it went on your side."

"Okay, well . . ." Alvar plopped down next to him. "The first blast of heat was kind of painful. It felt like you were zapping me with electricity, and I wanted to yank my hand away, but I could also feel the energy pulsing through my veins and zinging toward that empty pool that kept haunting me. So I gritted my teeth and made myself hold on. And then there was this weird sort of . . . crystallizing? I don't know if that's the right word. Honestly, it feels like there aren't really words to describe this stuff, you know?"

"I do," Keefe agreed. "But . . . I think I remember that too. It felt like the pool turned to glass."

"Yeah, that makes sense. Sort of. I'm guessing there isn't *actually* a glass pool of energy inside me, since that seems like something that would break into a zillion painful splinters. But assuming that's just the strange metaphor our brains came up with to try to make some sense out of all this super-abstract stuff, then . . . yeah, the pool turned to glass, sealing the crack you'd made earlier. And then there was this strange lull where nothing was happening and I started to wonder if you were done—but I also hoped you weren't, because I still felt super empty. I thought about asking if you needed to take a break, but then this huge, like . . . tidal wave of energy slammed against my senses and flooded me with warmth. The glass pool filled to the absolute brim, and then these tiny tingles erupted across my skin. It took me a few seconds to realize I was feeling the light again—you know that's how vanishing works, right? It's all about sensing the way the light is hitting your skin and letting it pass through instead of bouncing off. That's why glass looks invisible, even though it's solid, because the light can shine through it—"

"Yeah, I know," Keefe cut in. "I don't need a science lesson."

"Fine, whatever, my point is, I could feel the light again—and not like I had when we first got back, when it was just a faint itch that kept fading in and out. I can feel it all the time. I just have to concentrate and . . ."

He vanished.

"I could sit like this for hours," his disembodied voice told Keefe. "In fact, I pretty much have been. There wasn't a whole lot to do except listen to you snore, so I've been testing how long I can stay invisible. I don't have the control I used to have, but I feel like I'm probably going to be way stronger once I do a little more training—which isn't surprising, given how much energy you sent me. Did you mean to send that much? Or is that why you blacked out?"

"No idea," Keefe mumbled. "It might be . . . lots of things."

Alvar reappeared. "Lots of things, huh? You realize I'm the only person who can help you figure out what happened, right? And it's going to be way easier for me to do that if you actually, you know, tell me stuff."

He had a point, but . . .

Keefe wasn't ready to talk about those hidden reserves of energy he'd discovered.

Even thinking about them made his insides tangle.

"Is that it?" Keefe asked. "Is that all you remember?"

Alvar sighed. "Pretty much. After the big energy surge, you pulled your hand away and collapsed, and I tried to ask if you were okay, but your eyes rolled back, and your head slumped to the floor, and you were out. I checked your pulse and checked your breathing, and all seemed good, so I went to get a cold compress for your forehead—but then I heard you gagging and figured you wouldn't want to have to explain to house-keeping why their lovely sitting room was covered in puke. So I hauled you to the bathroom and . . . well, let's just say it'll be a while before I'm in the mood for pavlova again. Definitely *not* a pretty sight when it comes back up. I'll spare you the details—unless you want them. You did make me promise to share *everything*—"

"Yeah, I'm good," Keefe said, curling his knees into his chest. "Unless you want to watch me barf again."

"That's what I figured. Want a sip of water, by the way? I

offered you some earlier, but you swatted it away, mumbling something about dirty feet. Any memory of that?"

"Nope."

"So then . . . you probably also don't remember mumbling about Sophie?"

Keefe curled up tighter. "Do I want to know what I said?"

"Oh, you know, just your basic 'I miss you, I love you, you're my universe' kind of stuff."

Keefe groaned and looked around for something he could bury himself with.

Best he could find was a towel, which he pulled over his face.

"Wow, okay, I was kidding," Alvar told him. "I thought it might jolt you out of this sulkiness. But who knew you had *that* many feels for the lovely moonlark?"

"Remind me why I healed you?" Keefe asked, flinging the towel at Alvar's head. "I liked you better when you were all weak and flickery."

Alvar laughed.

But his smile faded just as fast, and he fidgeted with his shirt as he said, "I haven't really thanked you, have I? You didn't *have* to heal me—but you did. So . . . thanks. I know using that power was rough."

"It was."

Keefe could've left it there, but . . . he wanted Alvar to know: "I'm glad it worked."

"Me too. It's going to be weird having to remind myself not to vanish around any humans—but it might also make a few things easier. Especially since I don't have a handy human ID like *some* people." He nudged Keefe with his elbow. But his smile faded again as he added, "Mostly, I'm just glad that emptiness is gone. I've lived through some seriously awful stuff, and that was honestly one of the worst things I've ever felt. I hope no one else ever has to experience anything like it."

"They won't," Keefe assured him.

"Are you saying that because you think you're the one who caused it?" Alvar asked.

"Uh, I *did* cause it—you said so yourself."

"So what's your plan, then?" Alvar asked. "Never let anyone touch your hands? Maybe stay in the human world forever?"

"No idea," Keefe admitted—then stood and made his way out of the bathroom, hoping that Alvar would drop the subject.

"You're looking at this wrong," Alvar called after him, blinking in and out of sight as he followed. "Seriously, Keefe. I get that having a new ability is scary. Especially one that no one else has ever had. And I know you're still learning how to control it—and worried your mom is going to try to exploit it. So you think it's better to try to pretend it's not there. But . . . your mom is going to find you. We both know that. She's been planning this too long to let you just run off. And I'm sure a lot of people in the Lost Cities are wondering about you right now—maybe even worrying about what you can do. So why not go back there and show them, 'THIS IS WHAT I CAN DO!' I guarantee, everyone will be like, 'Wow, that's amazing!' Because it is! What you just did was incredible—and we haven't even talked about all the different implications—"

"And we're not going to," Keefe snapped, spinning around to face him. "We're not going to think about them either. In fact, let's just pretend the power doesn't exist, okay?"

"Why? Are you still thinking about trying to get rid of it?"

Keefe shrugged. "At this point, I'm not ruling out anything."

"Well, you should. Trust me, you don't want to get rid of this ability—and not just because you could seriously hurt yourself in the process. Remember: Your mom wanted you to have this power—"

"Which is exactly why I don't want it," Keefe jumped in.

"I know. But you don't have to use it to help *her*. You can use it to help the people you care about—and you might need to. Think about what Tam did to Ruy. Do you really think there won't be some sort of retaliation?"

Keefe . . . hadn't considered that.

"Aha!" Alvar said when Keefe shuddered. "You're finally starting to get it. I know it's easy to think, 'My mom planned this, so I don't want it.' But you have to remember that when she made those plans, she assumed you'd be on her side."

Her side.

The words sent Keefe's brain flashing back to the memory

he'd recently recovered, when his mom told him, *Someday you and I will do incredible things together, Keefe.*

She'd sounded so matter-of-fact.

So self-assured.

But it was the rest of that conversation that felt like icy needles stabbing down Keefe's spine.

She'd wanted him to store his rage, so he could draw on that power later.

Was *that* what that pool of energy was?

"Whoa—you just turned whiter than that tablecloth," Alvar said, pointing to the tray of untouched room service that must've been delivered while Keefe was passed out. "Another side effect from the healing? Or did you just remember something?"

Keefe shook his head—hard—even though that never actually shook away any of his dark thoughts the way he wanted it to.

"Nope," Alvar said, grabbing Keefe's shoulders and guiding him to the couch. "We're talking about this, whether you want to or not."

Keefe was too wobbly to resist.

He sank onto the uncomfortable cushions and stared at the little flowers embroidered on the fabric as Alvar dragged over one of the chairs and sat right in front of him.

"Tell me what just happened," Alvar ordered. "You can't keep holding everything in. That was my mistake. I bottled everything up, never let anyone fact-check anything going on in my head. If I had, I'm sure someone could've pointed out some of the ways I was overreacting, or misunderstanding stuff, and it probably would've saved me a lot of problems. So just . . . talk to me, okay? After everything we've been through, you *have* to know you can trust me—and if you still need more proof, remember: I could've run off the second you healed my ability. You were passed out on the floor—and I'm pretty sure I can light leap now. I could've grabbed your pathfinder and cleaned out your safe—because we both know the new combination is zero, zero, zero, zero, since you thought no one would think of zero as a number—"

"Okay, seriously, *how* do you keep figuring that out?"

Alvar smirked. "Because I know you. I know how you think. And I realize you hate hearing this, but . . . you're a lot like me."

The scary thing?

Alvar wasn't totally wrong.

Keefe just didn't know what to do with that information.

"You have to talk to someone," Alvar pressed. "Writing it all down in journals and sketchbooks isn't enough. Blank pages never question you or call you out. And you *really* need that, because whatever you just figured out can't possibly be as bad as you're thinking."

"Oh really?" Keefe snapped, well aware that Alvar might be baiting him.

But . . . he wanted to prove him wrong.

Wanted to share all the scary connections he'd made so Alvar would have to admit, *Okay, that's pretty creepy.*

So he told him about the two different reserves of power he'd found inside himself: the icy energy his mom must've put there, waiting for him to embrace it—and the endless bubbling rage he'd apparently been storing away.

"Pretty sure that's why I blacked out and barfed up everything in my stomach after I used the power," Keefe mumbled when he'd finished. "I've basically been storing up poison."

"Hmmm." Alvar dragged out the sound. "So . . . let's see if I have this straight. You managed to resist relying on the energy your mom gave you—even though that's where your instincts wanted you to go. And then you followed some sort of inner self-defense mechanism you must've created to a giant reservoir of power you've been secretly storing up for years and used that energy to heal me. And somehow all of that proves you're . . . evil?"

"Uh, how would *you* explain it, then?" Keefe demanded.

"Well . . . it's a little hard, since I'm sure I'm missing a ton of the pieces to this puzzle. *But* working with what I have, I'd say . . . first, awesome job resisting the energy your mom put there! I'm not saying I don't think you should ever use it, but I do think that's the kind of thing you'd want to do on your terms, when you're really prepared for it, since we all know there's going to be a trick. And second . . . so . . . that memory you mentioned. Your mom erased that, right?"

"I don't know. She might've erased it. Or I might've repressed it."

"Okay, but either way, you *just* got it back, right? So that means that all the time you've spent subconsciously storing that energy, you've been doing it without knowing why. You didn't have the memory. You just had the emotions connected to it. And what were those emotions? What were you feeling when your mom told you to store up your rage? Were you feeling a cold fury, like, 'Yes, I want to tear down the world, and this is how I will do it—mwahahahahahaha'? Or were you scared and confused and worried that you might need some protection?"

"Why does that matter?"

"Because intention matters. If I'm right about what you were feeling, then you weren't building an evil, rage-filled stockpile. You were building an arsenal from any power you could spare, hoping to protect yourself and anyone else you care about."

"Then why did using that 'arsenal' make me sick?" Keefe countered.

"*That*, I don't know. It could be because you're still learning how to use the ability. Or because tapping into that much power is always going to be overwhelming. Or maybe that's the price of using your own energy instead of your mom's energy. Or insert a million other logical explanations here. But take it from someone who got hit with a tidal wave of that energy—it wasn't rage. I know what rage feels like—and it's *not* warm and soothing. It also doesn't heal. It only destroys. Though, for the record? You're also entitled to a healthy amount of rage. In fact, you're going to need to let yourself get pretty furious if you want to win this."

Keefe closed his eyes, trying to believe him.

But his brain kept wanting to poke and prod at Alvar's reasoning.

"It must be hard," Alvar said quietly, "to see yourself for who you really are after a lifetime of being verbally battered and manipulated. That's why I keep trying to tell you you're one of the good guys. I knew that way back when I tried to recruit you—and saw it even clearer when you tried to pretend you'd switched sides. Do you always make the right choices? Of course not. No one does. Even the great Sophie Foster—and I'm sure she'd be the first to admit that."

"She would," Keefe agreed. "But that's different."

"No, it's not. Mistakes don't define who we are—unless we never try to correct them. That's where I went wrong. So don't be like me. Remember that the things you do or the things you discover are only a tiny piece of what makes you *you*. And at the end of it all, you get to take a look at all those pieces and decide who you want to be and what you want to do with them. If you don't believe me, think about the fact that you were will-ing to use an ability that terrifies you—an ability you'd rather keep completely secret—to fix the empty feeling you acciden-tally caused when we light leaped. We both know you didn't have to do that. And even though you had no idea what you were doing, you chose the safest way to heal me. So I know you're going to think this is cheesy, but will you please just go with me on this and repeat after me?"

Keefe rolled his eyes.

But Alvar's expression was so sincere—so compassionate—that Keefe didn't have to be an Empath to recognize it.

"Fine," he mumbled. "But if you try to get me to say anything embarrassing, I'm going to grab those room service trays and throw them at your head!"

"See . . . now I kind of want to, because a food fight sounds fun—especially now that my telekinesis is back. Did I tell you that? All my skills are fixed. You healed *everything*. Add that to the list of reasons why I want you to repeat after me. Ready?"

Keefe gave the world's most reluctant nod.

"Okay." Alvar cleared his throat. "I'm Keefe Sencen."

"Ugh, I'm already regretting this."

"Say it!"

Keefe sighed. "I'm Keefe Sencen."

Alvar nodded. "The only legacy I have is the one I'm going to make for myself."

Keefe raised one eyebrow. But he went ahead and said, "The only legacy I have is the one I'm going to make for myself."

Alvar nodded again. "This is fun! I kinda want to see how many sentences I can get you to say. But I don't want to risk ruining it before you say the most important one, so let's just skip to that to be safe." He waited for Keefe to hold his stare before he said, "I'm not afraid of my new abilities, because I'm going to master them."

"How?" Keefe demanded.

"Just say it," Alvar told him. "And try to believe it. Convincing yourself is the most important step."

Keefe didn't really see the point, but . . . he wanted to believe it was possible.

So he went ahead and told his mostly empty hotel suite, "I'm not afraid of my new abilities, because I'm going to master them."

Alvar applauded. "Do you feel better?"

"No," Keefe told him—even though he kind of did.

"Well then, I guess it's a good thing we're not done yet. Now comes the fun part."

"What's that?" Keefe asked.

"Now we figure out how to make all of that happen!"

THIRTY-THREE

RIGHT NOW?" KEEFE SAID, GLANCING out the nearest window, trying to figure out what time it was. Given how dark it looked, it had to be the middle of the night. "You want to work on my abilities *right now?*"

"Why not?" Alvar asked. "Do you have somewhere else you need to be?"

"Uh . . . bed."

"Oh please, you just got a ton of sleep!"

"I'm pretty sure lying unconscious on the bathroom floor doesn't count as *sleep*," Keefe argued.

"Sure, it does! You were totally snoring! Besides, we have this great momentum going. You healed me. I kept you from barfing all over the sitting room. You opened up and actually talked about some of the stuff you've been worried about. I gave you what many would consider to be the Greatest Pep Talk in the History of the Universe. So we can't slow down now! The next step is Total Ability Domination!"

"Okay," Keefe said, wondering if his friends ever thought he was this obnoxious.

Probably.

"But . . . *how?*" he asked. "Because I haven't heard an actual plan for how I'm supposed to achieve this Total Ability Domination."

"Working on it." Alvar leaned back in his chair, and his eyes narrowed as he studied Keefe from head to toe. "I guess the first thing we need to do is this."

He snatched Keefe's hand like a gremlin grabbing a shiny new gadget.

"Gah—what are you doing?" Keefe asked, trying to twist his palm free—but either he was still weak or Alvar was freakishly strong now.

"Feel any weird blasts of warmth?" Alvar asked. "Or is your head spinning? Stomach churning? Anything like that?"

"No—though I *am* feeling a pretty strong urge to punch you in the face."

"Good to know." Alvar dropped Keefe's hand. "For the record, I didn't feel anything either. And that awful emptiness also didn't come back."

"Well . . . that's good, I guess," Keefe mumbled, shaking his hand to get some blood back to his fingers. "But how does that help me?"

"Not exactly sure," Alvar admitted. "But it *might* mean the power only affects either someone who hasn't manifested yet or someone whose ability is damaged. Oooh, or someone waiting to manifest again, like a Polyglot who only has one special ability."

They both froze.

Keefe might've even let out a squeaky gasp.

Was *that* what his mom had been going for?

"Do you think . . . ?" he said slowly, wondering how he hadn't made the connection before. "Did my mom do all this because she wants me to trigger her second ability?"

He wouldn't be surprised at all if his big *legacy* turned out to just benefit her.

"It's possible," Alvar admitted. "Though . . . I don't know. I've always wondered if she already manifested something else forever ago and has been hiding it all this time because it's either really embarrassing or because she thinks it'll give her an advantage if people don't know what she can do. *But!* I could definitely be wrong about that. And if she thinks she has some sort of untapped potential, I can see how she might've tried to find a way to trigger it. I guess you won't know for sure until you see her again. But when you do, it might be smart to avoid any kind of physical contact."

"I might need to start wearing gloves," Keefe grumbled.

He hated gloves.

They were so itchy.

He seriously had no idea how Foster wore them all the time back when she didn't know how to turn off her enhancing.

Plus, if his mom saw him wearing gloves, wouldn't that immediately give away that her evil plan worked and he'd become exactly who she wanted him to be?

He could totally imagine her pointing at his gloved hands with a triumphant smile, shouting, *I won! I changed him!* right before she had some of her loyal minions pin him down and rip the gloves off so she could—

"Looks like your head is starting to sink into a dark place," Alvar noted, pointing to Keefe's white-knuckle fists. "So try to remember that we're going to master these abilities."

"Just because you say that doesn't mean it's actually going to happen," Keefe argued. "And even if we come up with a solid strategy, how are we going to test it to see if it works? I can't exactly go back to the Lost Cities, find someone who hasn't manifested, and say, 'Hey, would you mind grabbing my hand and seeing what happens?'"

"They probably would think that's pretty weird," Alvar admitted.

"Yep. And if our strategy doesn't work and I accidentally trigger their ability, it would only be a matter of time before word got out. And then—"

Keefe cut himself off, realizing he'd just steered the conversation down a very dangerous path.

But it was too late.

"And then . . . *what?*" Alvar asked. "What were you going to say?"

"I don't know. I'm still freaking out about the fact that Mommy Dearest might've put me through all this to turn me into her personal Ability Triggerer. What if she finds a way to force me into triggering her—and then manifests as a Mesmer? That'd pretty much be game over, wouldn't it? Or what if she's a Beguiler?" He shuddered. "Even if she became a Telepath—"

"Don't change the subject," Alvar interrupted. "We can debate the worst ability for your mom to manifest later. Right now I want to know what you think will happen if word gets out that you can trigger abilities. Because I'll be honest—I don't understand why you're so afraid. I mean . . . I'm sure it'd get a bunch of attention—but you love attention! And yeah, the Council would probably want you to go to Foxfire and shake the hand of everyone still in ability detecting, and that'd be pretty exhausting—but I bet you could set some boundaries. You'd have to, because parents with younger kids would probably start turning up all the time, kind of like what happened to Councillor Terik with his descrying. But—"

"STOP!" Keefe jumped to his feet and held out his hands. "We're done with this conversation."

"Uh, you realize that even if we do stop talking about it, that doesn't mean I'll stop thinking about it, right? I'm going to figure it out, Keefe. So you might as well tell me."

"Or what?"

"Or nothing—I'm not threatening you, if that's what you're implying. I'm just trying to help—and clearly there's a big problem here we need to tackle. So tell me what it is, and we'll start coming up with a plan—"

"There's no plan, Alvar. Not for this. It won't matter if I can control the ability or not. Once word gets out about what I can do, it changes everything."

"Why?"

"It just does. So if you really want to be my friend and really are trying to help me—then drop it. Right now."

"I just—"

"LET IT GO!"

Alvar sighed. "Pretending it doesn't exist isn't going to solve anything. Why don't we—"

"No! In fact, you know what? I can't do this."

Keefe rushed to the door, grabbing the first coat he could find—a short burgundy one that wasn't nearly as warm as some of his others, but he didn't have time to find anything better.

He had to get out of there.

Now.

Before Alvar put the final pieces together.

He raced down the stairs, through the lobby, out to the street, and just kept on running.

If he'd thought to grab his blue pathfinder, he might've leaped away right then—disappeared into a random human city and hoped no one ever found him.

Never looked back.

It'd mean giving up any hope of ever going home—but that was probably gone anyway.

Alvar was going to figure out what he was trying to hide.

And even if he didn't tell anyone, this was going to keep happening.

Every time anyone found out that he could trigger abilities, it was only a matter of time before they wondered what would happen if someone were Talentless.

And the Lost Cities would never be the same.

"What am I doing?" he asked, realizing his feet had steered him to the next street he was supposed to check if he'd kept going with his systematic search for the house where he'd delivered the letter.

Maybe it was out of habit.

Or maybe it was easier focusing on the past now that he was staring down such a bleak future.

Either way, he walked to the end of the block, checking every door. Then he turned down the next street.

And the next.

And the next.

Didn't matter that his feet ached and he couldn't stop shivering.

He kept walking and walking and walking.

Up one street.

Down another.

And another.

And another.

Mentally crossing each one off the map in his memory.

It took several more blocks before he admitted what was really happening.

He was stalling, of course, since he had no idea how he could ever go back to his hotel room.

But . . . it was also time to leave London.

He'd already stayed way longer than he'd ever meant to—and he'd known how risky that would be.

He needed to get out of there before his enemies caught up with him.

Or anyone else figured out what he could do.

And somehow leaving seemed easier if he could at least know he'd tried as hard as he possibly could to find the answers he'd gone to London looking for in the first place.

So he walked.

And walked some more.

Watching the sun rise and the streets grow more and more crowded.

He walked the entire rest of the day—until he'd finally

crossed off the last street on his mental map.

Then . . . that was it.

He'd officially searched every door in London.

And found nothing.

No surprise, of course—but he still had to stop himself from kicking the nearest lamppost and shouting in frustration.

There were too many people around for that.

Instead, he mumbled, "Okay, it really is time to go."

He even stopped to buy a big duffel bag, since the clothes he'd bought wouldn't all fit in his backpack.

Then he made his way to the same park bench he'd sat on the day he arrived in London and tried to figure out where he wanted to go next.

Should he visit the last few libraries on his list?

Or just spin the crystal on the pathfinder and settle in wherever it led?

A random city seemed safer—especially since Alvar had seen his library list. . . .

"Spin the pathfinder it is." He said the words out loud to make them official—and tried to be excited. "Let the adventures in Humanland continue!"

But first . . . one last meal in London.

He'd bought himself a cheese-and-pickle sandwich on his way to the park, in honor of the jogger who first helped him, and took a huge bite.

It wasn't *as* bad as he thought it would be—but the

pickles were weirdly sweet. So he was kind of relieved when he spotted a pair of familiar eyes peeking out at him from the flower bed.

"Yeah, you can have it," he told his fox friend, tossing him the rest of the sandwich. "But that really is the last meal you're going to get from me."

It shouldn't have made him sad.

But his eyes got super watery, and he turned toward the lake as he smeared the tears away.

He searched for the black swan he'd seen that first day, wondering if seeing it again would prove he was making the right decision.

But there was no sign of any swan.

Not that it changed anything.

Keefe was about to get up and head back to his hotel when he noticed the low fence running along the perimeter of the lake—and an idea sparked to life.

He'd been looking for a visualization exercise to help him switch off this horrible triggering ability, so . . .

What would happen if he imagined building huge mental fences around those pools of energy he'd found during the healing?

Better yet: What if he built enormous mental walls?

He closed his eyes and pictured brick and stone and mortar piling higher and higher and higher. Then he surrounded the walls with thick metal rails.

By the time he was done, he couldn't even see the pools anymore—and his hands felt very, very cold.

It might've been from the drizzle seeping through his thin coat—but Keefe didn't think so.

He'd felt another *click* when he added the last layer—just like when he unraveled those mental threads tied to his empathy.

And he was pretty sure that meant he'd just taken control.

THIRTY-FOUR

YOU'RE BACK," ALVAR CALLED from the couch as Keefe let himself into the hotel suite. "I was starting to wonder if you would be. I knew you'd left all your stuff, but as the hours dragged on . . ." He shrugged. "Looks like you're not planning on staying very long, though."

He pointed to the duffel bag Keefe was carrying.

Keefe nodded. "I think it's time to move on."

Alvar sighed. "Look—"

"It's okay," Keefe interrupted. "I know what you're going to say—and I'm not running away. I never meant to stay this long in one city. Especially London, since it's the first place my mom will come looking for me."

"You're right about that—and I've already said I think a change of scenery would help clear your head. You'll probably regret leaving without trying banoffee pie—but I'm sure you'll get over it. That wasn't what I was going to say, though." Alvar waited for Keefe to make eye contact before he told him, "I get it, okay? I understand what you're so afraid of."

Keefe wasn't surprised that Alvar had figured it out.

But his knees wobbled anyway, and he sank onto the nearest chair and buried his face in his hands.

"I'm not going to tell anyone," Alvar assured him. "I know that's probably hard for you to believe—but I swear, Keefe, your secret really is safe with me. For one thing, everyone thinks I'm dead—and even before that, I'd already lost any friends or credibility. But you still have my word that if I ever cross paths with anyone from the Lost Cities, I won't say anything about what you can do. I won't even tell them I saw you."

"But . . . ?" Keefe prompted. "Since I'm sure there's going to be one. . . ."

"Nope. I'm not my dad—I'm not going to try to convince you that there's no reason to worry when we both know there is. You're right: The implications of your ability *are* scary. I don't think it's hopeless—but it's definitely going to need to be handled strategically. That's why I hate that you're dealing with this alone."

"I'll be fine," Keefe assured him.

"You will. You're Keefe Sencen! But you know what I've

noticed? You're always at your best when you work with a friend."

"I can't go back to the Lost Cities."

"Maybe not yet—but that wasn't what I meant by 'friend.'"

Keefe frowned. "Are you . . . offering to come with me?"

Alvar collapsed back against the couch cushions. "You know what? I honestly don't know. I miss the tiny room I was renting back in my city. And the honey hotteoks—and yes, those are pancakes, in case you were wondering. I was also getting sorta okayish with the language—and the music there is incredible. But . . . that'll all still be there in a few weeks or months or whatever. Well, maybe not the room—but I could find another one. And even if they throw out my collection of sheet masks, it'd be worth it if I could help you find a way to go home."

"Home," Keefe repeated, leaning forward in his chair, trying to decide which surprised him more: Alvar's offer—or the fact that he was sorta tempted to take him up on it.

"I know you want to go back to the Lost Cities," Alvar told him. "And you should! You have a life there and people you care about. And I still think you can find a way to manage these abilities. I don't know *how* yet. But if Mesmers and Inflictors can have normal lives without constantly unleashing mind control and pain on everybody, then I'm sure you can figure out how to avoid triggering everybody. Especially if you have some help."

Keefe was trying to decide if he should mention the

visualization exercise he'd done in the park when Alvar added, "And if Councillor Terik was able to say, 'Nope—I'm not doing any more readings except in very special situations, because they're causing too many problems,' and people accepted it, why can't you say, 'Forget it, I'm not triggering anyone except in these specific instances'?"

"Huh." Keefe hadn't really considered how bold it probably seemed when Councillor Terik first started limiting his descrying. "But . . . I'm not a Councillor."

"No. But you have some powerful friends. Pretty sure all it would take is for the moonlark to back you up, and you'd be able to set whatever limits you want."

When he put it like that, it *almost* sounded possible.

"Except reading potential isn't the same as being able to tell if someone's Talentless," Keefe reminded him, wincing as he finally said the words they'd both been carefully avoiding. "Potential is just a chance. If you don't do anything with it, it doesn't matter. It doesn't hurt anyone. But everything in the Lost Cities is defined by talent. Where you go to school. Where you work. Who you're matched with—"

"Yeah, and it shouldn't be," Alvar interrupted. "Honestly, the whole talent-based system is even more broken than the horrible matchmaking process. Maybe you can help them realize that."

Keefe shook his head. "We both know that's never going to happen."

"Not *never*. Change is slow in the Lost Cities because there's been no reason to hurry. But the Neverseen and the Black Swan are forcing the issue. They have completely different solutions—and some are admittedly a lot creepier than I realized when I chose my allies. But they're both responding to the same problems. So if the wrong side wins . . . well, you won't want to stay in your mom's world anyway. Head on back to Humanland—we'll be waiting here with extra pancakes! But if *your* side wins, you should have the power to set your own limits—and I doubt anyone would argue. They made the rules of telepathy to keep Telepaths in check, didn't they? So you can all figure out the rules for triggering—or whatever you want to call it."

Once again, Alvar made some very valid points.

It was kind of a shame he'd wasted his talent and energy on the enemy for so long.

"So . . . what exactly are you suggesting?" Keefe asked.

"No idea. I'm totally making this up as we talk. But . . . maybe we could head to a new city. Settle in—hopefully somewhere with room service because, man, am I going to miss that otherwise. And we'll just . . . try different things. Sooner or later we *will* find something that gives you more control over your abilities. And when you're feeling like, 'YES—I'VE GOT THIS!' you'll head back to the Lost Cities and show them how powerful you are. I'm assuming you won't want to tell any of your friends that you've been hanging out with me—which would honestly be better. I still have no desire to ever go back, so it's easier if everyone thinks I'm dead—and it'll save you a ton of drama too. Then you can focus on saving the world with your friends and becoming celebrated heroes—blah, blah, blah." He rolled his eyes but also flashed a teasing smile. "Who knows? Maybe they'll even try to make you a Councillor—though I'm betting you wouldn't be a big fan of that idea, given the whole no-dating-or-getting-married thing."

"Yeah, hard pass," Keefe agreed. "Plus, their circlets are ugly."

"RIGHT? They totally squish their hair and make it look all bumpy."

"Yep, and this hair is way too awesome for that kind of abuse," Keefe said, dragging his fingers through it to try and coax it back to his careful style. "But . . . what about you?"

"Me?" Alvar asked.

"Yeah, what's your grand plan?"

"I don't have one. I might go back to where you found me. Or I might explore somewhere new. I have a few more options now that I can vanish, so . . ." He shrugged. "But if you'd rather skip all that and go our separate ways, I get it. Just . . . can you do me one favor? Don't decide right now, when you're exhausted and your head is still spinning from all these weird revelations. Take the night to think about it. And maybe take a shower, too—'cause, um, you totally stink. Between the Vegemite and the vomiting and whatever you've been doing all day that's made you so soggy and sweaty, there's a pretty potent plume around you." He sniffed the air and coughed. "Yeah, definitely shower. Then try to get some sleep. Have some breakfast—I of course recommend pancakes. And *then* decide. It's not even wasting time because you seriously need some rest. And that shower. Have I mentioned you stink?"

Keefe had to laugh as Alvar plugged his nose and fanned the air away from his face.

And taking the night to think things through probably was a smart idea.

"Fine," he said. "I guess . . . I'll see you in the morning."

"Only if you've showered. If not, I take back my offer. You can figure out your abilities all by your smelly self."

Keefe snorted, and his brain filled with a million snarky comebacks—which felt good.

He *wanted* to joke around with Alvar.

But he should probably wait until he'd truly made a decision before he started acting like they were besties.

And he still needed more time to think everything through.

Bringing Alvar with him when he left London would be very different than when he'd dragged him there in the first place.

It wouldn't be a test anymore.

He'd *have* to trust him.

He'd also have *way* more to hide from his friends.

Yeah, he was already going to have to avoid telling them that Alvar was alive and that he ran into him. But the longer he spent with Alvar, the harder it was going to be to tell anyone anything about his time in Humanland without constantly lying.

Showering didn't help him find any answers—but all the fancy soaps and shampoos at least had him smelling like a field of flowers, which was hopefully better than the Sweaty Thing That Rolled Around in Vegemite and Vomit.

He tried to go to bed after that—but he was feeling way too twitchy to sleep. His feet were also throbbing from all the walking, so packing was going to have to wait.

So he grabbed his sketchbook and journals and the different maps and lists and settled into bed to make some very important updates.

He stared at his hands, which still felt cold—even after all the hot water—and tried not to get his hopes up. But that mental *click* had seemed . . . significant.

He'd have to figure out a way to test if anything had changed without trying to trigger anybody.

Maybe Alvar will have some good ideas.

The fact that his brain went there first kinda made it seem like he'd be taking on a traveling buddy—but he still wasn't ready to call it.

Instead, he opened his sketchbook and wrote:

Be careful who you trust—but don't be afraid to go with your gut.

He also added:

Drop bears aren't real—but Fitzy would totally fall for that.

Pickles should never be sweet.

Try to find some banoffee pie.

Never listen to anyone who tells you beans on toast is delicious.

Keep your mental walls strong.

He put a bunch of stars around the last one as he imagined himself adding another layer of brick and stone to his mental barriers.

His hands turned a little colder when he finished, and goose bumps prickled his arms.

"Even if it doesn't work," he told himself, trying to manage his expectations, "I'm not going to let these abilities define me."

He made a note of that, too, in case he needed the reminder.

Then he set his sketchbook aside and grabbed his handy world map, trying to see if there was anywhere he'd rather go instead of leaving it up to chance.

He'd heard tacos were pretty amazing, so maybe he should head somewhere with lots of those?

Or dumplings sounded delicious too.

He made notes by a few possibilities—then wondered if he should let Alvar weigh in.

"Life is weird," he said as he tried to imagine spending weeks—or months—with Alvar Vacker.

He'd need to up his snark game if he did.

No more letting Alvar out-sass him.

And maybe he should plan some epic pranks.

But before he could think too far into the future, he still needed to tie up a few threads from his past.

He started by crossing off the final streets on his London map, leaving the entire city X-ed out.

"I tried," he told the empty room, wishing it made him feel like less of a failure.

He also made a quick sketch of the streets outside the British Library—and not in his sketchbook. Ethan and Eleanor belonged with the rest of his important memories in his silver journal.

But since he hadn't triggered anything at the scene, he could only draw the redbrick building and a bright red double-decker bus, plus a bunch of cars on the streets and faceless people on the sidewalks.

He studied the drawing when he'd finished—and it was detailed and accurate. But Ethan and Eleanor deserved so much more than a crossed-off map and a boring rendering of the place where they'd been murdered.

So he dug out the obituaries for reference and drew a proper portrait of the two of them, making sure to capture Ethan's smile, and the way Eleanor was snuggled into her dad's arm and grinning with huge dimples. Keefe wished the photo had been printed in color, so he'd know if he should make Eleanor a brunette or a redhead—but he went with red hair, since it looked more vibrant and alive.

Sadly, he'd never know if he got it wrong. . . .

Maybe that's why the drawing still didn't feel like *enough* when he'd finished—and as he tucked the journal away, he realized there was one final thing he could do to honor their memory.

One of the obituaries had listed where Ethan and Eleanor had been buried.

And wasn't it a human tradition to bring flowers to people's graves?

He wished he could go there knowing he'd uncovered the truth about what had happened to them.

But . . . he should pay them a visit anyway.

Tell them he was sorry.

Promise to make sure his mom couldn't hurt anyone else.

He doubted that would stop him from blaming himself, or wondering why his mom chose to target them.

But . . . it was worth a try.

If nothing else, he could say goodbye before he moved on.

THIRTY-FIVE

THAT'S A LOT OF HEADSTONES," Keefe mumbled as he stepped through the gates of the cemetery—which stretched on for what looked like miles and miles and miles.

He'd known death was way more common in the human world.

But he hadn't truly been able to grasp what that meant until that moment.

The Wanderling Woods only housed a few hundred Wanderlings—and that was the elves' *only* graveyard-type thing for the entire history of their species.

And yeah, Keefe was sure there were a few rogue elves like

Forkle's twin brother, who'd preferred to have his Wanderling planted elsewhere.

But still.

The cemetery he was standing in had thousands of graves.

And that was just *one* cemetery out of dozens of other cemeteries in London—and London was only *one* human city.

The amount of loss that added up to was truly staggering.

How did humans cope with that much grief?

They must be way stronger and braver and more resilient than the elves ever gave them credit for.

"Can I help you?" an unexpectedly cheerful voice asked, making Keefe jump as he turned to find a man wearing dark clothes and a dark hat, smiling at him.

Keefe hoped the guy was the groundskeeper, since he was also carrying a shovel.

"Uh . . . maybe?" Keefe tightened his grip on his flowers, trying to hide his shaky hands. The lady in the flower shop he'd stopped by on his way to the cemetery had recommended bouquets of tiny blue flowers called forget-me-nots—which had seemed fitting, given their name. "I'm trying to find a couple of graves, and I hadn't expected there to be so many."

He'd also thought they would be more spread out—like the Wanderlings were—but most of the headstones were so close, they were practically touching.

"Who are you here to visit?" the groundskeeper asked.

Keefe cleared his throat, trying to keep his voice steady as he said, "Ethan Benedict Wright II and his daughter, Eleanor Olivia Wright."

The man's eyebrows shot up so high, they disappeared under his hat.

"They're this way," he said, motioning for Keefe to follow him down a narrow path, past graves of all different shapes and sizes.

Some were plain and simple. Others were decorated with symbols and filigree. Others had big slabs in front of them, or even statues—usually of women with sad faces and giant wings. Some were old and weathered and covered in moss. Others were brand-new and almost gleaming.

All had names and dates and messages, and some even had pictures—which Keefe hoped *wouldn't* be on the graves he was visiting.

It was going to be hard enough staring at Ethan's and Eleanor's names, knowing they were right . . . underground.

He wasn't sure he'd be able to handle having them stare back at him.

Especially on a cold, dreary day in such a cold, dreary place.

Maybe he should've taken Alvar up on his offer to tag along for moral support.

He'd turned him down, feeling like this was something he needed to do alone. But it would've been nice to have someone to talk to.

Especially since the *crunch, crunch, crunch* of the leaves and

pebbles under his feet sounded way too much like he was stepping on something much more horrifying.

"So . . . uh . . . are the big fancy gravestones for famous
people?" Keefe asked, trying to drown out the sound.

"Not usually," the groundskeeper told him. "Just people who
spent more money."

"Riiiiiiiiiiight." Sometimes Keefe forgot that humans fell
into all different financial categories.

"How did you know Ethan and Eleanor?" the groundskeeper
asked, and Keefe was glad Alvar had made him come up with
a story before he left.

It'd taken a while to find a good answer, since claiming too
strong of a connection could give away that he was lying if he
ended up talking to someone who knew them. But too vague of a
connection might seem odd that he'd bother visiting their graves.

Eventually they'd settled on something short and sweet that
was also mostly true.

"I didn't actually know them," Keefe said quietly. "But my
mom did, and she would've wanted me to stop by while I'm
in town."

The groundskeeper nodded, and Keefe hoped that meant
the answer worked.

"Where are you visiting from?" he asked—which Keefe had
also prepared for.

"I'm kind of between places at the moment. I took a year off
to do some traveling."

The groundskeeper smiled. "I always wanted to do that. But my parents insisted I go straight to uni."

Keefe nodded, like he knew what that meant. "Well . . . there's still time, right?"

"For travel?" The groundskeeper shrugged. "Maybe for scattered holidays. But once you have a job and a family, time just . . . slips away."

He pulled back his hat, revealing thick gray streaks in his black hair—which Keefe definitely hadn't expected.

His dark brown skin barely had any wrinkles.

"You tell yourself, 'We'll all go on a big adventure someday!'" he continued. "But first the kids are so little—and traveling with all that baby stuff?" He shook his head. "Plus, the crying. And changing nappies on those tiny portable tables? Total nightmare! So you wait until they're older—but then work is so busy. So you say, 'Next year.' But then the kids have football practice every week, and violin lessons. So it's the year after that—but only a quick trip to visit your sick nan. And before you know it, your own kids are ready for uni, and you're telling them they should start right away too."

"Wow," Keefe mumbled, not sure what to say.

Part of him wanted to pull out his pathfinder and tell him, *Where do you want to go? I can take you!*

But that would be a very bad idea.

"It's okay," the groundskeeper told him. "There's more than enough joy in the day-to-day moments. That's why I like working here. Everyone always asks, 'Isn't it depressing?' And it can be, of course. But it also reminds you that it doesn't matter how much money you have, or how many exciting things you do. It's about having people to share your life with. People you'll mourn when they're gone—and people who'll mourn for you. So enjoy your travels. Have your adventures. Then go find yourself a home and fill it with people you love. That's my two bits of advice, anyway. Do with it what you will. We're almost there."

It took Keefe's brain a second to keep up with the rapid subject change.

The advice had sent his brain wandering to his favorite spot under swaying Panakes branches, staring into a pair of warm brown eyes.

But, right—he was also in a human cemetery, and the groundskeeper was pointing to a row of headstones up ahead.

"I can't believe you have all these graves memorized," Keefe said, trying to ignore the way his heart was slamming against his ribs.

"I wish. I mostly know the ones that no one ever visits—where I never have to clean up any dead flowers or gather up little notes. Feels like it's my job to remember those graves—to be a *person* for them, since they clearly don't have anyone else."

A lump lodged in Keefe's throat, and it took him three tries to choke it down so he could ask, "Does that mean no one has ever visited Ethan and Eleanor?"

The groundskeeper nodded. "It's possible someone slipped

by while I was busy elsewhere. But I doubt it. And if they did, they never left any trace."

Keefe sighed.

Honestly, that made sense.

His mom probably chose Ethan because he didn't have any friends or family, so it'd be cleaner if she needed him to disappear.

She probably even grumbled about how annoying it was that he had a daughter.

One loose end she had to deal with.

"You okay?" the groundskeeper asked, stopping to study Keefe. "Most people are a little shaky when they first get here. But you're looking very pale."

"I'm fine," Keefe assured him—then took a deep breath and tried again. "I'm okay. I've just never been to a cemetery before. It's . . . a lot."

"It is," the groundskeeper agreed. "So pace yourself. They're right over there whenever you're ready."

He gestured to two of the smallest headstones in the cemetery, sitting side by side in the middle of a bunch of other graves.

Keefe would've walked right by them if the groundskeeper hadn't been there to point them out.

"Take your time," the groundskeeper told him, patting Keefe on the shoulder before he stepped back. "I won't be far, if you need anything."

It took Keefe a few breaths to scrape together enough voice to say, "Thanks." And by then he was alone.

"You can do this," he told himself as he forced his legs to carry him forward.

The graves looked even smaller up close—and they had two of the shortest epigraphs in the entire graveyard:

Ethan Benedict Wright II	Eleanor Olivia Wright
Beloved Father	Cherished Daughter

No dates.

No descriptions.

Thankfully no photos.

Keefe also couldn't help noticing that there was no "Dr." by Ethan's name.

But he was done trying to solve giant mysteries with tiny, disconnected clues.

"I'm sorry," he whispered, wishing he could think of something better to say. "I know I can never make up for what happened, but . . . I brought these for you."

He bent down and rested a bouquet of forget-me-nots against each of the gravestones, even though he still didn't understand why humans had chosen that as their tradition.

Weren't the flowers just going to wither and die and make the grave look even more depressing?

But . . . at least the groundskeeper—and anyone else—would

see them and know someone cared about Ethan and Eleanor.

"I *do* care," Keefe told the silent headstones. "And I wish I could've done more."

Sadly, it was far too late to help them.

The most he could do was remember them.

So even though it was getting colder and drizzlier by the minute—and he could easily draw from his photographic memory later—Keefe pulled out his silver journal and a few colored pencils and made a detailed sketch of the gravesite, trying to capture the lonely feel of the cemetery.

He was shivering by the time he finished, and his hands felt numb as he stuffed the journal back into the pocket of his raincoat.

His eyes were also wet and his nose felt drippy, so he'd probably been crying.

But he also felt . . . lighter, somehow.

Like he'd set down some invisible burden along with those pale blue flowers.

All that was left was to say, "Goodbye."

He let the word hang in the soggy air.

Then he turned and walked away, ordering himself not to look back.

It was time to focus on the future instead of the past.

He even picked up his pace, cutting through parks and taking side streets.

He knew London well enough at that point to know all the

best ways to make good time. And the sooner he got back to the hotel, the sooner he could pack up and figure out where he and Alvar were going next.

But when he ducked down a narrow alley between two tall brick buildings, he started to get that familiar prickly feeling down the back of his neck.

"I told you I didn't need you to come with me for moral support," Keefe called over his shoulder. "You didn't have to follow me like a creepy Vanisher!"

Alvar didn't respond.

Keefe glanced over his shoulder and studied the empty alley.

Most of the windows were blacked out, and the doorways were all sunken into shadows.

"You're really going to keep hiding?" Keefe asked. "I know you're back there."

Alvar still didn't appear.

Keefe frowned.

He could've sworn he felt someone following him.

That's when he realized he was alone in a sketchy-looking alley in a world that was known for having thieves.

"If this is a joke," Keefe said, reaching into his pocket for his pathfinder, "it's not funny—and it's making me change my mind about letting you come with me."

Still nothing—which could mean that the prickly feeling had just been the drizzle or the wind.

But it wasn't worth the risk.

Keefe had bigger enemies than human thieves.

He pulled out his pathfinder, planning to leap somewhere far away and head back to London once it felt safer.

But as he held the crystal up to the light, someone screamed, "STOP!" and a figure leaped out of one of the shadowy doorways and slammed Keefe into the wall, knocking his pathfinder out of his hand.

The pathfinder skidded across the cobblestones, and Keefe tried to twist free and grab it—but the figure shoved him back and pinned him harder.

He turned to face his attacker, expecting to find a black hooded cloak with a white eye symbol on the sleeve.

Instead he found a girl about his age, with bright red hair and vivid green eyes, wearing a dull gray sweatshirt and dark jeans.

"You're human," he blurted out before he could stop himself.

"I am," she said, shoving him back when he tried to break free again. "And you're not going anywhere until we talk."

"Why? Who are you?" Keefe demanded.

"Doesn't matter. All you need to know is that I've been training in Krav Maga and jujitsu since I learned how to walk—and if you try to twist free one more time, I'm going to start breaking some bones."

She shifted position, pinning his chest with her forearm so she could grab one of his wrists with her free hand and give it a squeeze.

Not enough to break anything—but enough to prove she wasn't making idle threats.

"Okay, what do you want?" Keefe asked, gasping as a jolt of pain shot up his arm. "I don't keep much cash with me, but you can have all of it—"

"I don't want your money! I want to know who you are and why you went to those graves!"

"Graves?" Keefe repeated. "Why would you . . . ?"

His voice trailed off when he took a closer look at her face.

"Stop staring at me like that!" She slammed him into the wall again. "Just answer my question!"

But Keefe couldn't speak.

His brain was too busy screaming, *IT'S HER—IT HAS TO BE!* and also *NO WAY—THAT'S IMPOSSIBLE!*

Red hair.

Two shadows on her cheeks that probably turned into dimples when she smiled.

And she was the right age.

IT'S HER!

BUT IT CAN'T BE!

"Tell me who you are!" she demanded, squeezing his wrist harder.

"Okay," Keefe said, finally getting his voice to work.

He studied her face one more time to make sure he hadn't completely lost his mind before he said, "My name's Keefe. Are you . . . Eleanor?"

THIRTY-SIX

I 'M NOT HERE TO ANSWER YOUR QUESTIONS!" the girl—*Eleanor*—told Keefe. "You're here to answer *mine*. And you can stop looking longingly at your little crystal thing over there. You're not going anywhere until we have a nice long talk."

"Wait—you know what a pathfinder does?" Keefe asked.

She must, since most humans wouldn't see a small crystal attached to a stick and think it was something someone would use to escape.

If anything, they'd think he was holding a magic wand.

A fake one, of course.

So they'd probably also question his sanity.

"You said your name is Keefe?" she asked, ignoring his

question. "Great. Now tell me why you went to those graves!"

"If I answer your questions, will you answer some of mine?" Keefe countered.

She shoved her arm harder into his chest, pressing him into the cold brick wall. "You're not in a position to bargain."

"Are you sure about that?"

Keefe knew he was probably about to make one of those *What were you thinking???* kinds of mistakes—but he needed to take control of the situation before Eleanor started making good on her threats.

He also kinda wanted to see how she'd react if he made it clear that he might not be human, since it seemed like she had some suspicions.

Maybe it'd shock her enough to cooperate.

So he closed his eyes and reached deep into his core, wishing he'd practiced his skills a little more recently—and hoping his visualization exercise hadn't walled off the energy he was going to need.

Thankfully, he could still feel a reserve of pulsing warmth in the pit of his stomach and was able to channel it to his legs, giving them a huge burst of strength—enough to leap out of her grasp, launch over her head with a flip, and land in the middle of the alley in an awkward crouch, dropping to one knee to keep himself steady.

"Did you seriously just land in a superhero pose?" Eleanor asked, not sounding nearly as impressed as Keefe hoped she would.

Then she tackled him, pinning his arms to the ground with her hands and pinning his legs with her weight. "Did I mention I've also studied wrestling?" she asked, tossing her hair out of her eyes. "And boxing? Trust me, I can handle whatever weird tricks you try to throw at me."

"I believe you," Keefe said, reaching into that pulsing warmth again and shoving it out of his mind like it was an invisible arm. He used it to snatch his pathfinder and drag it through the air to his waiting hand. "But I can bring you with me when I leap, and not take you back until you answer my questions."

"Do it! Then I can finally see where you disappeared to that day."

"What day?"

And then it hit him.

"The day I delivered the letter?"

All the fight drained out of him when she nodded.

"Wow. You really are Eleanor," he mumbled, trying to sort through the hundred thousand questions that slammed into his head. "How are you still alive? Is your dad alive too? Why would you—"

"*Stop!*" she snapped, shifting her weight and wrenching the pathfinder out of his hand. She pressed the crystal against the cobblestones. "Answer my questions, or I'll smash this and you'll be stuck here forever!"

Keefe shook his head. "Pathfinder crystals are unbreakable.

Trust me, I've tried. But . . . you don't have to make any more threats. I'll answer your questions. Could you maybe just let me breathe a little first?"

Her eyes narrowed. But she shifted her weight again—just enough for him to suck in a wheezy breath.

"Now talk!"

Keefe coughed. "Okay, I'll try. Like I said, my name is Keefe."

"Keefe what?"

"Why do you care? I guarantee I'm not in any of your directories."

"Neither am I. But I still want to know."

"Fine. I'm . . . Keefe Sencen." He realized after he said it that it probably would've been smarter to say "Foster." "What was the other question you needed me to answer? My brain's racing, like, five thousand directions right now."

"Why did you visit those graves?" she reminded him.

"That's right." Keefe took another strangled breath. "Pretty sure this isn't the answer you're looking for, but . . . I went there because I thought you were dead, and I wanted to leave flowers since I guess that's what people do. It really is *your* grave, right? Can you at least give me that? 'Cause the only other explanation I can think of is that this is another secret-twin thing, and I've already lived through that twist—though I guess I also did the not-dead twist when I ran into Alvar. And when Fintan showed up again."

"What are you talking about?"

"I'm not totally sure. Like I said—my brain's going five thousand directions right now. It's just really starting to hit me that I've been blaming myself for the murder of someone who isn't actually dead, so . . ."

"You've been blaming yourself?"

"Why do you sound surprised? Isn't that why I'm on my back in a grimy alley with your elbow digging into my ribs right now? I'm assuming that's not how you treat your friends, so you must be blaming me for something. I'm not sure *what*, since it turns out you're alive, but . . ."

He had no idea how to finish that sentence.

"I don't . . . *blame* you," Eleanor mumbled, studying him for a second before she let him sit up.

She also rocked back into a crouch, clearly ready to pounce if he gave her the slightest reason.

"I'm holding on to this until we're done talking," she added, tightening her grip on his pathfinder. "But . . . I don't blame you for anything. You were just a little boy dropping off a letter. At least, I think it was you. You're older and taller now, but . . . same eyes and same hair."

"It was me," Keefe said quietly. "I didn't realize anyone saw me."

She shrugged. "I've always been good at sneaking. And I was out riding my bike that day and spotted you walking toward my house. I didn't like the way you kept glancing over your shoulder. Seemed rather sketchy. So I watched you slip the letter through the letter box, and then I followed you down the alley, trying to find out where you were going. I thought you'd made a wrong turn, since that alley is mostly for storing rubbish bins. But then you pulled a crystal out of your pocket and held it up to the light and just . . . disappeared in a shower of glitter. I screamed and ran inside and told my dad what happened—and he tried to tell me I'd imagined the whole thing. But I grabbed the letter—"

"Wait, you saw the letter?" Keefe jumped in. "What did it say?"

"I don't know. It was sealed—and my dad snatched it out of my hands before I could rip it open."

Keefe scooted closer to the wall and leaned his head against the damp bricks. "You're sure it was sealed?"

"Why?"

"I just really need to know, okay?"

She hesitated for a beat before she told him, "Yes, it was definitely sealed."

Keefe closed his eyes, feeling about a million pounds float off his shoulders.

He never opened it.

Apparently, he *was* capable of occasionally following orders. Who knew?

Though, sadly, that also meant he really had been wasting time trying to trigger his memories.

"And you never went back and stole the letter later—since you're so good at sneaking?" he asked.

"I tried to. But either my dad hid it super well—or he destroyed it. All I ever saw was the symbol on the outside."

"Two crescents forming a circle around a glowing star, right?" Keefe verified.

She nodded. "What does it mean?"

"No idea. I'm not even sure if I care what it means anymore—do you have any idea how many pointless symbols I've had to deal with?"

"No—but *I* care. I saw it on . . . other things."

Keefe sat up taller. "What things?"

"You tell me—you were the one making the deliveries."

"Uh, I only went there once. Or . . . I *think* I only went there once."

"What does that mean?"

Keefe traced his finger along the dark lines separating the bricks. "You're probably not going to believe this—and I probably shouldn't tell you. But, hey, we've come this far, haven't we? So . . . someone erased some of my memories."

"Who?"

"Huh, I would've thought you'd start with 'How?' But I guess it doesn't matter. I don't know who did the actual erasing. All I know is my mom was the one who gave the order."

"Your mom," she repeated, slowly standing up to her full height. "Blond woman, about as tall as me, wearing a fancy cloak?"

"Sounds like her," Keefe muttered, wishing he was surprised

that Eleanor knew about her. "I take it that means you've met Mommy Dearest."

"No—but I saw her."

"When?"

"Doesn't matter."

"See, but it really does." Keefe tried to dust some of the street grime off his raincoat as he stood up to face her. "Where did you see my mom? And how long ago was it?"

Eleanor shook her head and stared into the distance.

Her green eyes looked about a million years old.

"I told you, it doesn't matter," she said quietly. "None of this does because it doesn't change anything. In fact, I probably shouldn't have followed you. I'd just . . . never seen anyone visit the graves, and then I realized you were the boy who disappeared, and I had to at least try to get some answers."

Keefe cringed.

Maybe someday he'd laugh at the irony of him and Alvar both having the same nickname.

But right then, it didn't feel very funny.

"You really are good at sneaking," Keefe told her. "I mean, I was a little distracted at the cemetery. But I don't remember seeing anyone else there—especially someone with bright red hair."

"That's probably because I wasn't there," she admitted, tucking her hair behind her ears. "I can't sit in a cemetery all the time waiting to see if someone shows up, can I? So I hid a small camera in a bush with a proper view of the headstones, and it syncs with an app in my phone and sends me an alert anytime anyone stays longer than a few seconds. It's usually just people visiting the nearby graves, but today I saw you and . . . I'm not sure why I'm telling you this."

"What do you think I'm going to do? Go find the camera and steal it? I'd rather talk about why you have a grave. Also *how* you have one—since I'm assuming that's not an easy thing to pull off. Did you . . . ?"

His voice trailed off as a horrifying possibility hit him.

"Wait. Did my mom help you and your dad fake your deaths?"

If she did—and then let him blame himself for what happened to them . . .

"No, your mom thinks we're dead," Eleanor assured him before he had a total mental breakdown. "And it needs to stay that way. You can't tell her—"

"Uh, I would've thought the whole she's-been-erasing-my-memories thing would've made it pretty clear that my mom and I aren't really on speaking terms right now."

"That can change, can't it?"

"Trust me, it won't." He could tell she didn't believe him, so he added, "Let me put it this way. You know how some stories have supervillains? My mom makes those guys look cute and cuddly. So the next time I see her, we're not going to have a chat or hug it out. I'm going to do everything in my power to end her."

He would've thought Eleanor might look a little shocked by that kind of confession.

Maybe even a little scared of the guy openly talking about killing his mom.

But she stared him dead in the eyes and told him, "Good. The sooner the better."

She opened her mouth to say something else, then shook her head and said, "I should go. I've been here too long."

She started to hand him back his pathfinder but kept it just out of his grasp. "Before I give you this, I need to be *very* clear: You never saw me. We didn't speak. And you still think I'm buried in that cemetery. Just like I never saw you move anything with your mind or do any other tricks that I'm betting your kind—whatever they are—wouldn't be happy about you exposing. Deal?"

"No way. You don't get to decide when this conversation is over! Do you have any idea what I've been going through, trying to find the truth about what happened to you? I've walked every street in London searching for your old house, to see if going there would trigger any memories. I've been to libraries all over the world trying to learn something about your dad's research—"

"You need to stop that!" she cut in. "No—I mean it. Leave my dad out of this—especially his research."

"Why?"

She crossed her arms and looked away, taking several

breaths before she said, "Because . . . I'm pretty sure that's what got him killed."

Keefe cleared his throat, feeling like a total jerk for what he was about to say. But her emotions were too jumbled up for him to make any sense of them.

"I want to believe you," he said. "It's just a little hard to do when the same obituary said you were dead too, and . . . here you are."

"I know." She closed her eyes, wrapping her arms around herself. "My dad's the one who wrote that."

"I thought you said he's dead."

"He is!"

Tears streamed down her cheeks, and she tried to smear them away with the backs of her hands—but new ones kept trickling down.

Yep—he was definitely a jerk.

And he was pretty sure if he tried to hug her, he'd end up with a fist to his throat.

So he told her, "I'm sorry," even though that always sounded so empty. "Do you . . . want to talk about it?"

She wiped her nose and sniffled. "There's not much to say. My dad was always paranoid. Always preparing me for something he seemed afraid would happen. But he got much weirder toward the end. Started shutting himself in his office for days at a time. Wandering around the house muttering under his breath about power sources and how he should've spent more time studying geology. And then one night I came downstairs and found him smashing all his laptops and burning all his research in the fireplace—and when I asked him what he was doing, he grabbed my arms and told me he'd made a huge mistake, and the only way to fix it was for us to disappear. He said he had a plan that was going to sound scary because it would mean starting over with new names, but I had to trust him because it was the only way, and he promised he'd tell me more once he had everything arranged." She had to clear her throat a few times before she said, "Three days later a stranger showed up at our door and told me my dad was dead and I had to leave because I needed people to think I was dead too. I thought it was a cruel joke, but . . . they had a letter from my dad. Apparently he'd given it to them in case something like that happened."

"What did it say?" Keefe asked.

"A bunch of stuff I'm not going to tell you. But . . . he'd made all these arrangements. Obituaries. Graves. A new name. New guardian. A bank account. Lists of dos and don'ts and general survival skills. And he told me the most important thing I could do was forget my old life, forget about him, pretend I was an orphan, and never look back."

"I'm guessing the hidden camera at your grave doesn't really follow those rules," Keefe said quietly.

"Neither does trailing you—or telling you any of this."

Keefe nodded, deciding not to ask why she was doing it.

He was pretty sure it was the same reason he kept trying to trigger the memories his mom stole.

Some things you just can't let go.

"I'm sorry," he told her again.

"You keep saying that."

"I know." Keefe paced across the alley a couple of times before he said, "I just . . . can't help feeling like I did something—or didn't do something—that makes me responsible for all this, and I just don't remember it."

She fidgeted with the sleeves of her sweatshirt. "So that's why you brought us flowers and stood there drawing in your little journal."

Keefe nodded.

"Can I see it?"

"The sketch? It's nothing special."

"I'd still like to."

"You realize in order to do that, I'll have to reach into my coat pocket. Figured I'd mention that because I'd really rather not be tackled again."

Her lips twitched, like he'd almost gotten her to smile. "Move slowly, and we should be good."

Keefe reached for his pocket.

"Ugh, you can move faster than that!" she grumbled when he set his pace just slightly faster than a sleepy ghoul.

Keefe smirked and pulled out his silver journal, flipped to the sketch of the graves, and held it out to show her.

"Nope!" he said when she tried to grab the journal from him. "Lots of stuff in there you don't get to see."

She rolled her eyes and leaned closer, studying his drawing.

"Wow, that's . . . brilliant, actually."

Keefe's cheeks warmed. "Why do you sound so surprised?"

"I mean . . . it's a drawing of headstones. I figured it'd be boring. But I like the way you captured the shadows and the drizzle. Very . . . moody. Kind of like you."

"I'm not moody."

She snorted. "I think you're the moodiest boy I've ever met. The strangest, too—by far."

She reached out, tracing a finger gently across the tiny flowers he'd drawn in front of her dad's grave.

"I guess I should thank you for the forget-me-nots. It's always killed me that I couldn't put any flowers there myself—or even ask someone to do it for me."

"If it helps, that's what made the groundskeeper pay attention to the graves. He's making sure they won't be forgotten."

Her smile faded. "That's the last thing my dad would want. In fact . . ."

She grabbed the corner of Keefe's drawing and ripped it out of the journal.

"Hey!"

"Sorry! My dad wouldn't want something like that 'out there'—whoa, and he definitely wouldn't want *that*," she added, pointing to the portrait Keefe had drawn of her and her dad as Keefe tried to assess the damage to his journal. She ripped that drawing out as well, before Keefe could move the journal out of her reach.

"Hey—I based that off a picture in the obituary *he* apparently wrote, so why is that bad?"

"It probably wouldn't be, if you weren't the boy who disappeared," she argued. "But what if that journal ends up in your mom's hands?"

"That's never going to happen."

"I'm sure you want that to be true. And I hope it is. But we both know you can't guarantee it."

Keefe scowled but didn't argue.

"For what it's worth," she said, tucking both drawings into the pocket of her sweatshirt, "you're really talented. I hope you know that. And . . . you've actually done me a huge favor. I don't have any pictures of my dad. He burned them all when he was erasing our lives. And the newspaper article is so grainy. So . . . thank you."

"You're welcome, I guess," Keefe said, shoving his journal back in his coat.

"Wait—is there anything else about me in there?"

"Just a drawing of the British Library, but it doesn't have your names on it or anything. I went there to see if it triggered any memories, since that's where the obituary said you were killed."

"Wow," she mumbled. "You really did blame yourself for our deaths, didn't you? Why?"

He shrugged. "It's hard not to assume the worst when you recover a stolen memory and find out you delivered a letter to someone who ended up dead not long after."

Eleanor chewed her lip. "It was just a letter, Keefe."

"Easy to say when you don't know what was inside," Keefe said, shaking his soggy hair out of his eyes. The drizzle was turning into a light rain. "I wish I'd opened that envelope."

"Tell me about it. But that's the problem with the what-if game. All it does is make you feel guilty for things you can't change. Better to stick to the facts—so let's repeat them, okay? You were just a little boy delivering a letter. And . . . I don't blame you. So let it go. No more drawings. No more visiting graves. Destroy any other notes or sketches you've made about me and move on. I'm serious, Keefe. We both have to drop this. *Now.* I'm going to take down that camera at the cemetery, since I'm realizing how lucky I am that no one's used it to find me. And I need you to promise me something." She waited for him to look at her before she said, "You can't tell *anyone* you saw me. Ever. Eleanor Olivia Wright is dead. I need you to stick to that story. If anyone found out . . ."

"But this was about your dad—not you. Unless you knew what he was into . . ."

"I didn't."

"You sure?" His emotions kept clouding out hers, but he could still feel traces of fear. "You can tell me."

"I *didn't,*" she insisted. "But do you think that's going to matter to your mom? You said she's a supervillain, right?"

"Worse, actually."

Eleanor nodded. "So what do you think she'd do if she knew I was still alive?"

"I don't know."

But he didn't want to find out.

"That's what I thought. So we have to keep this simple: You never saw me. I never saw you. If anyone asks, I'm buried in that grave where you put those pretty flowers."

"Okay, but what if I need to find you?"

"You won't."

"Kind of sounds like I might. My mom tried to recruit your dad for a reason. You might be the only person who can help me figure out what it was."

"No, I can't. I know you think I'm hoarding all this information. But I was just a kid too, Keefe. And I was really good at tuning out my dad's conspiracy theories."

"And yet you still set up a camera at your grave."

"Hey—you try having a grave and see if you're not a little curious about who comes to visit!"

"I'm sure I would be—but come on, Eleanor, we both know you're hiding stuff."

"If I am, do you really think you're going to convince me to share it after I've protected it all these years?"

Keefe sighed.

So did she.

"Look," she said eventually, "I get the feeling you're used to working as a team. But that's not me. I work alone. Always have. Always will. And trust me, it's better that way. If you're still worried that you're letting some vital secret slip away . . . focus on stopping your mom. That'll solve everything."

"Easier said than done."

"Well . . . I believe in you."

The words could've easily been teasing.

But he could tell she meant them.

"So . . . do we have a deal?" she asked. "You'll keep my secrets, and I'll keep yours?"

"I guess," he said, even though he had no idea how he was going to hide something this huge from everybody.

But he'd have to.

If he told even one person, it would spread.

Secrets always did.

"Thank you," she said, flashing a sad smile that didn't show her dimples. "Pretty sure that means this is goodbye. And not 'see you soon.' Not 'until we meet again.' It's goodbye. Period. For good. Got it?"

She handed him his pathfinder when he nodded.

"All right," she said, giving an awkward wave as she turned to leave.

But she spun back around after a few steps.

"Okay, I have to ask. What *are* you? And please don't say an alien."

Keefe laughed. "You sure you want to know? The truth won't sound much more believable."

She considered that.

"You're right," she said, smiling for real that time—dimples and all. "I don't want to know."

THIRTY-SEVEN

SO, YOU LOOK . . . DRENCHED," ALVAR said as Keefe tried—and failed—to sneak back into his suite without being noticed. "Is that because you were standing in the rain staring sadly at a couple of graves this whole time? Or because you went for a sulky walk in the rain afterward?"

"A little of both," Keefe told him, since it was sorta true.

He was going to have to get used to half-truths and vague answers if he wanted to pull this off.

It wasn't like he'd never hidden anything before—but this definitely wasn't a normal lie.

This was a massive, game-changing secret.

Even bigger than the fact that Alvar was still alive.

And he had to hide this secret forever.

From *everybody*.

Even Foster.

The thought of all the lies he was going to have to tell her made him feel like he'd swallowed a basket of larvagorns.

But it was the only way to protect Eleanor.

Honestly, it was the only way to protect *everyone*.

Whatever Ethan Benedict Wright II had discovered was so terrifying and dangerous that he'd given up everything to hide it—including his life. In fact, Keefe wondered if he left the "Dr." out of his obituaries—and off his gravestone—as a final, desperate way of saying, *Please forget who I really was, and don't ask what I was working on!*

Keefe had zero doubt his mom would do *anything* to get her hands on that research.

Who knew? Maybe that was even why she'd tried so hard to make Keefe blame himself for Ethan's and Eleanor's deaths.

Maybe she'd hoped he'd uncover something useful in his quest for redemption.

If that'd been her plan—it'd worked.

Eleanor had obviously known *something*.

So if his mom found out she was alive, she'd unleash a whole new reign of terror until she tracked Eleanor down and found out what she was hiding.

Who knew how many people would get hurt in the process?

Keefe couldn't let that happen.

He just needed a solid secret-keeping strategy, or he'd never be able to keep track of this many lies. His story had to sound smooth and consistent—and he needed to start telling it now, so he could perfect every detail. Otherwise his very smart, very observant friends would figure out the truth someday.

And he'd hoped that if he sat on his lucky bench in the park with his little fox buddy nearby, inspiration would strike again.

But the light rain had turned to a torrential downpour, and his raincoat could only do so much.

"Anything you want to talk about?" Alvar asked, reminding Keefe that he was still standing in the sitting room, dripping all over the floor.

"Maybe later," Keefe told him. "Right now, I need a shower."

"Really? It kind of looks like you already took one."

"Haha—but that reminds me: Wherever we go next, let's go somewhere sunny—and not Australia."

Alvar grinned. "Still haven't forgiven them for the drop bears, huh?"

"More like the giant spider. I swear, I can still feel that thing crawling on me."

He shuddered and flailed.

Alvar laughed. "Fine, no Australia—for *now*. One day I still need to try a Tim Tam. But in the meantime, are you any closer to figuring out where we *are* going? Because if you're still wavering, I have lots more information about international pancake varieties that might help you narrow it down. I was also thinking we might want to take a day or two and explore a few different places before we settle on one. Try the food. Check out the hotels. Soak up the music and the art. It's not like we're in *that* big of a hurry, right?"

"I don't know," Keefe mumbled.

The sooner he got out of London, the easier it would be to pretend that Eleanor wasn't out there somewhere. He doubted he'd be able to see anyone with red hair without thinking, *OH NO—IT'S HER!*

"Seriously, Keefe. Are you okay?" Alvar asked, making it clear he needed to get a whole lot better at acting normal.

He tried to think up some excuse for his current mood—then realized he didn't need to come up with a big, complicated cover story.

He just needed to go back to being the guy who'd walked into that alley after spending some time staring at graves he felt responsible for—instead of being the guy who walked out after getting tackled by a dead girl.

"It was rough," he told Alvar. "But . . . I'm glad I went."

"Got some closure?" Alvar asked.

"I guess we'll see."

He headed toward the bathroom and jumped in the shower—and as he stood in the warm steam, he realized what he really needed was a reset.

A way of recalibrating his life to pre-Eleanor Keefe.

Physically.

Mentally.

Emotionally.

And it shouldn't be too hard since he could tackle each area individually.

In fact, he started with the physical as soon as he'd dried off and changed into his favorite blue flannel pajamas. He just had to make sure Eleanor hadn't given him any bruises and check his clothes for weird stains from rolling around a grungy alley.

But then he remembered that he also needed to fix his journal, since someone might notice the missing pages—even though the tears were fairly clean.

Half an hour of tedious trimming later, he was pretty proud of how pristine he'd gotten the binding to look.

But he also needed to replace his drawing of the graves.

He knew Eleanor hadn't wanted anyone to see it—but someday he'd have to tell Foster that he'd gone to that cemetery, and she'd expect him to have a sketch of the memory.

So he dug out his colored pencils and set to work—drawing the headstones smaller than he had the first time and showing more of the cluttered cemetery. Hopefully that would make it harder for anyone to recognize the graves if they ever went there. And he limited most of the detail to the forget-me-nots he'd brought.

He also started working on the mental component of his reset as he sketched, imagining himself showing Foster the drawing and trying to figure out what he'd say.

He'd tell her he brought flowers to put by the headstones—and probably discuss how weird that tradition was.

Maybe he'd also tell her about the groundskeeper, so he could make it clear he'd been the first person to visit those graves. Then they'd still be able to talk about how grossly strategic his mom had been when she chose Ethan, picking someone without anyone who'd miss him.

He could even show her the drawing of the British Library and let her know he went there and it didn't trigger any memories.

The less he edited the truth, the easier it would be to keep it all consistent.

But the bigger challenge was going to be the emotional component to the reset, since finding out Eleanor was still alive had changed the way he felt about pretty much everything.

So much of his time in London had been spent looking for a no-longer-green door and trying to trigger a nonexistent memory of what was inside the letter. And he was going to have to make sure that when he talked about those quests, he sounded like the Keefe who *didn't* know he'd never opened the envelope and the Keefe who *hadn't* heard Eleanor tell him that she didn't blame him for what happened.

He needed to sound sad and frustrated and doubting himself and kind of desperate and more-than-a-little broken—which shouldn't be hard, since he still felt all those emotions.

He just felt them for different reasons.

He hated that Eleanor was out there all alone, hiding from his mom.

Hated that he was stuck lying to everyone to protect her.

Hated that he didn't have any clues to what Ethan had been working on, since he was sure it had something to do with stellarlune.

Eleanor said her dad mentioned something about geology in those final days—and wasn't geology the study of *rocks*?

Keefe didn't see how that could be a coincidence.

And yet, all those fragments still didn't add up to anything useful.

So the trick was going to be matching all those genuine feelings with facts that used to be true but were now a little outdated and then sharing only the outdated version of the story.

It was definitely going to hurt his brain.

But Keefe was sure he could handle it.

He'd just have to practice.

Run the stories over and over in his mind.

And he'd need to do the same thing when it was time to hide the fact that he ran into Alvar.

"You okay in there?" Alvar asked, peeking his head through the doorway. "I thought you might be coming back out to debate possible cities."

"Sorry," Keefe said, setting down his colored pencils. "I wanted to make sure I recorded my memories."

Alvar nodded. "And I'm assuming you still don't want to talk about it?"

"Not yet."

Not until he'd rehearsed it a few more times.

"All right, then I think I'm going to get some sleep," Alvar told him. "It's getting pretty late. And tomorrow's going to be a big day, right? Lots of packing and planning. Maybe even taking a quick trip to the city I was going to tell you about. I'll save most of the sales pitch for the morning. But I'll leave you with two words: churro pancakes."

Keefe laughed as Alvar mimed dropping a microphone.

"Come on, you know we *need* to try those," Alvar pressed. "Doesn't mean we have to move there. Just treat ourselves to an awesome breakfast! You deserve it after a rough day."

"Maybe," Keefe said, wondering if he'd made the right call when he agreed to bring Alvar along with him.

It was going to be even more complicated now that he had so much to hide.

But . . . maybe it would be good practice.

Either way, it was happening.

So he should probably try to get some rest.

He crawled into bed and closed his eyes, but his brain kept racing, racing, racing.

And the rain was pounding, pounding, pounding—or, wait.

Was that the rain?

He listened closer and . . .

No—that was knocking.

He got up and threw on his slippers, assuming Alvar ordered fresh towels or room service or something.

But when he opened the door, he didn't find any hotel staff.

His eyes stretched as wide as they could go as he stared at three very drenched figures.

Some part of his brain recognized all three of them—but his gaze stayed locked on the girl in the middle, who was watching him with nervous brown eyes.

His lips curled into a smirk as he whispered, "Foster?"

THIRTY-EIGHT

FOSTER'S HERE!

Keefe wasn't sure if he should be happy-dancing or hiding, but before he could decide, Foster lunged for him—and after the Eleanor tackle, Keefe fully expected to get slammed into the wall.

Instead, it turned out to be the Most Amazing Tackle-Hug of All Tackle-Hugs!

Keefe didn't even care that her clothes and hair were soaking wet, or that he had to hug her back without making any contact with his hands in case his abilities weren't as controlled as he wanted them to be.

All that mattered was: *FOSTER'S HERE!*

And she actually seemed happy to see him!

He couldn't tell for sure, because his own emotions were clouding out everything—but it seemed like a good sign that she kept on hugging.

Part of him would've stood like that forever—but his slightly more practical side forced him to kill the moment and say, "Um . . . not that I'm not glad to see you, Foster, but . . . *how did you find me?* Is everything okay? Also: At some point, I'm going to need to breathe."

She dropped her arms and stumbled back with adorably bright red cheeks. "Sorry!"

"No need to apologize," Keefe assured her, coughing to catch his breath as he flicked on the lights and stepped aside to let her in. "I had a feeling you were going to strangle me if I ever saw you again."

It was totally the wrong joke to make.

Her smile vanished and she turned away, fidgeting with her cape. "You really weren't planning on coming back, were you?"

Keefe knew he needed to fix it—but it was hard to know what to say because . . . he still couldn't feel what she was feeling.

Even when he *tried* to read her emotions, all he could pick up was a weird, dull ache.

"I thought I explained that," he mumbled, trying not to worry that something was wrong with his empathy. "I don't *want* to stay away. It's just not safe for me to be in the Lost Cities, between my mom and . . . everything else."

"But it seems like you're able to talk without giving commands now—so that's some major progress," a new voice reminded him.

Keefe jumped—even though he shouldn't have been startled.

He'd totally seen that Foster wasn't alone when he'd opened the door.

He'd just gotten so distracted by all the hugging that he'd forgotten: Dexy was there!

So was Bangs Boy, which seemed like an odd choice for a Keefe Sencen Search Party—but he could wonder about that later because he'd also remembered that Alvar was in the next room, and it would be so, so, so, so, so, so, so, so bad if anyone figured that out.

Hopefully, Alvar was smart enough to stay hidden.

In the meantime, Keefe felt like everyone was waiting for him to say something.

Right!

He hadn't responded to Dex!

"It's not as much progress as you think," he said, realizing he couldn't read Dex's emotions either, so he had no idea if Dex was still as upset as he'd been during their last conversation. "Plus, there's still all the other stuff, you know?" he added, to at least acknowledge the weirdness between them.

"I *do* know," Foster jumped in, holding his stare. "About everything."

Keefe's mouth went dry. "Dex told you?"

"She guessed a lot of it," Dex explained. "And I didn't tell anyone else."

Keefe frowned at Bangs Boy.

Tam shrugged. "I'm super good with not knowing. Feel free to keep all your secrets to yourself."

"Deal!" Keefe said before turning back to Dex, wanting to make sure he was okay. "Um . . . how is your family, by the way?"

"Kinda the same." Dex glanced at Bangs Boy again, and the dude finally got the hint and wandered over to the windows at the far end of the room. But Dex still lowered his voice when he told Keefe, "You know what happened isn't your fault, right? I've had a lot of time to think about it, and I realized . . . you didn't *change* anything. Everything is exactly the way it was always going to be."

Keefe wanted to grab the words and hug them.

But he wasn't sure they were true, now that he knew he could *trigger* abilities.

"Yeah, but—"

"No," Dex interrupted. "There's no 'but.' I'm not saying you don't still need to learn how to control that ability—and the fewer people who know about it, the better. But I don't think you need to hide, either."

"Especially since you've already made a ton of progress controlling your voice ability," Foster added. "If you can do that, I'm *sure* you can control the others."

Keefe dragged a hand through his hair, wishing he could share her confidence.

But he was starting to worry that all the visualization stuff he'd done had made his abilities worse, not better.

Like . . . he could see the cute little crease between her eyebrows—but he couldn't feel whether it was an *I'm being serious!* crease or an *I'm really stressed!* crease or a *How do I look so cute when I worry?* crease.

He sighed. "It's just . . . It's hard to tell if I'm really controlling the whole command thing or if I only think I am because . . ."

"Because what?" Sophie pressed.

"I don't know."

He tried to scrape together a solid explanation, but his brain was too busy shouting a million DON'Ts.

Don't mention that you can heal abilities.

Don't mention Alvar.

Definitely don't mention anything about Eleanor.

So what *could* he say?

"Maybe my brain instinctively realizes that controlling humans would be a nightmare," he blurted out—then wanted to smack himself because that wasn't even true!

But the words were already out there, so the best thing he could do was just change the subject.

"I swear, the longer I'm here, the less their world makes any sense. Do you know they have a food called bubble and squeak— and it has zero bubbles, and definitely no squeaks? And don't even get me started on the way they decorate." He waved his arms around the suite. "What's with all the flowers? Vases of them. Paintings of them. Carvings of them. Even pillows and curtains and comforters printed with them. I think humans might be more obsessed with flowers than elves are with sparkles."

Was he seriously rambling about decorating?

Apparently, since Foster told him, "Most places aren't decorated like this. Which reminds me—uh . . . how can you afford to stay here?"

Keefe tried to figure out the best way to explain that—then realized he should probably stick with the same story he gave Alvar, since Alvar had to be eavesdropping.

"Technically, Mommy Dearest is paying for it," he said, adding a smirk to sell it. "I raided her jewelry box at Candleshade before I left, and the stuff I took turned out to be worth a *lot* of human money."

Thankfully, they all looked impressed—but then Foster had to get all logical and start asking stuff like, "How did you know where to sell everything? And don't hotels require some sort of ID before they'll check you into a room—especially a room like this?"

"It's been a lot of trial and error," Keefe said, scrambling to redirect the conversation. "Took me a few days of pretty much nonstop light leaping to find the facet on the pathfinder that got me to London. And then I just kinda wandered around, trying to figure out how everything worked—and I realized it's all about who you know. Ask the right questions, make the right friends—"

"Friends?" Foster interrupted. "You have friends here?"

Great, why did he say that?

Now Dex looked super curious, and Foster looked . . .

Was she sad?

Or maybe she was hurt.

All he knew for sure was that it definitely wasn't going to be good if they knew he'd been talking about Alvar.

This was exactly the kind of slip he needed to avoid.

"Let's just say I've had a little help and leave it at that, okay?" Keefe begged.

He could tell Foster still had at least a hundred zillion questions, so he added, "I promise, someday I'll tell you all about my adventures in Humanland, including a particularly awesome anecdote involving a giant spider and a horrible paste called Vegemite."

At least that earned him a smile.

And hey, now he'd *have* to share his drop-bears humiliation—and he could easily tell the story without mentioning Alvar.

He just had to get used to choosing his words *strategically*.

"But right now," he said, realizing it'd be safer to make them do more of the talking—especially since they had some serious explaining to do! "I think I've been very patient, waiting for you to tell me why you're all here—soaking wet, in the middle of the night—and how you found me when I've done a *really* good job of staying hidden. I'd also love to know how you managed to ditch Gigantor for this little adventure, since I'm guessing that was a pretty epic struggle."

"That's a really long story," Foster told him with a slightly smug smile that totally made his heart skip a beat.

He loved it when Miss F was proud of herself.

"Well then, I guess it's a good thing my room has all these chairs!" He waved his arms around the sitting area. "Warning: They're not as comfortable as they should be. Nothing is, honestly. What I wouldn't give for a gnomish-made bed. And maybe a slice of mallowmelt. Oh, and some bottles of Youth! Human water is *terrible*. I can't decide if it tastes like feet or dirty rocks. Should we do a taste test at some point and take a vote? I have a bunch of bottles."

"Actually," Bangs Boy said, making his way back over like a dark cloud ready to dump a ton of rain on their cheerful little conversation, "what we *should* be doing is getting rid of your tracker."

Keefe glanced at Foster, hoping she'd shake her head and tell him, *Don't worry, it isn't what it sounds like.*

But she'd gotten all pale and serious.

And Dex was rolling up his sleeves.

And Bangs Boy was watching him with something that looked annoyingly like pity.

"Um . . . I have *a tracker*?" he said, giving them one more chance to deny it.

None of them did.

THIRTY-NINE

HE HAD A TRACKER.

The words played over and over in Keefe's head—along with a billion questions, like . . . "*How? And more importantly, from who?* Also: *Please tell me getting rid of it isn't going to require melting off my skin!*" Keefe begged.

"No skin-melting," Foster promised with a wide-eyed, gentle stare that calmed a little of his panic—until she ruined it by adding, "But Tam's right—we should've started working on that immediately. Any idea what you're going to need, Tam? Should he lie down or sit or—"

"Whoa—Bangs Boy is doing what, now?" Keefe cut in. "Because the last time he used one of his little Shade tricks on me, I kinda ended up almost dead and woke up with a bunch of freaky new abilities—and I'm not blaming you for that," he clarified, since Tam actually looked a little guilty.

Keefe was never going to be a fan of the guy—but he did get that Tam hadn't really had a choice that day.

"I told you to do it, remember?" he said, waiting for Tam to relax before he added, "But that doesn't mean I'm ready to repeat the process."

"I get it," Tam assured him, sounding like he meant it. He even shook back his bangs and looked Keefe in the eyes as he said, "But this will be different. I'm not sending any shadow-flux into you—I'm just drawing some out."

Keefe crossed his arms over his chest. "Yeeeeeeaaaaaaaah, see . . . that doesn't actually sound any better."

And it got a whole lot worse when he had to sit through a super-confusing explanation about something called a ripple.

Then Dex started rambling about some special Spyball-Imparter contraption he'd made, and talking about how next time he needed to make sure it would warn them about the weather so they wouldn't get drenched, and Keefe was only half listening because his brain was stuck on the fact that he'd had this weird tracker inside him the entire time he'd thought he'd been hiding.

"So . . . ," Keefe said, trying really, really hard not to freak out—but he could feel the meltdown coming. "You're telling me that Fintan had Umber lace my food with creepy shadows and move them to my heart—and then my mom stole his special Spyball, so now she can find me anytime she wants and show up at my door just like you all did?"

"Well, she'd have to wait for the eleventh hour, but . . . yeah," Dex admitted.

Keefe laughed—the kind of screechy sound that wasn't funny at all.

But . . .

Apparently he could've been ambushed any day, any place, regardless of what precautions he'd taken.

And every person who'd been around him had been in danger.

Including Eleanor.

"You know," he mumbled, "sometimes I think, '*Surely* I've found all the messed-up ways my mom and her creepy little minions have been manipulating my life.' But NOPE! There's always another fun surprise just waiting to be discovered! Anyone want to guess what it'll be next time? Maybe there are light beams hidden in my eyeballs that let her see everything I'm seeing! Or maybe the Neverseen's Technopath made some sort of tiny listening device that's hidden in one of my teeth! Think they can hear us talking right now?"

"I doubt it," Dex said. "The teeth would be a *terrible* place to hide a listening device—you'd have to hear every time someone chews or . . ." His voice trailed off. "Sorry, you meant that hypothetically, didn't you?"

"The sad thing," Keefe said, "is that we probably *should* treat those ideas like possibilities. I mean, *there's a shadow-ripple-tracker thing hidden in my heart!*"

"Not for much longer," Foster promised.

Keefe wished he could reach for her hand to see if she was feeling even a fraction of the confidence she was pretending to have—but that wouldn't be safe with his ability.

Plus, he didn't know if she'd want him to do something like that after reading his letter.

So he sighed and said, "Well . . . I guess the sooner we get rid of it, the better."

He started unbuttoning his pajama shirt.

"Uh, what are you doing?" Bangs Boy asked.

"You said it's in my chest, right?"

"Yeah, but if I'm already drawing the shadowflux through skin, bone, and muscle, I can also pull it through a little bit of fabric," Tam reminded him.

"I suppose that's a valid point," Keefe said, dropping his arms to his sides.

He tried to tell himself that at least he hadn't taken his shirt all the way off—especially with Foster there.

But he was still tempted to bury himself in pillows and hide.

"So . . . should I sit? Lie down? Do a little dance?" he asked, hoping the joke hid at least some of his embarrassment.

"Sitting might be wise," Tam told him, and Keefe plopped down on the nearest chair, finally risking a glance at Foster.

"It's okay to be nervous," she told him, reaching for his hand

and then stopping herself—then staring at him with a crease between her eyebrows that kept getting deeper and deeper and deeper.

He could tell there was some serious emotional turmoil going on in her head—but he still couldn't read a single thing she was feeling.

Was she worried about him?

Annoyed that she was stuck there helping with this when she had way more important things to do?

Or was she just awkward because of his confession?

Whatever it was, she was so distracted by the noise in her head that she totally missed Tam's question.

"You with us, Foster?" Keefe teased, trying to snap her out of it. "Tam just asked if you wanted to enhance him for this."

"Oh! Sorry." She hid her flushed cheeks behind her soggy hair. "Whatever you think would be best," she told Tam.

"Might be a good idea," he decided. "Since I'm not really sure what I'm doing."

"Just so you know, that's *not* making me more excited for this," Keefe said, hoping it sounded like a joke.

But this was all starting to remind him way too much of Loamnore.

"It'll be quick," Tam promised. "I think."

He reached for Foster's hand.

"One second." She closed her eyes and took a slow breath before she nodded.

Apparently that was all she needed to switch on her enhancing.

"You've gotten pretty good at that," Keefe noted, trying not to feel super envious. "Maybe you can teach me some of your ability-controlling tricks."

"Sure—but only if you want."

She said it with a shrug and an eye roll, and Keefe had to stop himself from shouting, *SERIOUSLY—WHAT ARE YOU FEELING RIGHT NOW?*

He definitely wasn't a fan of this new emotional obscurity.

"Ready?" Foster asked, taking Tam's hand when he nodded.

"Wow," Tam breathed. "I forgot how intense that is."

"Foster has that effect on people." Keefe said it with a smirk that hopefully hid the fresh wave of jealousy that crashed over him.

He wasn't necessarily worried that there was anything going on between Foster and Bangs Boy—but he couldn't *completely* rule it out.

Mostly he just wished he could hold her hand—or anyone's hand—without worrying about what he might sense or trigger in them.

But he should probably be focusing on the fact that Tammy Boy was doing that creepy whispering thing he did when he used his power.

His brows were also scrunching together, and he was curling his fingers like he was grabbing something only he could see.

"Okay. I think I know how to call the darkness free," Tam murmured. "You might feel a little pull."

"Little" was definitely an understatement.

Tam flicked his hand in a strange pattern, then yanked his arm back like he was playing tug-of-war, and Keefe jerked forward, letting out a startled grunt as pain slammed against his ribs.

A tiny whiff of darkness blasted out of his chest and hovered a few feet in front of him as the pain slowly faded.

"It's kinda sad that this isn't even in my top five weirdest experiences," Keefe said, rubbing his chest as he squinted at the shadowy cloud.

"Does it hurt?" Foster asked.

"Not anymore. But that tug was like getting kicked in the ribs."

"Sorry," Bangs Boy mumbled. "I was worried if I went slow, it'd drag out the pain."

"It probably would have. It's all good—thank you for, uh . . . Huh. I can't think of a non-weird way of saying, 'Thanks for dragging the freaky ripple-tracker thing out of my heart,'" Keefe admitted.

Tam flashed one of his still-mostly-surly grins. "You're welcome."

"You're sure you got it all?" Foster asked—beating Keefe to the question.

Tam nodded and called the shadowflux closer, letting it hover over his palms.

"What are you going to do with that?" Dex asked.

"No idea," Tam admitted. "It'll probably evaporate if I release my hold, but there's a chance Umber did something to it that'll make it unwieldy."

"Oooh—I know!" Keefe jumped up and raced for the trash can, returning with an empty water bottle. "Trap it in there. Then it'll go out with the recycling, and if the tracker is somehow still working, it can lead my mom to a big pile of trash."

"Works for me," Tam said, taking the bottle from him and filling it with the puff of darkness before sealing the lid.

Keefe called the front desk and buried the bottle in the bottom of the bin before leaving it out in the hall for housekeeping.

Then he plopped back onto the couch, trying to pretend like he wasn't freaking out—but he couldn't stop thinking about the fact that his mom could've ambushed him any day she'd wanted.

That had to mean she was waiting for some sort of opportune moment.

And even though the tracker was gone now, Keefe doubted that would stop her.

She always had a backup plan.

"Soooooo," he said slowly, "does this mean you're ready to tell me the rest? And don't give me the confused eyebrow crinkle, Foster. You told me about the tracker, but you've conveniently *not* told me how you came across a bunch of very specific information about ripples and eleventh hours and altered Spy-balls. So hit me with it—what's going on? What is my darling mommy up to now?"

"Honestly, we're not sure," Foster said, hesitating a second before she sank into the armchair across from him and told him about a ton of memories they'd found in Kenric's cache.

Also about something called Elysian—and all the dead ends they'd been hitting, trying to find out what it was.

The more she talked, the more Keefe couldn't decide if he felt left out or impressed by how hard everyone had been working.

And when she shared a fun little story about a memory his father had recovered—and the possibility of there being a third step to stellarlune—Keefe wanted to shove his head in a pillow and scream and scream and scream.

But there was no time for that kind of pity party because Foster had saved the scariest stuff for last.

Apparently there'd been a meeting with the Neverseen.

And in that meeting, Vespera had proposed that they form a temporary alliance and team up against his mom because it was in all of their best interests to stop her, so they might as well work together.

Keefe waited until Foster finished explaining all of that madness.

Then he jumped to his feet, fighting the urge to grab his stuff and flee to the farthest human city.

Instead he slowly crossed the room and stopped in front of Foster's chair, wishing he could reach for her hands—but her shoulders were safer, since they were covered by multiple layers of fabric.

He placed one hand on each shoulder, making a squishy sound as his fingers sank into her soaked cape. And he waited for her to look at him before he said, "Please tell me you didn't agree to this horrible plan. I know you're the queen of huge risks, but—"

"I didn't agree," Foster assured him. "We're going to find Elysian on our own."

Keefe nodded and stepped back to pace as she explained that Wylie was trying to find the starstone, and how she was convinced they'd be able to see through the illusions.

Then Dex chimed in, saying he had plans for a gadget to separate beams of light and help them.

Keefe let them finish, watching the rain streak down one of the windows.

"We'll be careful," Foster promised. "And once we get that power source—"

Keefe spun back to face her, no longer able to stay quiet.

She was talking about rocks.

Probably the same rocks Ethan Benedict Wright II died trying to protect.

"You have to destroy it, Sophie!" Keefe hoped using her real name would prove how serious he was. "I mean it. I need you to listen to me on this. If you actually do find Elysian and track down these special glowing rocks—or whatever they are—you *have* to destroy them. Otherwise *everyone* is going to come after you. The Council. The Neverseen. My mom. Who knows—maybe the other species will even get in on the action. Sounds like the trolls definitely will. And there's no way you're going to be able to protect it through all of that. So you have to destroy it. Otherwise you'll put yourself—and everyone you care about—in worse danger than they've ever been in before. And the power will probably still end up in the wrong hands."

"No, it won't," she argued. "I'll hide it—"

"And they'll start hurting people you love until you tell them where it is," he insisted, moving back to her side and taking her by the shoulders again. "You know I'm right."

She shook her head, holding his stare as she mumbled, "The thing is . . . you might need it."

And there it was.

The *real* reason.

She was willing to take all these huge risks . . . for him.

He had to smile at that—even though it made him want to scream into his pillow again.

"I had a feeling you were going to say that," he said quietly. "And I appreciate it—you have no idea how much. I've never had anyone try to take care of me the way you do, and . . ." He started to say something else, then changed his mind, taking a deep breath before he added, "But this is bigger than me,

Sophie. And it's bigger than you. It's bigger than *everyone*. So I need you to promise me that if you get anywhere near that power source, you'll do everything possible to destroy it."

"Fine. I promise."

She really was a terrible liar.

Even without being able to read her emotions, Keefe could tell there was no way she was going to keep that promise.

Which meant it was time for a change of plans, even though he'd barely had time to think it through.

"Clearly you still haven't learned that you can't lie to an Empath," he said, feeling his lips curl into a smile as the reality of what he was about to do settled in. "So I guess that only leaves me one other option."

"Wait—where are you going?" she asked as he marched toward his bedroom.

"To get my stuff. I'm coming with you."

FORTY

WOW, AM I REALLY DOING this?" Keefe asked as he fumbled around his room, hastily filling his new duffel bag with all the little human snacks and souvenirs he'd been accumulating—plus his journals and sketchbook and maps.

He kept his voice low, hoping no one could hear him doubting the decision—especially since he wasn't going to change his mind.

He couldn't.

But wow, had it all happened superfast!

A couple of hours ago he'd been figuring out which human city he wanted to move to—with Alvar Vacker, of all people—and trying to prepare himself for a future filled with lots of awkward lying.

And now . . .

Foster was there—along with Dex and Bangs Boy.

He'd had some sort of weird shadow tracker ripped out of his chest because his mom could always sink to a new level of creepy.

And he was heading back to the Lost Cities.

It wasn't that he didn't trust his friends—or thought they couldn't handle this horrifying new project without his help.

Honestly, they'd probably be better off without him.

But . . . he needed to make sure they didn't take any huge, unnecessary risks trying to fix him.

Even if there was a third step to stellarlune.

Even if his abilities would never work right without it.

None of that was worth the nightmares that could happen if this awful new power source fell into the wrong hands.

And since he'd be the one most affected by its destruction, he should be the one to destroy it.

He just wished he'd had more time to perfect the careful wording he was going to need to protect all of his scary new secrets—especially given all the slips he'd already made.

And he wished he had some clear control over his new abilities.

He also wished he had some elvin clothes to change into—but he'd left the tunic and pants he wore when he ran away back at his father's cabin, since they were wet and dirty from the waterfall-boat debacle.

So apparently he'd be returning to the Lost Cities in a pair of dark jeans and his favorite blue hoodie.

Honestly, though? It actually felt kind of fitting.

A little proof that he wasn't totally the same guy he'd been when he ran away.

After all, he wasn't as scared anymore.

He'd also learned a few tricks.

And . . . he had a whole lot more secrets—and hiding them was going to be one of the hardest things he'd ever have to do.

Maybe that was why he packed the rest of his human clothes, just in case he ended up needing them.

It probably *would* be safer for everyone if he only stuck around long enough to destroy the power source and then disappeared—at least until it was time for the final showdown with Mommy Dearest.

And then he wouldn't have to lie all the time.

But . . .

He was pretty sure that no one would forgive him if he ran away *again*.

In fact, it wasn't totally clear if they'd forgiven him for running off *this* time.

He was one thousand percent *not* a fan of not being able to read Foster's emotions—particularly since it turned out she was actually pretty good at hiding what she was feeling.

He'd always thought he could read all her inner turmoil by studying the little creases and crinkles around her eyes and on her forehead—but as it turned out, he'd been relying on the Foster-feels bombardment way more than he realized.

Or . . . she was working extra hard right now to keep her emotions in check.

And if that's what was happening, it wasn't good news for his sappy, hopeful heart.

She knew exactly how he felt—no more Great Foster Oblivion.

So if she was trying to hide where she was at, that probably meant they weren't in the same place.

And that was fine.

He'd always known she deserved so much better.

But, wow, did it hurt.

Keefe sank onto his bed, staring at the tiny stuffed elf he'd bought her, wondering if he should even bother bringing it.

"Just take it," Alvar's disembodied voice told him from the other side of the room. "She's going to love it."

Keefe barely managed to stop himself from shrieking.

"Uh, how long have you been there?" he whisper-hissed.

"Long enough to see a whole lot of pouting," Alvar said as he blinked into sight over by the window. "And I figured you were over there convincing yourself you shouldn't bring that adorable gift because you think she'd be better off with my brother or something. So I thought it might be a good time to show up and say, *nope*! Fitz is a selfish snob with a terrible temper, and he's never going to treat her the way she deserves."

"You just hate your brother."

"I do. But it's also super obvious that she'd be way happier with you. And you know what?" He tiptoed across the room and whispered, "She's starting to realize it too."

Keefe looked away, checking the bedroom door to make sure it was closed—glad he could hear the TV on out in the sitting room and a whole lot of giggling. Hopefully that meant no one was eavesdropping.

Alvar must've understood his concern because he vanished again.

But he didn't go away.

"I saw that tackle-hug she gave you," his voice whispered. "And all those sly looks she kept sneaking when she thought no one was looking. You're both insecure and terrible with crush stuff, so it's probably going to take a little bit longer for you two to get in sync. But don't give up! I guarantee Team SoKeefe will have its victory."

"Oh please," Keefe mumbled, hating how red he could feel his cheeks turning when Alvar started making kissy sounds.

He glanced at the door again.

Then shoved the stuffed elf in his duffel bag.

"Good." Alvar cleared his throat a couple of times before he said, "So . . . big night for you."

"Yeah . . ." Keefe fidgeted with the zipper on his hoodie. "I take it you heard everything?"

"Yep. Figured I should probably make sure they weren't here to grab me and drag me to an elvin prison."

"I wouldn't have let them," Keefe promised. "I mean, that's not why they're here. But . . . if it had been, I would've made sure you got away. I'm also not going to tell them—or anyone else—that I saw you, or that you're alive."

"Probably smart since I'm sure they would *not* be excited to hear how much time we've been spending together."

"They wouldn't," Keefe agreed. "But . . . they'd be wrong. And for what it's worth . . . I'm glad we ran into each other."

Alvar reappeared just long enough to flash a huge grin. "Look at that. I passed your little test."

"You did," Keefe admitted. "You definitely proved that you deserve a normal life. Just don't forget that we're all only as good—or as bad—as our next decision. I'm trusting you. Don't make me regret it."

"Is that your way of telling me you'll be keeping an eye on me? You know, after you completely abandon me?"

"I—"

"Relax." Alvar's voice drifted toward the windows, as if he'd gone to watch the rain. "I knew you'd be going back eventually. I'd just been looking forward to sharing a few more pancakes before you left—especially those churro ones. Missing out on those really will be a shame."

"It will be." Keefe had to agree.

"But . . . I get it, okay? You belong with your girl. And your friends. And I hope you make your mom pay for putting a freaky shadow tracker in your chest." He blinked back into sight before he added, "I didn't know about that, by the way. In case you were wondering."

"I figured," Keefe said quietly. "Otherwise you wouldn't have hung around me."

"I wouldn't have. In fact, my first thought when I saw that darkness seep out of you was 'Get that thing far away from me!' Though clearly your mom is waiting for something." He vanished again before he said, "You're right to go back to try to figure out what she needs—and hopefully take control of it before she can. I also couldn't help noticing that my little 'rocks' clue isn't looking so pointless anymore."

"It isn't. Leave it to Mommy Dearest to come up with the weirdest plans ever. Though that's probably why she wins."

"She's had her share of victories. But you *can* beat her, Keefe. You have to believe that. You're stronger and smarter, with way better allies and much better hair."

"It's the hair that really clinches the victory, isn't it?" Keefe agreed.

"Totally."

Keefe's smile faded. "But . . . what about you?"

"I can't go with you," Alvar said immediately.

"Yeah, I know. Wasn't going to ask. I can take you back to

your city if you want—but I'll have to wait until later tonight, otherwise they'd know I leaped somewhere because I'd reappear back by the clock tower. I'm sure I can sneak away after everyone goes to bed if that's what you want."

Alvar blinked back into sight. "I guess that could work. But I was actually thinking I might try traveling around on those human train things, now that I can vanish and don't have to worry about having a passport. Maybe I'll do a . . . Pancakes of the World tour! You know, focus on the important things."

That actually sounded amazing—and way more fun than anything Keefe was about to do.

But . . . it wasn't about fun.

Not for him, at least.

"Hey—Sir Serious Face," Alvar said, "I know you're going to miss me—"

"I am," Keefe cut in. "Believe me, I'm more stunned about that than anyone. But it feels weird saying goodbye. Especially since it's not like I have any way of finding you again."

Alvar shrugged. "I don't know. We both seem to spend a lot of time in libraries. Might be a good place to check—you know, if you ever need snack recommendations. Or feel like taking me to get that Tim Tam you owe me. Particularly if the library is in a city known for having amazing pancakes."

Keefe grinned. "Good to know."

He glanced at the door again.

"You should probably head out," Alvar said, following his

gaze. "They might start to wonder why it took you so long to shove some stuff in a duffel bag."

"True." Keefe packed up his mom's jewelry—but left a couple of the biggest, sparkliest pieces for Alvar, just in case.

He also left him the rest of his cash.

"Oh, and I'm not going to check out of this room," Keefe told him. "They have my card on file, so you should be able to stay as long as you need. Order all the room service you want."

Alvar smirked. "I was already planning on it. But I feel like I should repay you for your generosity. So how about I give you one last piece of brilliant advice before you go do all your hero stuff?"

"You're going to, whether I want you to or not, right?" Keefe asked.

"You bet," Alvar agreed. "Should I wait for you to get your sketchbook so you can write this down?"

Keefe rolled his eyes. "I think I'll be able to remember it."

"Let's hope." He held Keefe's stare as he said, "Stop doubting yourself. You can handle anything that's about to be thrown at you."

"I guess we'll see."

"Seriously, Keefe. You've got this. You just have to believe."

He vanished again, and something about the look in his eyes told Keefe that was the last time he was going to see him—for now, at least.

Only time would tell if that would change.

In the meantime, Keefe slung his duffel bag over his shoulder. "I think . . . I'm finally ready."

For what, he wasn't sure.

But that was kind of the point, wasn't it?

He took one last look around his fancy human bedroom before he headed toward the door and said, "Okay. Let's do this!"

Hello again, dear readers!

I'm not sure if you're back here because you were a good little rule-follower who started on page one and have now gone with Keefe on all of his human adventures (and learned some of his enormous secrets!)—or if you skipped straight to the back because you couldn't wait to get to this scene.

Either way . . .

YES, WHEN YOU TURN THE PAGE, YOU WILL FIND A RETELLING OF STELLARLUNE *CHAPTER 42 FROM KEEFE'S POV!*

(And if you don't know why that's so exciting, you might want to stop reading RIGHT HERE because, you know . . . SPOILERS!)

I knew as soon as I decided to write *Unraveled* that one of the biggest fan reactions would be something along the lines of, *Yay, we're going to get to read THAT SCENE told by Keefe!!!* But I *also* knew that Keefe really only needed to tell "his" story from the moment he ran away (at the end of *Unlocked*) to the moment Sophie, Dex, and Tam came to find him in London. Everything he did after that was covered by the rest of *Stellarlune* (and, of course, the story will continue in book 10 . . .).

So I wrote *Unraveled* the way it needed to be written, because I always trust the story first—but then I had to include this special bonus chapter at the end, because I love you all too much to disappoint you.

And so, without further ado, I give you a hearty dose of SOKEEFE!!!

Happy reading!
(And swooning!)

xoxo

EVERYTHING

HEY, GLITTER BUTT . . . CAN I ASK
you a question?" Keefe said as he stared into
the eerie black nothingness.

He hated the void—and not just because
he'd almost gotten trapped in it once.

It was too quiet.

Too empty.

Too . . . lonely—and he'd been battling that feeling enough
already.

Maybe it was because he had to keep so many secrets about
his time in Humanland, so he was always lying or dodging
questions or avoiding conversations.

Or maybe it was because his abilities seemed to be getting worse instead of better.

Or maybe it was because his friends had all been busy making memories without him and seemed different now that he was back.

Whatever it was, he just felt . . . out of sync.

Which was probably why he was now turning to an overprotective mama alicorn for advice and asking, "Does Foster seem different to you lately?"

SOPHIE! SOPHIE! SOPHIE!

Keefe sighed. "Yeah . . . that's what I thought you might say."

Silveny's conversation skills weren't necessarily the greatest.

"I don't know," he mumbled, not sure if he was talking to himself or Silveny at that point. "It could just be because I can't really read her emotions right now—which is *the worst*, by the way—but . . . it feels like she's avoiding me. I've barely seen her the last few days, and the few times I have, she's been super quiet and fidgety, and that cute little crease between her eyebrows never seems to go away. And I don't think she's like that around anyone else. I think it's just me."

KEEFE! KEEFE! KEEFE!

"Is that your way of telling me that you agree, that it's just me?"

KEEFE! KEEFE! KEEFE!

Keefe took that as a yes.

And he shouldn't be surprised.

He was pretty sure he even knew *why* Foster would be awkward around him. . . .

They'd never talked about his letter.

He'd thought about bringing it up at least a zillion times, but . . .

It didn't feel like he should be the one starting that conversation.

After all, he'd already made his embarrassing confession.

Wasn't her silence . . . kind of her answer?

And wouldn't forcing her to talk about it just be pushy and rude?

Or was he being a wimp and looking for excuses to avoid having the last tiny shreds of his hope drowned in a pool of sadness?

TALK! TALK! TALK! Silveny told him, making Keefe wonder if she'd been able to hear what he was thinking. *SOPHIE! KEEFE! TALK!*

"Maybe," Keefe said, hoping it would silence the exuberant transmissions.

But Silveny kept right on repeating *SOPHIE! KEEFE! TALK!* as she cracked open the void and teleported them back to Havenfield—where a familiar blond figure just so happened to be waiting for him under the swaying branches of the Panakes tree.

SOPHIE! SOPHIE! SOPHIE! FRIEND! FRIEND! FRIEND! Silveny announced helpfully.

"Is everything okay?" Keefe asked as he hopped off Silveny's back and rushed over.

Foster nodded, taking a deep breath before she told him, "Yeah, I was just . . . waiting for you."

Keefe's heart did a few backflips—and then sank with a thud when she added, "And I was starting to think you weren't coming back."

He fidgeted with his cape, wondering if he'd always be the Guy Who Kept Running Away. "Sorry. I wanted to see what would happen if I had Silveny fly me around in the void while I talked in my mom's voice. I thought maybe if I managed to say at least a couple of the right words while I was in there, whatever she hid would come crashing toward me."

"Did it work?"

"Not particularly. And in case you were wondering, the void never gets any more exciting. It's just darkness and more darkness—and oh, hey, even more darkness! I'm sure Tammy Boy would love it, but, man, I'm glad to see color again."

He couldn't help stealing a glance at her tunic.

Foster looked amazing in *any* color.

She even looked adorable covered in ooze.

But there was something particularly special about the way she looked in red.

Almost like the color existed just for her—which might've been the most ridiculously sappy thought he'd ever had. But it was hard not to feel a tiny bit sappy when Foster's cheeks blushed after she caught him admiring her.

"You could've taken me with you, you know," she said quietly, which made his heart do a couple more backflips—until she added, "Or at least left me another note telling me where you went."

They both froze—and Keefe's brain screamed, *QUICK! MAKE ONE OF YOUR FUNNY JOKES!*

But . . . they needed to have this conversation eventually, didn't they?

If she was finally ready, then . . . he'd have to deal.

He dragged a hand through his hair and chewed his lower lip while he let her decide.

"Do you want to go for a walk?" she asked.

His heart went *thud* again, since he was pretty sure "go for a walk" was code for *Hey, let's go somewhere quiet so no one will see you crying.*

But . . . at least then he'd finally have an answer.

This is good. This is how we save our friendship, he tried to tell himself—and Foster looked so relieved when he nodded that he wondered if she was thinking the same thing.

He tried to get a reading on her emotions as she led him into the pastures—but all he could feel was a jumbled-up, pulsing hum.

Definitely something intense and significant.

But he couldn't translate it.

"Are we heading anywhere in particular?" he asked, trying to fill the awkward silence.

"Not really," she admitted. "I just need to move. I've been stuck in one place for way too long."

"I know the feeling," Keefe mumbled. "And if you don't have a specific spot in mind, then follow me—I found the coolest place the other night after training with Grady."

If he had to have his heart crushed—might as well do it somewhere with a little style, right?

He led her into the Grove, rambling about which of the weird trees he was currently sleeping in and how one of them had tiny glowworms inside, covering the walls with flecks of blue light.

"Sounds amazing."

He might've believed her if she hadn't also started scratching her arms, like the thought of a room full of worms made her itchy.

Keefe was trying to decide if he should tease her about it when her toe clipped the edge of a root and she crashed into his back and clung on like a drop bear.

"Sorry," she said—and it took him a second to realize . . .

She wasn't letting go.

"You okay?" he asked. "Did you hurt your ankle?"

"No. Just . . . uh . . . getting my bearings."

Her voice was adorably squeaky.

"Will this help?" he asked, taking one of her hands and shifting so they were walking side by side.

It took his brain another second to realize what he'd done—and he held his breath, hoping he wasn't about to get hit with a weird blast of heat and trigger another ability for her.

But the only warmth he felt was gentle and soothing.

Meanwhile his brain started screaming, *AHHHHHH—WE'RE HOLDING HANDS!*

And they were.

Foster wasn't pulling away.

WHAT DOES THAT MEAN???

"It's so weird," she mumbled. "I'm so used to having you feeling everything I'm feeling. It's strange not having you call me out on it all the time."

"Tell me about it," he grumbled.

"Sorry—I didn't mean—"

"It's okay, Foster. I know what you meant. And just so you know, I can still pick up on certain things—especially from you. Pretty sure your emotions will always be stronger than everyone else's."

"Really?" she asked, grinning when he nodded.

"I just . . . wish I could get back to how it used to be," he admitted. "It's hard not getting the whole picture. Makes me not want to trust anything I'm feeling—if that makes sense."

She nodded, and they fell silent again.

But the silence felt charged that time.

Like some sort of energy was building between them.

And Keefe felt his heart pick up speed as he guided her toward a wall of vines.

"Here we go," he said as he brushed the leaves aside like a curtain.

"Oh wow," Sophie breathed as she followed him into the clearing, craning her neck to take in the full effect.

Keefe had thought elves were the masters of sparkle—but clearly that title belonged to the gnomes who'd trained the hundreds of delicate vines covered with sheer, twinkling flowers to create a shimmering canopy.

The ground was also dotted with colorful, glowing toadstools.

Honestly, it felt like the kind of fairyland humans were always dreaming about.

"Did you know this place existed?" Keefe asked.

"Flori mentioned it—but I haven't had a chance to go looking for it. She was trying to convince Sandor to bring Grizel here for a date, since it's so romantic."

They both froze again, and Keefe felt a jolt of emotions where their palms were connected.

It almost felt like fear and regret—but that didn't make any sense.

He was about to ask her what was wrong when she tightened her grip and told him, "I'm glad I got to come here with you. Even if it was kind of an accident."

Keefe sucked in a breath.

"I know you said you got over a bunch of things after you left the Lost Cities," she added, blurting out each word faster and faster, like she was trying to force them all out before she could change her mind. "And I'm sure that probably includes the stuff you told me in your note."

Wait—what?

IS THAT WHAT SHE THOUGHT I MEANT?

He wanted to tell her how wrong she was, but she was still going.

"And I know you said you're not looking for a relationship right now—and I get it," she added quietly. "But . . . it makes me a little sad. Mostly because it means I missed my chance to be with this really incredible guy who makes me laugh and always finds ways to be there for me when I need him. And that's fine. It's my fault—and I'm not trying to, like . . . guilt you into liking me again. I just felt like you should know why I might get a little awkward around you right now. I'm trying to figure out how to go back to only seeing you as a friend, and it's not easy, because I'd just started realizing how much I care about you."

Somewhere along the way she'd squeezed her eyes shut.

Keefe, meanwhile, had completely stopped breathing.

If it weren't for the warmth pulsing through their clasped hands, he might've thought he'd nodded off somewhere and was going to wake up and realize he'd dreamed the whole thing.

But this was very, very real.

And his next words were going to be very, very important.

"Sophie?" he whispered, needing to use her actual name.

He leaned closer, breathing her name again before she slowly opened her eyes—looking so real and sweet and fearless and gorgeous and . . .

How?

How did he get this incredible girl to look at him like that?

He didn't deserve her.

He'd never deserve her.

But that didn't mean he wouldn't try—with every breath and every second of every day that she was willing to be with him.

"You realize," he whispered, because he needed to give her one last chance to change her mind, "that if we do this . . . it could get *very* messy."

She looked away, kicking her toe against one of the glowing toadstools. "Because I'm unmatchable?"

He would've laughed at the absurdity of that—but this moment was way too serious.

"No—the Council can feed their match lists to the gorgodon, for all I care," he assured her. "But . . . I wasn't lying when I said my mom will try to use anyone I care about to hurt me."

"Yeah, but I'm pretty sure I'm already at the top of your mom's list of targets," she reminded him. "And I'm ready for her."

She patted the holster of her dagger.

He caught her hand before it returned to her side, cradling her palm in his—and he could feel the steadiness in her grip.

Keefe had zero doubt she'd fight with every weapon in her arsenal. But . . .

"That might not be enough to stop her."

"It might not," she agreed. "But I'm not afraid of her. And I'm not going to let her control my life. So if she's the only reason—"

"I think we both know she's not," Keefe interrupted, needing her to be *really, really* sure.

But he couldn't bring himself to mention Fitz's name.

And he couldn't stop himself from stepping a little bit closer—close enough that he could feel her breath on his cheek when he asked, "Would you like me to list off all the complications?"

She shook her head. "All I care about is how you feel. If you're only doing this"—she held up their clasped hands—"because you don't want to hurt my feelings—"

Keefe twined their fingers together and shook his head.

Time for words—and he needed to get this right because if he ruined it now, he would never be able to forgive himself.

"Trust me—this is what I've wanted from the moment I first saw you, wandering through the halls in the middle of session covered in alchemy goo," he told her. "I knew right away that I'd just met someone incredibly special—and every minute I've spent with you since then has proven how true that is. But is this really what *you* want?" He squeezed her hand, wondering if she could feel him shaking as he added, "I can't tell what you're feeling—and it's seriously terrifying."

A long second passed, and Keefe was pretty sure neither of them was breathing.

Then Foster tilted up on her toes and leaned forward, meeting his eyes and lining her lips up with his—but she left the tiniest sliver of space.

For a second he worried she'd changed her mind.

Then he realized she was leaving it up to him.

Giving him a choice.

And he knew *exactly* what he wanted.

He closed the distance between them, pressing his mouth to hers, and . . .

It was perfect.

The way their lips fell into sync as his brain screamed, *IT'S ABOUT TIME!* and he had to stop himself from raising one arm and pumping his fist.

He'd always known kissing her would be amazing.

But he hadn't realized it could be *everything*.

A single perfect moment he never wanted to end.

But of course it had to.

He was even the one to pull away, leaning back to study her in the shimmering light because he had to know. "You're okay, right? No regrets?"

Her grin was glorious.

And he could tell she meant it when she told him, "Absolutely none."

He leaned his forehead against hers, hoping he could deserve that trust.

"I don't want to mess this up," he whispered. "Please don't let me mess this up."

"I won't," she promised, tilting her chin up to steal another quick kiss.

But someone cleared their throat, and they both flung themselves apart.

PLEASE DON'T BE GRADY!!! Keefe begged the universe.

Thankfully it was Flori—and her huge smile made it pretty clear she knew exactly what they'd been doing.

"I'm *very* sorry to interrupt," she told them. "But you have a visitor, Miss Foster. And I thought you might want a moment to collect yourself."

"Is everything okay?" Foster asked, tugging at her hair and wiping her mouth.

"I believe so, yes," Flori said. "But they wanted to come find you, and since I knew where you were, I thought it would be best if I came to get you myself."

"Yeah. Um. Thanks." Foster glanced at Keefe, looking equal parts stunned and smug—and maybe a tiny bit nervous.

Keefe smirked and blew her a kiss, hoping to lighten the mood.

"Are you ready?" Flori asked.

Foster took one last look around the twinkly clearing, and a crinkle formed between her brows, like she was worried about how much had just changed. So when she turned back to him, Keefe whispered, "I'm ready for anything."

"Good," Flori said, motioning for them to follow her, "because I'm not sure how much longer we should keep them waiting."

"Them?" Foster asked, fanning her cheeks and smoothing her hair as she scrambled to keep up. "Who's them?"

"You'll see."

Keefe trailed a few feet behind her, wiping his mouth and fixing his hair and trying to keep a safe distance—and avoid breaking out in any happy dances—until they knew who this mysterious visitor was.

And, boy, was he glad he'd stayed back, because when he stepped into Havenfield, he found Grady and Edaline—and the Fitzster.

ACKNOWLEDGMENTS

Since this is a different kind of Keeper book, I'm hoping you won't get *as* mad at me for the cliff-hanger ending. After all, you can always go grab your copy of *Stellarlune* and start at chapter 38 to see how the story continues.

(Or start at the beginning and enjoy all those adventures again!)

(Though I do realize that will inevitably lead you to the ENORMOUS cliff-hanger at the end of *Stellarlune*, which will probably feel even huger now that you know these additional secrets, so . . .)

(*goes into hiding*)

(I promise, I really am writing book 10 as fast as I can!)

Writing this book was both an absolute joy and a nonstop struggle, thanks to the fact that I had two kiddos under three who apparently have a gift for catching every cold/flu bug they possibly can. I never would've survived the intense deadline schedule without a seriously enormous support network. Thank you, Annah, Ashley, and Emily, for all the extra hours you covered so I could squeeze out those additional pockets of writing time. And thank you, Grandma and Nana, for giving me some desperately needed work hours during those deadline weekends. Daddy also deserves the Best Daddy in the Universe Award for covering every middle-of-the-night wake-up or feeding when I reached the drafting-late-into-the-night stage. You all have my undying gratitude. (And I'm so sorry for how often you ended up covered in boogers or vomit. . . .)

My undying gratitude *also* goes to my editor, Kara Sargent, who immediately jumped on board the "Yes, we need an entire Keefe book in this series!" train and patiently Zoomed with me each week to talk through every aspect of Lord Hunkyhair's adventures. And when the deadlines started to drown me, she was right there to cheer me on and supply anything else I needed, even if it was just patiently listening to me talk about an abundance of baby vomit.

And of course Kara is only one piece of my incredible Keeper team at Simon & Schuster, who not only turn my drafts into beautiful book-shaped things but who also do everything in their power to help me share this story with the world, whether it be trusting me when I said, "I think we need to add another .5 book to the series," to giving me the extra weeks I needed when the perfect storm of deadline and baby vomit crashed down on my life.

(Side note: Is anyone counting how many times I've mentioned vomit in these acknowledgments? Still not even close to how much vomit there's actually been!)

But back to my S&S team! Thank you, Valerie Garfield, Anna Jarzab, Jon Anderson, Mike Rosamilia, Art Morgan, Rebecca Vitkus, Elizabeth Mims, Olivia Ritchie, Adam Smith, Jen Strada, Bara MacNeill, Julie Doebler, Sara Berko, Alissa Rashid, Caitlin Sweeny, Mitch Thorpe, Michelle Leo, Nadia Almahdi, Ashley Mitchell, Nicole Russo, Ian Reilly, Jenn Rothkin, and the entire sales team. I also can't thank Karin Paprocki enough for designing another breathtaking cover. And thank you, Jason Chan, for creating a piece of art that was perfectly *KEEFE! KEEFE! KEEFE!*

Tremendous gratitude also goes out to my long-suffering agent, Laura Rennert (and the rest of the Andrea Brown Literary team), as well as the Taryn Fagerness Agency, who help me share the Keeper series with the world in every possible format. Publishing is a complicated, confusing business, but they take care of all the hard parts for me so I can focus on the writing thing.

I also wish I had the space to thank all of my amazing foreign publishers and translators—but since I don't, please imagine me giving you all an enormous group hug (and be glad you haven't had to suffer through any emails from me about baby vomit).

And I have to give a special shout-out to Rebecca Caicedo for supplying all kinds of fun details about Munich—and to Amie Kaufman, who possibly betrayed her people by telling me all about drop bears. Anything accurate and amazing in those scenes is all their doing. Any mistakes are totally my Google failings.

Thanks also to Deb and Amy, since I probably wouldn't have made it through the final deadline days without our writing sprints and check-ins. And to my assistant, Katie, for keeping up with all the emails and social media things that quickly become overwhelming. I also have to give a huge high five to Cassie Malmo at Malmo Public Relations because I'm so, so, so, so, SO excited we get to work together again! And thank you, Faith, Brandi, Eric, Kasie, Jared, Kelly, and Elyse, for just generally being amazing. Also: giant tackle-hugs to the rest of my family and extended family for putting up with how often I disappear during deadline times.

And to my incredible, energetic, brilliant, inspiring, and exhausting kiddos: I realize I've mostly talked about your vomit in these acknowledgments. So I hope you also know that I cherish every single one of your snuggles (even the ones where I end up covered in yuck). You have stretched my heart to fit in more love and joy than I ever thought possible, and it is an honor and a privilege to be your mom. I love you infinity plus infinity.

Last, but definitely not least, to the man who truly is the most wonderful support for our family. I promise you'll be able to get a little more rest soon. In fact, I'll wrap this up quick so I can go in and take a turn on rocking-the-baby-back-to-sleep duty. I love you. Thank you for everything you do and everything you are, and here's to hopefully less vomit-y years ahead!